EARTH RISING

EARTH RISING

EARTHRISE, BOOK III

DANIEL ARENSON

This novel is a work of fiction. Names, characters, places and incidents are either the product of the author's imagination, or, if real, used fictitiously.

CHAPTER ONE

Colonel Yardley was enjoying a rare sunny day in Vancouver when the sky fell.

At eighty-six, he rarely left the nursing home anymore. It was too damn rainy most of the time, too damn cold, and his damn joints ached whenever his dear friends Jack and Daniels weren't nearby. He had to walk with a cane, damn it. He told people it was purely for style, a bit of dapper sophistication in these days full of green-haired kids with too-tight pants. Perhaps he told himself the same thing. His twisted legs, regardless of his pride, were thankful for the sturdy stick of oak. Those legs still carried shrapnel in them from the war fifty years ago. They had never stopped hurting.

Fifty years today, the colonel thought. He rolled up the sleeve of his uniform and checked his watch. *Well, fifty years in two hours and seven minutes.*

It was unlikely he'd make it to the ceremony without needing to find a place to pee first. Another pleasure of old age.

He walked on, tapping his cane. His medals jangled across his chest. He wore his old uniform today for the first time since retiring twenty-five years ago. It was too large on him now. He had shrunk several inches since last wearing it, and the uniform billowed like an olive-green tent whenever the wind gusted. But he had refused to replace or tailor it. No. This uniform was the one he had led men in, had killed scum in. And it was the same old rifle that now hung across his back, the very rifle he had shot the enemy with. He wouldn't swap them for one of the fancy new uniforms soldiers wore today. He would wear the same set of greens he had won the Battle of Amsterdam in. The same uniform he had worn when pulling children out of the ruins, saving lives, giving Earth a chance to fight on.

Tap, tap. His cane pattered on. He had walked only a few blocks, and he had to pee already.

But at least I'm not on Depends, he thought. Which was more than could be said for some of his friends back at Oceanview Retirement Manor.

The legion had offered him transport to the ceremony, a bus full of other creaky old farts like him, but damn it, Yardley didn't want to spend all day--his first day out of the nursing home in years--with other veterans. He didn't want to listen to them drone on and on about the old war. He had been living that old war for fifty years now. No. Yardley wanted to see the world. To see this city he had saved. To see the young ones, the lives he had made possible.

They were all around him on this sunny street between sea and mountains. Children raced along the boardwalk, laughing and chasing seagulls. Sailors were spending their Sunday on their boats, and white sails filled this harbor on the Pacific. In a nearby park, families were enjoying a rare day out. They all carried their boxes of gas masks, but there hadn't been an attack on this city for three weeks, not since the scum had blasted apart a school bus, consuming twenty-three children. Yes, the war still ebbed and flowed. They were still fighting across the deserts of Africa, the forests of South America, on the streets of every major city. Thousands of starships still battled the scum up in space. But the true war--the Cataclysm, that horrible year when billions of people had perished in the poison and fire--that war was over. That war Colonel Yardley and his friends had won. There was a semblance of life now, moments of sunlight between the long days of clouds. There was hope. There was humanity.

As he walked down Vancouver's sunny streets, Yardley passed by hundreds of soldiers. Soldiers patrolled every neighborhood in every city in the world these days; you never knew where the scum pods might land. As Yardley walked by them, the soldiers saw his insignia. Three stars on each shoulder. The young ones rarely saw anyone higher ranking than a captain in the field, and many had never seen a colonel up close. They stood at attention as he walked by. They saluted. Yardley nodded at them all.

"Good lads," he said. "Good lasses." Yes, they let women fight these days too, and damn good warriors they were, as tough as the men. "At ease, my friends."

He could see the ceremonial park now. His back was bent, his legs were frail, but his eyes were still sharp. A hundred old geezers were already gathering on the grass. Every year there were fewer. Yardley remembered the ten-year anniversary of the Cataclysm. There had been thousands of veterans there. Why, just a decade ago, there had been thousands. But over the past few years, more and more of his comrades had succumbed to old age. Some lay buried underground. Some simply no longer had the will to battle their nurses and escape their retirement homes.

Fifty damn years, Yardley thought. *Fifty years since the scum nearly destroyed the world. And still we fight.*

He turned his head and saw the memorial for the school bus on the roadside, a hill of flowers and teddy bears and cards. Tears stung Yardley's eyes to think of the children who had died only days ago, crushed by the aliens' jaws.

Even now, those asshole scum won't leave us alone.

He limped onward, leaning on his cane, until he reached the memorial park. A massive starship rose in the center, as old as he was. The HDFS *Constitution*, the flagship of the North American fleet back in the days of the Cataclysm. Today it was a relic. Holes gaped open on its hull, remnants of the scum attacks. They had never patched up those holes, leaving this starship blemished, its scars a memory of the war. Colonel Yardley had served on this ship. He had been a captain back then, commanding the starboard's artillery cannons, and they had blasted eighteen scum pods in Earth's orbit before the bastards had knocked them down onto the Mongolian plains. The *Constitution*. Old, beaten up, scarred, and tough as hell--just like the veterans of the Cataclysm who gathered around her.

His friends approached him. A few leaning on canes. One man using a walker. Two in wheelchairs.

"Hullo, old farts," Yardley said to them.

"'Ello, you bastard," said Major Taber, a grizzled old war dog, medals clanking across his chest. He liked to brag that he was descended of Viking warriors.

"Is that any way to address a superior officer?" Yardley growled at the man.

Another one of their comrades, Captain Garza, barked a laugh. "The only way you're superior to us now, you son of a bitch, is your superior crankiness. We're all relics now, just like that ship."

Yardley snorted. "That ship's still tougher than any of the tin cans they're launching into space today. And we old geezers are still tougher than these pups they're sending up there."

"What are you talking about?" said Sergeant Lora Buroker, walking toward them. "I'm only sixty-nine. I'm still a kid!"

They all huffed and snorted at her. "You were a pup back then, and you're a pup now!" Yardley said, waving his cane at her, but he couldn't help but smile. He remembered Lora from those days, a fresh-eyed teenage private who had served under his command, blasting scum ships apart with her cannon. She was still a loose cannon, even now, her hair gone to white.

The others were congregating on the grass. The HDF had arranged plastic seats, but few of the veterans were sitting. Their legs were tired, but they were busy moving toward their old comrades. They rarely saw other souls during the year. Some had brought their families. Many had no families left. There was certainly no family here for Colonel Yardley. He had dedicated his life to the military, taking no wife, fathering no children. He had loved a few women in his day--there had been the woman he had courted while stationed in Bangkok, and there had been Melissa, slain by the scum. But never a wife. Never a family. He reached over his shoulder to pat the stock of his rifle. That gun was the closest thing Colonel Yardley had to a wife.

"Well, the old farts are all together again," he said, looking around him. "Smaller crowd than usual."

"Just the toughest bastards remain," said Major Taber.

Yardley nodded, but he wasn't so sure. He thought back to the great battles fifty years ago when the scum had first attacked. To his gruff sergeant, slain holding back the scum with his own body, ripped to shreds to let his soldiers flee. To young privates, some as young as fifteen, who had charged into the ranks of the enemy, knowing they would die, knowing they had to die to let others live. Were the old farts the toughest bastards? No. They were the commanders. Those who had led from bridges and bunkers. It had been the young ones, the brave boys and girls, those who had sacrificed their lives--they had been the toughest. Their sacrifices had let Earth survive.

He looked around him at the crowd of veterans. The others saw their old brothers and sisters-in-arms. But Yardley saw the millions who had died. His friends who could not be here. The finest souls he had known.

A handful of young soldiers approached, and a trumpet blared, and the veterans moved to their seats. A young officer--damn it, anyone under sixty seemed young to Yardley now--stepped toward a podium. Yardley recognized her dimples and butterfly pendant from countless posters and propaganda reels. Here stood Captain Edun, the latest speaker of the HDF. The officer stood in the shade of the HDFS *Constitution* and spoke to the crowd.

"Fifty years ago," Edun said, "we awoke to a terrible reality. Earth had made first contact with an alien species, and they were hostile. Their pods rained down. Their poison polluted our air. Their claws cut our children. Billions died. Entire cities, entire nations fell. But from the ashes rose brave souls. The soldiers of the world's armies united. In blood and fire, they formed the Human Defense Force. They told the enemy: No more."

"No more!" rose voices in the crowd.

Captain Edun continued. "Your courage, your sacrifice, your strength, your leadership--they let us deal the scum a devastating blow. They showed the enemy that we could strike them on their own soil. That we will not tolerate their aggression. That we will live. That we will fight."

Yardley looked around him at the crowd. Like every year, he hoped to see him. The hero of the war. The legendary pilot. Earth's greatest soldier. But like every year, he had not come. Fifty years ago, it had been Evan Bryan, a brash young pilot, who had made it through the scum's defenses. As thousands of starships had burned, Captain Bryan alone had flown through the gauntlet, whipping his way around the scum vessels in a small, one-man starfighter. That day fifty years ago, Evan Bryan had unleashed the fury of Earth upon Abaddon, homeworld of the scum. The nuclear inferno had slain millions of the scum, destroying entire hives on their planet. It had ended the Cataclysm. It had elevated Bryan to the status of a hero. Since that day, the scum had dared not launch mass destruction against the earth. Since that day, the enemy had waged a war of attrition, slowly stabbing the earth time after time, hoping to destroy the planet with countless small attacks. Since that day, Earth had stood--bleeding, suffering, losing people every day--but saved from complete annihilation through a new doctrine of mutually assured destruction. A doctrine Bryan had birthed in furious flame and devastating vengeance.

Yardley had met the young pilot, fifteen years his junior, during that war. He had not seen him since. Few people had. The hero had gone into isolation, allowing no interviews, writing no books, remaining in the shadows. All they had to worship was the old photo of a smiling, twenty-one-year-old kid, a photo taken the day before the assault on Abaddon. It was the most famous photograph in the world. It was the photograph that appeared on posters, mugs, T-shirts, flags. The photograph that inspired action figures, video game characters, romance novel covers. The photograph of a smiling, handsome face that gave humanity hope.

"Just this morning," Captain Edun said, "we received news from deep space. A brave company of soldiers defeated a hive of *scolopendra titania* on the moon Corpus, killing its king. The spirit of you veterans continues to inspire the younger generation of fighters, leading them on to victories."

The captain continued speaking from the lectern, now recounting stories of the great battles of old, of the soldiers' heroism. Yardley soon found his bladder so full it consumed all his attention. To distract himself, he looked around at the civilians who had gathered for the ceremony. Some were families of the veterans, others just people who had come to the park for a sunny day out, who now peered at the old geezers around their rusty rocket. Some of these civilians were missing limbs. One man wore bandages around his face, and a tube in his neck was helping him breathe. They too knew war. They had known war all their lives. A young boy stepped closer to the crowd and saluted the veterans. He was missing one arm.

It's for them that I fought, Yardley thought. *Not for glory, not for heroism. For these people. For life.*

"Look, Mama!" said a boy in the crowd, pointing at the sky. "It's raining purple!"

Eyes rose to the sky. A woman cried out.

Air raid sirens wailed.

Yardley looked up. He saw them in the sky as he had seen them fifty years ago. The pods of the *scolopendra titania.* The scum.

For the past fifty years, the scum would send one or two pods a week into this city--just enough to terrorize the population, not enough to risk another nuclear assault on their world. Today thousands--tens of thousands--of pods screamed down toward Vancouver, this jewel of the Pacific.

So, Yardley thought as people stared, screamed, fled. *We destroyed one of their hives. So they will destroy one of ours.*

With flashes of light and roaring fire and clouds of poison, the pods crashed into the city.

Outside the park, pods slammed into a glassy skyscraper. The tower shattered, belching out dust and debris. In the port downhill, purple pods slammed into the water, boiling it, raising tidal waves. Ships burned and sank. More pods slammed down across the city, and towers fell one by one like houses of cards. In the distance, pods rained onto the mountains, spilling out noxious fumes that rolled toward the city.

This was not an attack to terrorize, to punish. This was an attack like those fifty years ago. An attack to utterly destroy.

People were fleeing the park. Pods slammed into trees, and fires raged. Across the park, the slimy eggs--each the size of a car--cracked open, and the massive centipedes emerged.

"Run to the shelters!" cried Captain Edun, leaping off the podium.

"Stand back, veterans, stand back!" shouted young soldiers, racing into the park, firing their T57 assault rifles and falling to the swarm of scum. Blood sprayed the grass.

For the first time in decades, Yardley--eighty-six years old, with bent legs full of shrapnel, with a crooked back and just a few wisps of silver hair--unslung his rifle from his back and aimed his weapon.

"What say you, fellow old farts?" he said to his friends. "One more battle before the end?"

They looked at him. Old men and women, some in their nineties, two of them older than a hundred, only one among them a spry spring chicken at sixty-nine. They too raised their weapons. Some leaned on canes, others on walkers. A few sat in wheelchairs. But all raised their trusty old rifles.

"T57s?" said Major Taber. The old man scoffed. "Let's show these young whippersnappers what a good old R14 can do." He hefted his rifle.

"Let's teach these kids a thing or two," said silver-haired Captain Garza.

"Like in the old days?" said Master Sergeant Jensen, tossing aside his cane.

"Like in the old days," agreed Yardley.

Across the city, pods kept slamming down, and towers kept falling. Thousands more pods kept hailing. In the park, the young soldiers fell. The centipedes swarmed toward the old veterans from every side, forming a noose around them.

"For Earth, friends," said Colonel Yardley. "One last time. For Earth."

"For Earth!" they replied, a hundred raspy voices.

As the scum scurried forth, tens of thousands of the creatures, as the city collapsed around them, a hundred veterans, relics of the old war, fired their guns. For one moment, for this last battle, they were young again.

CHAPTER TWO

Marco stood on the bridge of the HDFS *Miyari*, watching the great bastion of humanity's might shine among the stars.

"Nightwall," he said. "The mightiest military fortress we have. Our light in the dark. Our fist on the frontier. Our bright sword in space."

Standing beside him, Addy scratched her backside. "You think they got beer there? Fuck me, I haven't had beer in months."

It was only the two of them on the bridge. Three if you counted Osiris the android, who sat at the controls, piloting the ship onward. Four if you counted Sergeant Stumpy, the Boston Terrier they had rescued from the ravaged mining colony on Corpus. It felt too empty here. Too silent. Too many gone, too many left shattered on that dark mining hell. They had traveled to Corpus as a company of two hundred armed, deadly warriors. They flew onward as a handful of haunted survivors.

Marco kept expecting to hear Benny "Elvis" Ray, one of his best friends, announce he would drink Addy under the table. He kept waiting for Sasha "Beast" Mikhailov to burst onto the bridge, to speak of how Russian vodka was far superior to beer. He wanted Caveman to be here, to speak of his flowers, for

Jackass to talk to him of books, for Corporal Diaz and Sergeant Singh to offer Marco wisdom and guidance.

But his friends were gone, some lost in the ashes of a desert base on Earth, others buried forever in the mines of a dark moon.

He looked at Addy. His best, his oldest friend. The girl whose parents had died with his mother. The girl who had lived in his library since they had been eleven. The woman he had trained with, fought with. She was tall, brash, blond, and tattooed, but he knew that deep inside she was sensitive, kind, noble.

I'm glad you're still with me, Addy, he thought, looking at her. *I can think of no finer friend to--*

She punched his shoulder. "Stop staring at me all weirdlike! What, do I still have barbecue sauce on my face?" She belched. "I told you I only ate ten chicken wings. Fine, fifteen." She groaned. "Okay, I ate all twenty, but somebody needed to finish them before we reached Nightwall."

Marco turned back toward the viewport. He watched the massive outpost grow closer and closer as their starship approached. Nightwall was the headquarters of Space Territorial Command, the space corps of the Human Defense Force. The STC only had about one percent of the military's manpower but over ninety percent of its budget, and as the *Miyari* flew closer, Marco could see every dollar spent.

Nightwall was built around--and inside of, according to the stories--a rogue planet. The black sphere of rock and metal orbited no star, instead floating freely through space like a massive, Mercury-sized asteroid. Nuclear reactors worked deep within the planet, powering entire cities on its surface--cities dedicated to war. Even from here, Marco could see the lights of those cities on the dark planet. It was here that humanity's greatest generals devised their plans, that the greatest scientists developed new technologies, that the greatest warriors trained for battle.

Thousands of spaceships flew around the planet. Marco had never seen so many in one place. Small, one-person starfighters flitted around the *Miyari*. Bulky transport ships, large enough to fit ten *Miyari*s in their hulls, lumbered above and below them. Slick battleships lined with cannons, some large enough to hold thousands of marines, floated back and forth. A hundred space stations orbited the planet among a sea of satellites, offering ports for ships to seek maintenance and repairs.

"I've never seen anything like this," Marco whispered. "Back on Earth, even fifty years after the Cataclysm, everything is so . . . run down. At Fort Djemila, our tents were full of holes, our guns thirty years old, our armored vehicles covered in rust. But this . . ." He shook his head in wonder. "It's like the Cataclysm never happened. Like we're living in the future."

Addy nodded. "Yep. That's what happens when the STC sucks up all our taxes. Down on Earth, we only get the scraps. The chicken wing bones, my friend. But up here, this is the juicy meat."

Marco rolled his eyes. "Will you stop talking about chicken wings?"

"What?" She patted her belly. "I'm still hungry!"

He looked at her flat stomach. "I don't know where you tuck it all away."

"I use up all the energy killing scum," Addy said. "That and it goes into my ass."

Osiris turned around from the controls to face them. The android's platinum hair flowed down to her chin, and her lavender eyes blinked. In every way, Osiris looked human, a perfect imitation. But there was something--Marco couldn't put his finger on it--that seemed eerily *wrong* about her, like a doll that was disturbingly lifelike. Perhaps she was too perfect, too beautiful, missing the flaws flesh and blood humans possessed.

"We've been assigned docking rights at Station 57, Terminal B, Pier 47, master and mistress," Osiris said. "It will be thirteen minutes and five seconds until we dock." The android rose to her feet, looked to the back of the bridge, and saluted. "Hello, ma'am!"

Marco turned too and saw Ben-Ari enter the bridge. Like him and Addy, their commanding officer hadn't yet integrated into the STC, and she still wore the tattered drab fatigues of Earth's corps. The uniform was in shambles--the knees torn, the shirt stained with blood, the beret burnt--but somehow Lieutenant Einav Ben-Ari still managed to look regal. She wasn't particularly tall, not like Addy, and not much older than them. But something about her squared shoulders, her raised chin, and the calm determination in her eyes made Ben-Ari, even in her ragged uniform, look like a commander through and through.

"Emery. Linden." The lieutenant approached them. "As soon as we emerged from hyperspace, I sent my report to Nightwall of what happened in the mines. They're going to have a lot of questions for us. Mostly, I suspect, about Private de la Rosa." Her eyes softened. "Marco, you know that Lailani won't integrate into the STC with us."

Marco nodded, his throat suddenly feeling tight. "I know," he whispered.

It still pained him to think about it, about what Lailani had done, who she was. He had met Lailani Marita de la Rosa at basic training, at first mistaking the young Filipina, with her shaved head and small frame, for a boy. He had grown to love her. He had made love to her. He had comforted her, held her close in his arms as she told him of her childhood, growing up homeless and hungry in the slums of Manila, the daughter of a thirteen-year-old prostitute and a father she had never met.

And then, only weeks ago . . . Marco winced. After the battle in the mines of Corpus, Lailani had grown claws. Had stabbed him, nearly killed him. Had spoken in a deep, inhuman voice, revealing that she had been planted in her mother's womb by the scum. An agent of the creatures, imbued with their DNA.

She could have killed us all, Marco thought. *She killed Elvis. She sabotaged our engines, killing dozens of us. Yet I still know that Lailani--the woman I love--is in there somewhere.*

"Ma'am, may I go speak to her?" Marco said. "One last time?"

Lieutenant Ben-Ari nodded, and she placed a hand on his shoulder. "You have ten minutes. Go to her. But . . ." Her eyes hardened. "Don't get too close."

Marco left the bridge. He walked through the narrow halls of the *Miyari* as the ship limped toward the port. The corridors showed the signs of her battles: dented walls, severed wires, shattered viewports. Marco climbed down a ladder, squeezed through a crawlway, and made his way to the brig. He unlocked the heavy metal door and stepped inside.

Here, in the small chamber, she sat on the bed.

"Hello, Marco," Lailani whispered.

For the first couple of days, Lailani had remained on the bed, all four limbs strapped down, with an armed guard always outside her door. When she had not gone hostile again, Lailani had been allowed some modicum of freedom. Her feet were now hobbled, and a chain ran from one ankle to the wall, but she was free to sit up, to lie down, to stretch and move around the chamber--as far as one could move in a chamber only seven feet wide. Lailani no longer wore her military uniform, just boxer shorts and a white T-shirt, and her black hair was growing longer, long enough now to cover the tips of her ears and fall across her forehead.

Marco stood at the doorway, heeding Ben-Ari's advice. "Hello, Lailani."

She smiled wryly at him. "You can step closer. My chain is long enough that I can reach you anyway. Look."

She stood up and leaped toward him. Marco started and instinctively took a step back. The chain tightened. Lailani reached both arms toward him, grabbed him . . . and pulled him into an embrace. She playfully bit his nose.

"Chomp!" she said. "Don't wet your pants."

Marco relaxed and wrapped his arms around her. He chomped down on her own nose. "At least I'm wearing pants, unlike you."

They sat together on the bed. There was no viewport in the brig, but Marco heard Osiris's voice emerging through the speaker system. "Six minutes to docking." It wasn't enough time. Marco had spent three weeks on this ship, but now there wasn't enough time. He held Lailani's hands, and she gazed into his eyes.

"Lailani," he said softly, "when we arrive . . ."

She nodded and looked at her lap. "I know. Ben-Ari told them what happened, told them what I am. They're going to take me away. To study me. To experiment on me." Her eyes hardened. "I won't let them. I'll fight! If they kill me, they kill me. I--"

"Lailani, listen to me." He tightened his grip on her hands. "I promise you--I will get you back to me. It won't be forever. They will cure you, Lailani. Ben-Ari wouldn't have told the STC what happened if she'd thought they'd harm you. They'll find a way to . . . to cut out whatever is inside you."

Tears filled Lailani's eyes. "They can't, Marco. Don't you understand? They can't. The scum . . . They're a part of me." Her voice trembled. "I've been dreaming of them. In my dreams, I'm one of them, a centipede in a tunnel, following the orders of their emperor. It's who I am." She let out a sob. "I killed him, Marco. I killed Elvis. Our friend. I killed him. I'm a monster. I'm a scum."

"It is not who you are," Marco said. "Look into my eyes. Look at me." He caressed her cheek. "You are Lailani de la Rosa. You are human. You are the woman I love. They will heal you. They will remove the creature inside you. And you will come back to me. I promise you. I promise."

She nodded, head lowered, and held him close. "I wish I could be here with you forever," she whispered.

He kissed her cheek, then her lips. "I ruv you."

She nodded, tears spiking her lashes. "Ruv you."

Osiris's voice emerged from the speakers. "Docking in Nightwall Station 57."

Thuds sounded across the ship as the *Miyari* connected with the dock.

"Will you walk with me to the exit?" Lailani said.

"They want you to stay in the brig," Marco said. "They want to send a team of people here to accompany you. I'm sorry." He embraced her. "Be strong, Lailani. Wherever they take you, I will find you. I will bring you back to me."

A voice spoke from the doorway. "Emery, it's time."

He turned to see Ben-Ari standing there, staring at him with hard eyes, but he saw a softness there too, a little bit of pity. He nodded, then turned back toward Lailani. She held his hand. As he stepped away from her, their arms stretched out, out, until only their fingertips touched, until he was apart from her, until he was in the hall, until he left his heart ripped out and bleeding on the brig's floor. Ben-Ari slammed the door shut and locked it, and the sound pounded through Marco's chest.

"Come, Emery," the lieutenant said. "We're at Nightwall. We have a lot to do."

As they walked down the corridor, Marco's eyes stung, and he couldn't curb the anger inside him. "Ma'am, you didn't have to report what Lailani did." He hated that his voice shook, that it was so hoarse. "It just happened once. Just because we were so close to the scum. Now they're going to take her away, experiment on her, and--"

Ben-Ari paused from walking and turned toward him. Her eyes blazed with sudden fury, all pity gone from them. Ben-Ari was shorter than him, maybe even physically weaker, but now she seemed to tower like a giant.

"De la Rosa killed one of my soldiers with her own hands," she said. "She sabotaged the engines of this very ship, crashing us onto Corpus, which killed a hundred others. She is infected with scum DNA, Emery, and I will make sure she never endangers anyone again. Regardless of feelings you think you have for her."

"Think I have?" he said. "Ma'am, Lailani is more than just a scum agent. She's my friend. She's more than a friend. It's bad enough we kept her tied up, we--"

"Private, watch your tongue!" Ben-Ari said. "Have I been too lax with my discipline that you would speak to me as a friend? I'm your commanding officer, Private, remember that. I've made my decisions. The right decisions. I don't doubt that. If you do, keep it to yourself. Understood?"

He nodded, stiffening. "Yes, ma'am."

Ben-Ari's voice softened. "You've been emotionally compromised, Marco. It hurts you. I know that. But we have to be professional. We are at war. We cannot let our personal feelings interfere with our duty."

"Yes, ma'am." He nodded. "I'm sorry to have argued back. I not only respect your authority, ma'am. I also respect your wisdom and your leadership."

She squeezed his shoulder. "Thank you, Marco. You're a good soldier. I never doubted that. Now come on. They'll have many questions for us."

They walked into the exit bay of the ship, where Sergeant Stumpy greeted Marco with a wagging stump and a lick to his fingers. Two other soldiers were waiting there, the two other survivors of Corpus. Addy stood in her tattered old uniform, chewing gum, which Ben-Ari promptly made her spit out. Beside her stood Kemi Abasi, once Marco's girlfriend, now a cadet of Julius Military Academy, who had come here to train with Ben-Ari . . . and be near Marco.

Kemi gave him a small, shaky smile, her eyes damp. Marco knew that this day was goodbye from Kemi too. She had come here to reignite their love, had instead found horror and torture in the depths of Corpus. Now she would go home, back to Earth--scarred, afraid, without him.

Marco stepped closer to her. "Will you stay a few days in Nightwall, Kemi?"

She shook her head. "I received confirmation only a few minutes ago. There's a ship heading back to Earth today. In only five hours. I'll be heading home on it."

Marco nodded. This too hurt. He was still grieving for his losses in battle. Now he would lose Lailani, now he would lose Kemi, perhaps never to see them again in the maze of this vast military that spanned star systems.

The galaxy is falling apart, he thought. *I'm losing everyone I love.* He took a deep breath. *I cannot let myself fall apart too.*

The exit bay door opened, revealing a jet bridge connecting them to one of Nightwall's space stations. As they walked across the bridge, Marco looked around him. Aside from a narrow metal path below his feet, the walls and ceiling were a transparent tube, giving him a panoramic view of Nightwall. It felt like walking through open space, and his head spun. At his left side loomed the surface of the rogue planet, this starless sphere of rock hurtling through space. Military bases and towns for soldiers' families sprawled across its surface, all alight, powered by the nuclear reactors pumping underground. Marco could see roads, clusters of buildings, runways, massive star ports, and radio dishes the size of towns. Lined with lights, cables rose from the planet surface, hundreds of kilometers long, finally connecting with several space stations in orbit, forming space elevators. Marco could see rounded carts traveling up and down the cables, transporting people and goods between the space stations and the planet.

When Marco looked below, above, and to his right, he could see the many structures orbiting the planet. There were several space stations, mushroom-shaped and lit with countless lights. There were starship cruisers, some nearly as big as the stations themselves. He even saw a starfighter carrier--it looked like a floating runway with a hundred Firebirds on its deck. Many other Firebirds were zipping all around, following paths outlined by floating buoys.

Marco felt like a medieval peasant who had wandered into the modern world. He had never seen, had never imagined such technology. As he walked along the jet bridge toward the space station, strangely, along with his awe, anger filled him.

Earth is falling apart, he thought. *We're still struggling to climb out of the Cataclysm. We live in poverty, surviving on scraps. And here in space the wealth of humanity flows!*

The bridge led them to one of the orbiting space stations. As soon as they stepped through the door into the gleaming hallway, a crowd of STC soldiers intercepted them, wearing hazmat suits and holding guns.

"Remove your uniforms and raise your hands for decontamination!" boomed one man.

"Where is the hybrid?" shouted another soldier in a hazmat.

"Private de la Rosa is in the ship's brig," Ben-Ari said. "Is this really necessary? We--"

A team of soldiers barreled past the lieutenant, racing into the ship, holding chains and heavy guns. Their faces were invisible within their helmets. Marco winced. They were going to Lailani.

"Uniforms off!" shouted the first man. "All clothing, equipment, and weapons--into these bins."

Marco, Addy, Kemi, and Ben-Ari all glanced at one another. Reluctantly, they placed their backpacks, their weapons, and finally their clothes into the bins, which were quickly sealed and rolled away. Marco was glad he didn't have time to see the others naked. Within instants, the men in hazmat suits blasted steam from hoses. The mist flowed across them, stinging, so hot Marco winced and struggled not to cry out. Sergeant Stumpy too got blasted, and the dog howled.

Medics inspected their wounds and gave the approval. They were handed fresh uniforms--green uniforms of Earth Territorial Command, though of better make than their tattered old fatigues. They did not get their equipment back. Marco had placed his copy of *Hard Times*, along with the photo of Kemi, into the bins. Now he wondered if he'd ever get them back.

"All right, follow us," said a man in a hazmat. "Come on. Hurry now."

As the soldiers shepherded them down the corridor, Marco glanced back toward the *Miyari*, wondering if the men were decontaminating Lailani, if they were hurting her, if she was scared.

Be strong, Lailani. I'll find you again. I promise.

The corridor split into several branches, and Marco found himself dragged down one way, while other hazmat men pulled his comrades down other paths. One man placed Sergeant Stumpy in a crate and carried the dog off.

"Addy!" Marco said. "Kemi!"

They gave him glances before the men dragged them out of his sight. Gloved hands gripped Marco's arms.

"Come with us, Private Emery, and quietly. Your friends won't be hurt."

He followed the man, feeling like a prisoner. He had defeated a hive of scum. He had fought the very king of the creatures. He had survived while so many others had fallen. He didn't expect to be greeted as a hero, but damn it, he didn't appreciate being treated as a prisoner either.

They whisked him into a small white chamber where they sat him by a desk. It felt a lot like an interrogation room. He waited for a long time alone, pacing, locked in the chamber. Finally, two officers entered, wearing the STC's navy blue service uniforms. The men smiled at him. They gave him a bottle of water.

For a long time they asked him questions, and Marco answered.

They asked him about why the *Miyari* had accepted the mayday call from Corpus.

They asked him how they had navigated the mines, finding their way to the queen.

They asked him how he had freed Kemi from the scum's network.

Over and over, they asked Marco to draw what he had seen. Of the tubes flowing into Kemi. Of the strange creature with his face. Of the hybrids in the scum's labs, created from stitching human and scum bodies together.

And mostly they asked him about Lailani. They asked over and over about how Marco had met her, how close they were, how Lailani had behaved in training, whether she had killed scum in the Battle of Djemila, whether he had seen any markings on her body, whether she had ever communicated with scum agents, and a thousand other questions.

The interrogation grew more and more bizarre over time. "What did the specimen tell you of her past? Were there ever any discrepancies in her stories? Have you noticed her hoarding food or eating one particular type of food more often than others? Have you noticed her preference to face any one particular direction? Have you ever dreamed of rotten meat when sleeping next to her? Have you ever thought you heard voices, maybe those of fellow soldiers in a crowded room, speaking of the Scorpius constellation when near the specimen? Have you noticed any strange color to your urine or stool after coming in contact with the specimen?"

Marco replied honestly whenever he could, but two facts he kept secret.

He did not speak of his relationship with Lailani, of making love to her. He hoped that if Kemi, Addy, and Ben-Ari were being interrogated, they too were hiding this fact. He couldn't imagine that making love to an alien agent would impress his interrogators very much.

The second secret was just a suspicion, just a few words Ben-Ari had spoken in the hive.

They knew.

According to the android Osiris, the mayday signal from Corpus had been four years old when the *Miyari* had picked it up. If that was true, surely somebody in the HDF must have known of the scum invasion, had kept it under wraps for years. But what proof did Marco and his friends have? Just a bad feeling was all. This too he kept hidden. If somebody in the HDF top brass was somehow involved with the scum, the last thing Marco wanted to do was reveal his suspicions. That seemed like a real quick way to end up forgotten in some brig for the rest of his life.

"If you're lying to us about anything, Emery, that is a serious offense," said one of the officers.

"I'm telling you everything I know about Lailani," Marco said.

"Please refer to her as the specimen. Have you noticed unusual behavioral patterns among insects who came near the specimen?"

"Well, I once saw a bumblebee put on a top hat and coattails and tap dance. Does that count?" Marco sighed when the interrogators only gave him harsh stares.

The questioning continued for hours. Halfway through, a new set of officers entered, only to repeat the same set of questions. Marco felt more and more like a criminal as time went by. Finally--it must have been eight or nine hours into it--he stood up and said, "Have I broken any laws? Why am I being kept here?"

"Sit down, Private," one of his interrogators told him.

"I've been sitting down all day, sir. We fought bravely on Corpus. We defeated the scum."

The interrogator nodded. "And we're very proud of you, Private. You're also one of the few living soldiers who's seen a *scolopendra titania* laboratory, a queen, a king, as well as a cloned agent."

"Lailani isn't a clone," Marco said. "She's my friend. Where is she kept? I want to see her."

The interrogators glanced at each other, then back at him.

"You will never see the specimen again, Private."

Marco felt his heart hardening, then cracking inside him. "What are you doing to her? Are you hurting her? Are you going to . . . to kill her?"

"That is none of your concern, Private. Now sit down."

"I will not sit down!" Marco said. "Lailani is my friend. She fought with us. She--"

"According to your own report, Private, the specimen killed over a hundred HDF soldiers. Were they not your friends?"

Both officers were staring at him, and Marco realized he was in trouble here. If they thought he was an accomplice . . . The HDF didn't execute prisoners, not since those first chaotic years following the Cataclysm, but they could sure as hell make sure he spent the rest of his life in a dank cell on a forgotten asteroid. He sat down.

"Sorry, sirs. Ask me your next question."

But inside, he was trembling. Fuming. Terrified. The words kept echoing through his mind. *You will never see the specimen again.*

Finally, after what felt like days, they let Marco leave the room. Guards escorted him, holding his arms, through a back corridor, a dark tunnel that brought back visions of the hive under Corpus, brought back the smell of the creatures, the screaming of the dead. The guards took him to a heavy metal door, and they guided him into a room with a handful of empty bunks. They closed the door. A moment later the door opened again, and other men in navy blue shoved Addy--she was grumbling and cursing--into the room. The door closed again, then locked.

"You fucking bastards!" Addy shouted at the door, pounding at it, then spat on the floor. Finally, she turned around with a groan and seemed to notice Marco for the first time. "Oh hi, Marco. Did they ask you that question about insects behaving weirdly too?"

He nodded. "Several times."

"I told them I saw a cockroach do 'La Cucaracha'," Addy said.

"I told them I saw a bumblebee in coattails doing a tap dance," he said.

"They're such fuckers." Addy embraced him, then sat down on a bunk. "Any word from the others? Ben-Ari? Kemi?" Her voice dropped. "Lailani?"

He shook his head. "I haven't seen anyone but you until just now."

"They're treating us like criminals." Addy punched a pillow. "Fucking hell, Poet. We defeated an entire scum hive. We saw our friends die in the dirt. They should be giving us medals. Instead they locked us in here."

"Addy." He hesitated. "Did you tell them about . . . about how Lailani and I . . .?"

"About how you slept with her? Hell no." Addy pulled a pack of cigarettes from her pocket and lit one. "I'm not stupid. Don't worry, Kemi and Ben-Ari won't say anything either. They know that would get the STC to chop off your cock and study it in a lab." She rose from her bunk and paced the room. "La Cucaracha, La Cucaracha . . . damn, now that song's stuck in my head. Want to dance? Conga line?"

"Too hungry to dance," Marco said. "I haven't eaten anything since you polished off those chicken wings on the *Miyari*."

Addy nodded. "I'm so hungry I might just rip off your arms and eat them. Marco-wings."

"Eat me," he said. "Wait. No. Addy! Ow!" He rubbed his arm. "God, you bit me!"

"I'm hungry!"

He shoved her away. "Stay on your bunk. Stay, you rabid beast."

Addy flopped down onto the bunk. The chamber was so small that Marco, sitting on his own bunk across the room, was close enough to reach out and touch her. He lay down too and stared up at the ceiling. He was silent for long moments.

"I miss home," he finally said. "I miss seeing blue sky. I miss feeling the sun on my face. I hated Fort Djemila when we were there, but now I miss even that place. Spam sandwiches with our friends. Talking at night in our tent. Sneaking off to find the vending machine. Just . . ." He sighed. "Just being safe. Not being so scared all the time. I thought basic training would be the hardest part of military service. I thought nothing could be worse. But it *is* worse, Addy. I wish we had never gone into space."

"I wish I could bite your arm again," Addy said. "My first bite only whetted my appetite." She turned her head toward him and grinned toothily. "At least we have each other, right? Best buddies?"

Marco nodded. "Best buddies." He reached toward her bunk and let their fingertips touch. "I remember that day. That horrible day back in Toronto, the worst day of my life. The day when we were eleven, when the scum killed my mother and your parents in the snow. I cried at the funeral, but you never cried. I remember that. Not a tear throughout the ceremony. You were so angry. So strong. The worst day of my life." His voice was hoarse. "But that's also the day you came to live with my father and me in our little apartment above the library. The day you became my best friend."

"We fought all the time, Marco," Addy said. "Don't you remember? And for a long time, we ignored each other."

"I know," he said. "Maybe it took the second worst day of my life--joining the army--to really make us true friends. And Addy, I'd have gone mad here without you. Just mad. I'm so grateful that you're with me. I love you a ton."

She smiled and stuck her tongue out at him. "Oh, you. Such a tasty little poet." She pulled his finger to her mouth and gave the tip a bite. "Chomp."

Chomp. Like Lailani did. And pain stabbed him.

A key rattled in the door. Marco and Addy rose from their beds, expecting another round of interrogation. But when the door opened, it was Lieutenant Ben-Ari who stepped inside. Her face was ashen, her eyes haunted. She closed the door behind her, then looked at Marco and Addy, silent. She looked like she had aged a decade.

"Ma'am?" Marco said. "Is everything all right?"

"Sit down, Marco, Addy," the lieutenant said softly.

They sat together on one bunk, and Ben-Ari sat on the opposite bunk, facing them. She placed her hands on her lap. "When we received the distress call from Corpus, we had no way to report it to Nightwall. This headquarters still lay hundreds of light-years away. Even if we had sent out a signal, it would take centuries to reach this place."

Marco nodded. "I remember. We had no way of calling for help."

"For a long time," Ben-Ari said, "humanity has colonized space, fought in space, without faster-than-light communications. In science fiction novels, you sometimes read about ansibles--devices that let you communicate instantly across vast distances. But when our species ventured into space, we found that the only way to travel faster than light was using azoth engines on massive starships, bending the fabric of spacetime around us. That's how the *Miyari* traveled from our solar system to here, the frontier, within only a month. And that is how, for years, we communicated with Nightwall. By sending messages on heavy starships, traveling at warp speed, bringing news back and forth between Nightwall and Earth. A message would take three weeks to deliver, and it would require a starship and a brave captain. But those days are in the past."

Addy raised her eyebrows. "Did somebody invent those ansi-thingies?"

"They invented wormholes," Ben-Ari said. "They actually invented wormholes."

Marco's eyes widened. "Like in the stories? Great tunnels through space you can fly spaceships through, instantly arriving across the galaxy?"

"Smaller," Ben-Ari said. "Wormholes large enough to fly a spaceship through would require massive amounts of energy to remain open for only a single journey, more energy than Earth uses in an entire year. But the HDF has developed a very small wormhole, only a few atoms wide, I'm told. These portals through spacetime are just wide enough to send messages back and forth. In the future, the HDF wants to open a network of these atomic wormholes, connecting every one of humanity's colonies across the galaxy. In fact, we copied scum technology; they've been using wormholes to send their pheromones between star systems. Just a week ago, while we were still flying here, the first human wormhole opened. One end by Earth. The other end here at Nightwall. We can now communicate with Earth in real time."

This was incredible technology, Marco thought. Revolutionary technology. It could change human civilization the way the internet had in the late twentieth century. But he saw the dour expression on Ben-Ari's face.

"And through this wormhole, you received news from Earth," he said slowly. "Bad news."

Ben-Ari nodded. "The scum heard of our attack on Corpus, of the destruction of their hive. Their retaliation . . . has been beyond anything we've seen since the Cataclysm. Marco, Addy, I'm sorry. The attack was on your country. Vancouver was hit. Vancouver was destroyed."

They stared at her, silent for a moment.

"Destroyed?" Marco said. "You mean, the scum hit it hard? They killed thousands, they--"

"Vancouver is gone," Ben-Ari said. "We don't have a casualty count yet. But we estimate that half a million people have died, the entire city's population. I'm sorry."

Marco stared at her, barely able to process the news. Addy and he were from Toronto, on the other side of Canada, but Vancouver was still dear to them, still part of their country. His mouth went dry. His head spun. Addy reached out and clasped his hand, her face pale.

"This will mean a major escalation in the war," Ben-Ari said. "This will no longer be a war of attrition. Not like it has been for the past fifty years. We're entering a period of full war. And we will strike back. Hard. Already the generals are planning our retaliation, a major strike against Abaddon, the scum's homeworld. Tomorrow morning, both of you will officially integrate into the STC and begin an intense month of training. When that month ends, our assault on Abaddon will begin." She stood up and approached the doorway, then paused and looked back. "Try to sleep tonight. I know this news is hard. Mourn tonight. Comfort each other. But in the morning, be strong. You will need your strength to win this war."

The lieutenant left the room.

Addy and Marco remained sitting on the bunk for a long time, silent, trying to process the news.

"It's our fault," Addy whispered. "If we hadn't attacked Corpus, the scum wouldn't have done this. Oh God, Marco. It's our fault."

"Addy!" He held her shoulders. "It's not our fault. None of this is. The scum did this. Only them. The scum who killed our parents. The scum who killed billions. The scum we will fight, we will--"

She wouldn't let him finish his sentence. She pulled him into a crushing, desperate embrace, one that knocked the air out of him. Her tears flowed.

"I'm so sick of this," Addy said, tears flowing. "I want to go home. I'm so scared. I can still see them, Marco. I can still see the scum in the hive."

He held her close, and tears burned in his own eyes. "We have each other," he whispered hoarsely. "Always, Addy. Always. We'll get through this."

And suddenly he was kissing her, or she was kissing him, and it tasted of tears and cigarettes, and her lips were soft, desperate, and her fingers dug into his back. She trembled in his arms, tears still flowing, eyes closed, their lips locked together, and Marco knew it was wrong, and Addy knew it was wrong, he could feel it, but he felt her fear too, the fluttering of her heart against his chest, a bird caught in a cage. They needed each other. They needed this comfort. They needed companionship, love, affection, sex, tears, kisses, heat, digging fingers, beating hearts--needed these things like air when all lay dead around them, with the cosmos burned, when the nightmares screamed inside.

She stared into his eyes, cupping his cheeks in her hands, her eyes damp. She spoke to him without words. She spoke of their need for this. For human contact before the fury of the aliens. It seemed like a dream when they made love--no, not love but hypnotic, dreamlike sex, in darkness and heat and sweat, something that couldn't be real, something that felt like floating through an astral realm, and Addy cried out, clutching him, fingernails cutting him as they climaxed. Afterward she slept by his side, sharing his cot, her back toward him, holding his hand to her breast.

Marco didn't know if this was wakefulness or a dream. He felt caught in some hyperspace reality, still lost in a labyrinth. His friends, dead. Lailani, gone. The world, burning. Addy, naked in his arms. He did not know when he slept, when he slid into true dreams, and he was lost again in the hive, seeking a way out, seeking a path home but finding only darkness, only a thousand screaming creatures with his face.

CHAPTER THREE

Cadet Kemi Abasi walked through the corridors of the space station, seeking the port, seeking a flight back home. She had already missed her first flight home due to hours of interrogation. Come hell or high water, she was boarding the next starship heading back to Earth.

I was stupid to ever leave Earth. Her eyes stung, and she touched the pi pendant Marco had given her. *I was just a stupid, lovesick girl, chasing her boy into hell.*

She paused for a moment to steady herself, looked through a viewport, and beheld the vastness of space. Hundreds of starships floated above a rogue planet. Nightwall. Headquarters of Space Territorial Command. She should feel safe here, in this bastion of humanity's might, but her fingers trembled and her heart pounded. Beyond this space station, these starships, and the fortresses on the planet below--there, among those stars, lurked horror.

I should never have come into space, Kemi thought. *None of us should have. There is evil here.*

She grimaced, the memories pounding through her.

The claws grabbed her.

The antennae poked her.

The centipedes dragged her through the tunnels, bound her to the slab with sticky membranes, thrust tubes inside her, licked her, poked her, cut her, as the others screamed around her, and they flailed, half human, many legs kicking, and--

Kemi forced herself to take deep breaths, to clear her mind, to let those nightmares flow away. When her brother had died in the war, she had learned this technique, learned to focus on her breath until the anxiety faded. Breathe in. Breathe out. She stood for long moments until the horror retreated to the back of her mind like a crab retreating into its shell.

She turned away from the viewport. She walked onward through the space station. Soon she would board a starship. Soon she would be home on Earth. Soon she could forget about all this.

Yes, she had been a fool. She had been accepted into Julius Military Academy, the most prestigious officer school on the planet. She had told her superiors that she wanted an internship program, to shadow Lieutenant Ben-Ari on a mission. Kemi could have earned several credits doing so, gained real experience in the field, she had told them. The truth she had kept hidden from her school. She had come here chasing Marco. Chasing the boy she loved, the boy she had broken up with, the boy she had desperately wanted back.

A fool. A fool.

Yes, it hurt. It hurt Kemi to arrive here, to find Marco again, only to learn that, over the past few months, he had forgotten her, had sought comfort in the arms of another. Yet it hurt that he had chosen another, chosen the petite, pretty Asian girl, tossing Kemi aside. But Kemi had always been a fighter, a survivor. It was bred into her. In the aftermath of the Cataclysm, her grandparents had been poor immigrants from Nigeria, struggling to sell fruit on the streets of a cold, snowy city across the ocean. Her parents had worked hard, had built a life of moderate wealth, and they had never spoiled her, had taught her to never take their middle class life for granted. They had pushed her and her brother hard--to prove themselves in a world that could so easily descend back into chaos. And so her brother had become an officer, had become a pilot, had fought the scum in space and sky, had fallen fighting over South America. And so Kemi had joined a military academy, determined to become an officer too, to make her parents proud.

But she had found heartbreak. She had found terror.

Again those images flared. The hybrids in the lab. Half human, half centipede. The visions of the hive. The chemicals flowing through her, connecting her to the vast consciousness of the creatures. The pain. The horrible visions of herself becoming one of them, metamorphosing into a creature. Claws. Mandibles. Slime. Maggots.

Breathe in. Breathe out.

She walked on.

She reached the dock, a long corridor that thrust out into space from the station, and--

The mandibles thrust out. They hurt me. They--

--and Kemi waited there, gazing out the viewports, watching the hundreds of ships outside, waiting for hers to arrive.

In only three weeks she would be back on Earth, and she vowed to never leave again. Once she graduated from Julius Academy and became an officer, she would serve in Earth Territorial Command. She would refuse to return to space. She would find a cozy office job where no terrors could reach her, where she could bury herself in her work, where she could *forget.*

A slender starship came sailing toward the port, reminding her of a graceful fish, and Kemi wondered if this was her transport back home. She hefted her duffel bag across her back. Soon space would be nothing but a memory, then nothing at all, not even a memory, not even a chill at night.

"Cadet Abasi?"

The voice came from behind her. Kemi turned to see three men there, wearing the navy blue service uniforms of the STC. Sergeants. She nodded.

"Yes?"

"Good," said one sergeant. "We found you in time. You're summoned to room 507, to report at once."

He handed her a piece of paper, stamped with an STC seal. She frowned at it, then back up at the sergeant.

"I'm to catch transport back to Earth in only fifteen minutes," she said. "I don't have time."

"Orders come from Major Robert Verish," said the sergeant. "They trump your transfer for now. Report to 507 at once."

Kemi glanced back at the slender silvery ship. It was now docking, and a jet bridge was extending from the port toward it.

She winced. Her flight home. Yet the sergeant was right. She could not disobey an order from a major, a senior officer, not unless she wanted a heap of trouble back home. With a sigh, she nodded.

She left the port and caught an elevator up to level five. STC interrogators had already questioned her for a full day after arriving here on the *Miyari*. She had thought that interrogation complete, but apparently, they wanted to escalate it now. Kemi cringed. She didn't think she could handle more of their questions, didn't think she could describe her ordeal on Corpus again, reliving the terror yet another time.

Just let me go home, she thought.

Finally she reached room 507, where a guard stood at the door and accepted her summons. Kemi knocked on the door, called out her name, then entered the room and saluted.

She found herself in an office with a view of space. Nautical antiques hung on the walls, sealed in shadow boxes: an old compass, a scope wrapped in leather, a frayed parchment chart of the seas, and an astrolabe with brass gears. A major sat behind a desk, probably in his late thirties, the first hints of gray just touching his temples and the thinnest of crow's feet tugging at his eyes. A photo on the wall showed him as a younger man, only a captain then, shaking hands with a white-haired general in front of a badly damaged fighter jet. Beside it hung two framed diplomas, one a university degree in astronautics, the other a commission from Julius.

The major rose from behind the desk and returned Kemi's salute. "Good morning, Cadet Abasi. I'm sorry to have torn you away from your flight home. My name is Major Robert Verish, and I command one of our L16 Firebird squadrons here at Nightwall. Please have a seat."

L16 Firebirds. Kemi knew them well. Her brother had flown one. She had sat in the cockpit of his starfighter as a child; the photograph still hung in her parents' apartment. The Firebirds were the workhorse starfighters of the military, able to fly both in air and space, large enough for just a single pilot, deadly and fast enough to take the scum head-on. Her brother had been a lieutenant when falling in battle. Perhaps if he had lived, he could have risen to major too, commanded a squadron of his own.

She sat down, folded her hands on her lap, and stared at the major.

"Abasi, I heard of what happened on Corpus," Verish said, and his eyes softened. "Lieutenant Ben-Ari wrote you a very enthusiastic recommendation, speaking of your courage and determination in the face of horrible adversity. Are you all right?"

Kemi blinked several times, struggling not to cry in front of him. She didn't know this man, but something in his kind eyes made her soften, made the armor she always wore melt away. She wanted to tell him about her nightmares, about how the scum had bound her, infected her, forced her to live inside their minds. About the hybrids, the woman with the body of a queen, the babies who had burned. But she could not. She was not ready to speak of these yet. Back on Earth, she would request sessions with a psychiatrist, would work through her trauma. But not yet. Not here. She just wanted to go home quickly.

"I'm all right," she whispered.

Verish turned in his seat and gazed out the window at the fleet. Several large carriers hovered outside, each the size of a skyscraper. Suddenly five Firebird starfighters zipped just outside the window, leaving trails of light. A hundred or more were drilling in the distance, small lights.

"For years now, we've been building up our fleet of Firebirds," Major Verish said. "Each starfighter is among the galaxy's greatest feats of engineering, a true marvel of military might. When I joined the military twenty years ago, we had only a couple thousand of them. Today our fleet includes fifty thousand Firebird fighters." He turned back toward her. "And not nearly enough pilots."

Kemi nodded. "My brother was a Firebird pilot. I know how rigorous the training is, how few graduate from flight school."

Major Verish nodded. "I knew your brother well. I flew with him, fought with him. He was my friend."

Kemi's eyes widened. "You knew Ropo?"

"I did." He lowered his eyes. "I'm the one who retrieved his body when he fell, who brought him home."

Kemi too lowered her head, remembering that horrible day, that day her world had crashed around her. "Thank you."

The pilot rose to his feet and looked at a black-and-white photograph on the wall, showing an antique airplane. "This is a photo of an Ilyushin Il-2 fighter aircraft, built in 1942. During the Second World War, the Soviet Union built a staggering 150,000 fighter aircraft. Within only a few years! Even today, with a larger population, with vastly superior technology and resources, we struggle to produce as many fighter craft. But the USSR had the same problem we have today, two hundred years later. Where do you find enough pilots?" He nodded. "For many years, we indeed had only the strictest standards for our fighter pilots. Only the very best and brightest could assume this role. And for many years, that was good enough. We rarely had operations involving more than a few hundred Firebirds at a time. The other starfighters waited in hangars, ready for some remote possibility--an impossibility, many thought--that someday we'd need to fly all of them at once." He smiled thinly. "It seems nothing is impossible in war. Something big is coming. Something on a scale such as we've never seen. We need more pilots, so we're going to lower our standards a little bit."

"And you immediately thought of me," Kemi said.

Major Verish's smile grew. "When you put it that way, it doesn't sound very good, does it? But yes, Kemi. I want you. I want you to fly in my squadron. I want you to fly where your brother once flew. And I want you *soon.* Tomorrow morning you will begin flight school. The program normally takes six months. You will complete it in six weeks."

She rose from her seat. "Sir! I'm not a pilot. I'm not even an officer yet. Flight school? I haven't even completed military academy! I'm just a cadet."

Major Verish opened a drawer in his desk. He pulled out the insignia of an ensign, the most junior rank of officer. He held out the golden bars in his palm. "Accept my offer, and I'll grant you your commission here and now."

Kemi's eyes widened. She stared at the gleaming golden bars he held, bars that could shine on her shoulders, that could mean that she, Kemi Abasi, was a true officer of the Human Defense Force.

Marco would have to salute me. The thought popped into her mind, strangely satisfying.

But she forced her gaze away from the insignia.

"Sir, I can't," she said. "I'm sorry. I must return to Julius Military Academy. I must earn my commission the proper way."

"Kemi, six weeks from now, there might not *be* a Julius," Major Verish said.

She blinked. "Sir?"

"The end of this war is near, Kemi. Utter defeat or final victory. And I need you with me. I need you flying by my side as your brother did. You've received excellent marks at your first semester at Julius, an excellent recommendation from Lieutenant Ben-Ari, and your aptitude scores are off the charts. You've earned your commission. In six weeks, I want you flying by my side."

She narrowed her eyes, staring at him, and tilted her head. "But that's not it, is it, sir? Not all of it. There are millions of soldiers who serve in the HDF. Many of them are more experienced than I am. Is this because . . ." She thought she finally understood. "Because of what happened, because of Corpus, because . . ." She covered her mouth, unable to say anymore.

Verish stepped closer to her. He spoke in a low voice. "You were part of the scum hive for several hours. You were able to lead Lieutenant Ben-Ari to the queen of Corpus. Our scientists think that some of that ability is still inside you. Right now we have only one other soldier confirmed to possess such an ability, and she's being saved for another task. Go to flight school, Kemi. In six weeks, fly with me. We need a pilot who can speak the scum's language, who can understand how they think, how they feel, how they perceive reality. Only one pilot--Evan Bryan--ever made it through the scum's defenses to reach their homeworld. We believe that you can do it too."

She closed her eyes. Those images danced before her. The scum in their hives. A baby with a centipede body. A woman giving birth to maggots. Myriads of scuttling creatures, so angry, so vengeful, so cruel.

"If I do this, sir," Kemi whispered, "I need to know one thing." She opened her eyes. "That we're going to kill them. Not just retaliate, punish, or scare them. That in six weeks, we will kill them all."

Major Verish nodded and pinned the insignia to her shoulders. "Ensign Abasi, I promise you. We will kill them all."

CHAPTER FOUR

Ben-Ari stood in the space station's gymnasium, barefoot, stripped down to her combat uniform pants, a black tank top, and her dog tags. She balanced on the balls of her feet, fists raised, eyes narrowed. Her opponent stood before her--an MFR, Mechanical Fighting Robot, essentially a punching bag with padded limbs. The machine swung one of its "legs"--a bar of padded iron--in a swift roundhouse kick. Ben-Ari ducked, dodging the blow, then swerved sideways, avoiding a swing from the robot's arm. She pressed an attack, but the robot raised its arms, blocking her blows. Ben-Ari was of average height and weight, but she had chosen an MFR the size of a heavyweight prizefighter.

"You will lose," chimed the robot, for some reason speaking with a Russian accent, and kicked again. She caught the blow on her arm. It hurt. Badly. "I will crush you."

Whoever programmed this robot obviously watched Rocky XII too many times, Ben-Ari thought. She had raised the setting to eleven, its highest mode of aggression. Its padded limbs swung in a fury, emulating various martial arts, everything from kung fu to capoeira to Chun Kuk Do.

As for Ben-Ari, she used just a single martial art. Krav Maga. It included everything she needed. Other martial arts, she thought, were showy, as much about the theatrics as functionality. But Krav Maga just meant business.

"I must break you," intoned the robot, launching into a furious attack, fists and legs flying. Ben-Ari grunted as blows slammed into her. She knew they would leave ugly bruises. But she refused to fall. She swung her fist, hit the robot in the chest, and smiled as red lights flashed.

It had been too long since she had trained like this. As a teenager, she would spend hours in the gym, sparring with her father's soldiers. Even as a scrawny fifteen-year-old, she would come home with bruises dealt by beefy sergeants. And she would deliver them bruises twice as bad. Many of her opponents underestimated her, not thinking that a young blond girl could defeat larger fighters. But Ben-Ari was quick, dedicated, fast, strong for her size, and able to suffer many blows without falling. The mark of a true fighter, she knew, wasn't just how many blows she could deliver. A true fighter could take more pain than her enemy and stay standing.

And what was physical pain to Ben-Ari? She had known pain all her life. The pain of her family's burden and history. The pain of growing up motherless, her father an officer who had traveled the cosmos, leaving her in the hands of his soldiers on desolate bases. The pain of having no home but the army, no life but fighting. So what were bruises? Nothing. A reminder that she was still human. Blows to make her forget the demons inside her.

As Ben-Ari sparred on the mat, she knew nothing but the fight. Not her grief. Not her burdens. Just her enemy and herself.

Finally, taking another blow on the shoulder, Ben-Ari found her way through the MFR's defenses. She delivered a massive punch to its punching bag chest. Lights flashed. The machine dinged like one of those carnival games where you swung a hammer to ring a bell. The robot's limbs slumped, and the letters "KO!" popped up on its LED display.

"A winner is you," said the robot, then shut down.

Ben-Ari panted and wiped sweat off her brow. She had needed this. Here on the frontier, in this space station on the border of scum territory, weeks away from an invasion, she needed pain, needed sweat, needed forgetting.

"Fighting robots is one thing, ma'am." A rumbling baritone voice spoke behind her. "Fighting humans, quite another."

Ben-Ari turned around. One of the largest men she had ever seen was walking across the gym toward her. He must have stood closer to seven feet than to six, and his arms were wider than her entire body. He seemed to be in his mid-thirties, quite a bit older than her. He had dark skin, thick eyebrows, and a bald head, and the insignia on his sleeves denoted him a Gunnery Sergeant.

He was an NCO--a noncommissioned officer--a seasoned commander who had never gone to officer school, had never earned a commission, but who had spent years serving and fighting, rising through the ranks of the enlisted. NCOs were older and more experienced than Ben-Ari. As a commissioned officer, even just a junior one, she still outranked NCOs. No matter how old, experienced, and tough, NCOs had to salute and serve officers, even young lieutenants like her, only a couple years out of officer school. Many of them, she knew, resented that.

Ben-Ari had once had an aging, grizzled master sergeant refuse to salute her, refuse to call her "ma'am." She had been just a hesitant twenty-year-old ensign at the time, him a warrior who had been fighting the scum for decades. He had not recognized her authority. Some ensigns would have chewed out the older man, like little nobles out to humiliate a peasant, but Ben-Ari had let it slide. She had doubted her own authority in those days, had felt too meek, too young, too inexperienced, had trouble realizing that she was an officer through and through, part of the commanding class of this military, that the "butter bars" on her shoulders *did* denote her as army nobility. So she had let that gruff, scarred, older man grunt at her, insult her, call her "girl." She had fled from him. Later that year, Ben-Ari had learned, the master sergeant had tried the same attitude, this time on a vindictive lieutenant who got the man court-martialed, demoted, and transferred to a desolate asteroid.

Since that experience, Ben-Ari had been a little wary of NCOs, especially one as tall and powerful as this one. The man in the gym looked like he had survived battling hordes of scum. But then she saw the smile in his eyes, and she saw warmth on his face and no hint of condescension.

"So you think you can fight better than this robot, Sergeant?" she said to him.

"The name's Bo Jones, ma'am," the man said. "I'm to be your new platoon sergeant." He bowed his head. "I'm here to assist and advise you, to act as your second-in-command, your right-hand man. But at the moment . . ." His smile grew. "I'm here to teach you a few things about hand-to-hand combat."

Her new platoon. Ben-Ari suppressed a shudder. Yes, the orders had come from the top brass, from this fleet's admiral himself. She was to form a new platoon here, all battle-hardened warriors, the best in the fleet. She was to lead them on a critical mission during the upcoming invasion. What mission, Ben-Ari had not been told. All she knew was that the admiral was sending her the best warriors he could muster. Why he had chosen her to lead this new platoon, among the many capable officers here at Nightwall, she could not imagine.

She took a closer look at Gunnery Sergeant Jones. Her old platoon sergeant had been Amar Singh, a tough but kind warrior, a dear friend to her. It was still hard to believe that Singh had died in the mines of Corpus. Replacing him would not be easy, no matter how capable Jones was. This tall, bald man was still somebody different. He was still not her friend.

But we'll see if he can fight, Ben-Ari thought.

She widened her stance and raised her fists. "Very well."

Sergeant Jones removed his boots and uniform shirt, remaining in a tank top and trousers. By God, the man was huge.

He was probably over three hundred pounds of rippling muscle, far larger than the robot Ben-Ari had fought.

If the admiral wanted pure strength for our mission, Ben-Ari thought, *he chose the right man.*

The NCO lunged into a wild attack. Ben-Ari retreated at first, dodging his blows, but he was relentless. He would not let her win because of her gender, size, or commission. That much was obvious. He attacked in a fury, kicking, punching, and it was all Ben-Ari could do to dodge his blows.

"You're quick," he said.

"I have to be."

He leaped toward her, making to grab her shoulders. She sidestepped and shoved him over her leg. He slammed down onto the mat with a great *thud* and *crack*, sounds so loud Ben-Ari winced.

"You all right?" she said.

The giant lay on his back, groaning. She reached down and helped him up.

"Looks like I'm more about brute force than speed or agility," Jones said.

"That's good," said Ben-Ari. "I could use some brute force in my new platoon."

His eyes darkened. "Ma'am, if I may ask . . . There's talk. Talk of something big, that our platoon will be going far up shit's creek. Where exactly are we going?"

Ben-Ari had not received any more information, but she thought she knew. And that thought chilled her. She stared up into the tall man's eyes.

"All I can say is this: I need you to be ready. I need you to train our warriors well. And when the time comes, Sergeant Jones, I'm going to need every last drop of that brute force of yours."

*****

"Full war."

The words echoed through the halls of the space station, hovered in the eyes of soldiers, rose from the air vents, dripped from the walls, filled the eyes and ears of all who served here. No longer a war of attrition, a slow grinding down of the enemy, a slow pain beneath their claws. Full war. Full fury. The days of the Cataclysm--returned.

Marco and Addy walked through the corridors of the station. They wore new uniforms this morning. No more would they wear the olive green of Earth's corps. They now wore black fatigues, the sturdy fabric bristling with belts and buckles and pouches. Black helmets topped their heads, complete with dark visors. They carried new guns, no longer the T57s of Earth but the newer, lighter Fyre-7 plasma rifles, their barrels shorter but their fury deadlier. The gun had three modes: safety, semi to fire bullet-sized bolts of plasma that could rip through steel, and automatic to spray an inferno like a flamethrower.

"These make our old assault rifles seem like pellet guns," Marco said.

"They're almost as deadly as my old hockey stick," Addy said.

They were to begin training today as STC warriors. Soon they would descend down toward the dark surface of Nightwall's rogue planet, and there they would spend a month training before the great assault on Abaddon began.

As they walked through the station, a thousand thoughts filled Marco's mind. He thought about Lailani, wondering what she was undergoing. He thought about Kemi, wondering if she was already on her way back to Earth. He thought about what he and Addy had done last night, that night of scared, lonely sex they had not spoken of since. He thought about the war ahead, about humanity's looming assault on the scum's homeworld, about the fire and death he would witness. Soon that war would begin. Full war. Full fury.

But first--before the war, before their training--Lieutenant Ben-Ari had asked to meet them in the officer's lounge. They entered the room, a round chamber with floor-to-ceiling windows affording a view of a hundred starships, two other space stations, and millions of stars. Ben-Ari was there, and she too wore a new STC uniform. Hers was not battle fatigues but a navy blue formal uniform with brass cuff links and golden insignia on her shoulders. With her stood another officer, a mustached man with the insignia of a major--a single star on each shoulder strap.

Marco and Addy slammed their heels together, saluted, and reported for duty. Ben-Ari and the major nodded and returned the salutes.

"Private Marco Emery," Ben-Ari said. "Private Addy Linden. Both of you have served in the HDF for only a few months, but both of you have served admirably. You fought bravely in Fort Djemila. You fought bravely at Corpus. You both displayed valor and sacrifice and defeated your enemies."

Marco and Addy listened quietly to this praise. It felt so hollow to Marco. Valor? He had been scared shitless. Defeated his enemies? Those enemies still haunted his dreams. He said nothing.

"You have earned your spots in Space Territorial Command," Ben-Ari continued, "and in an hour, you will begin your integration and training into these prestigious corps, and you will fight bravely when the time comes to assault the enemy. But first I have a gift for you." The hint of a smile touched her eyes, and she held out insignia in her palm. "Wear these proudly, Corporal Emery and Corporal Linden."

Marco had heard that during promotions, soldiers laughed, sang, sprayed water from bottles, champagne if they could find it. But he and Addy could summon no mirth here, no joy. They stood still, faces blank, as Ben-Ari attached the insignia--two chevrons--onto their arms. They were now corporals, seasoned warriors, no longer green privates. But Marco did not feel like a warrior, not like Corporal Diaz had been. He felt as young and afraid as he had on his first day in the army.

Full war. Full fury.

"It's strange," Marco said to Addy after they had left the officer's lounge. They were walking down a corridor, passing between thousands of other soldiers walking to and fro, everyone from teenage privates to white-haired colonels. "When we were first drafted, when we first met our corporals--Diaz and Webb and St-Pierre--I thought them like gods. I thought them impossibly wise and strong. Now I realize they were like us. Just kids. Barely into their service, just with one or two battles under their belts. I don't feel as mighty as I thought corporals were back then."

"You're still the same old Poet," Addy said. "Some new piece of cloth on your sleeve can't change that."

But she was wrong, Marco knew. He wasn't the same old person. He wasn't who he had been when joining the military. He would never be that person again. He had seen too much, lost too much. They both had. He glanced at Addy, saw her look away hurriedly. She too, he knew, was thinking about last night. The quick averting of her eyes told Marco that yes, it had truly happened, had not merely been a dream. They walked on in silence.

As they traversed the space station, Marco kept looking around him, hoping to see Kemi or Lailani, knowing it was impossible, knowing that Kemi was on her way back to Earth now, knowing that Lailani was confined to some lab. He would have even welcomed seeing Osiris now, but the android was back on the *Miyari*, returned to her duties. Thousands of faces were here, young and fresh, old and stern, all strange to him.

Addy and he got lost several times, finally found their way toward the bottom of the space station, and saw a sign to the space elevator. They walked down a carpeted hallway between clear windows. Below them loomed the black surface of the rogue planet, lit with countless lights of the military bases and towns below. Marco could just make out the cables running down toward the distant surface. It was as if the space station were a balloon on a string hundreds of kilometers long.

Guards stood at the elevator doors. Marco and Addy showed the electronic passes they had received that morning. A guard scanned the chips, then nodded.

"You're clear. Next elevator in twelve minutes."

As Marco waited, he wondered if Lailani was being kept on this space station, down below on the planet's surface, or perhaps had been ferried somewhere else entirely. He hated the thought of potentially moving farther away from her.

Are they hurting you, Lailani?

Perhaps he should feel rage toward Lailani, maybe even disgust. His interrogators yesterday had felt such things. Lailani had killed people. Had killed Elvis, their friend. But Marco still couldn't believe that had been her. A different voice had emerged from Lailani's throat, deep, inhuman.

You were possessed by them, controlled by the enemy, Marco thought. *It wasn't you. It's not who you are. I know this. You have to tell them, Lailani. You have to show them who you really are.*

Finally the elevator doors opened. Marco had expected an elevator like those down on Earth, a simple metal box, but instead he stepped into a transparent globe with a ring of seats. On one side, the globe was attached to the cable--and that cable was, Marco now realized, a good ten feet in diameter. A few other soldiers shuffled in and sat down, all in black battle fatigues, carrying Fyre-7 plasma rifles. At first Marco felt a moment of awe, of respect, even a little intimidation being next to these warriors, and it was strange to think that he was one of them now, perhaps indistinguishable from the others. He had never wanted this, to be a fighter, to battle the scum in space, and he felt like an impostor here.

But that's who I am now, he thought. *That's who I've become. I fought the scum. I survived while hundreds died. I'm not like Ben-Ari, not like Addy. I never wanted to fight. Yet now I'm on the front line, gearing for total war.*

The elevator began to descend. Marco looked through the rounded, transparent walls. He could see hundreds of starships floating around them, some massive vessels the size of aircraft carriers, others small jets the size of cars that flitted back and forth. He could even see the *Miyari*, and he nudged Addy and pointed. They stared at the starship together. The damage looked terrifying from here. The hull was dented and cracked, one turbine dangled like a bad tooth, and the solar panels had shattered and hung in ruins across the hull like scabs. It was hard to believe this ship had ferried them here; it looked ready to collapse. More than ever, it dawned on Marco how close to death they had come on Corpus.

"Come on, move faster!" Addy said, pounding the elevator floor. "It'll take an hour this way."

"Just be grateful there's no elevator music," Marco said.

Addy's eyes lit up. "Now there's an idea!" She began to hum "The Girl from Ipanema," stopping only when everyone in the elevator was groaning and threatening to shoot her.

They kept descending, leaving the space stations and starships above, rushing down toward the black planet. Nightwall orbited no star. Here was a rogue world, hurtling aimlessly through space, no sun to warm it. But this world was not dark. Countless lights spread below, lining roads and airports and shining from thousands of buildings. There was no fire or so much as a tremble of reentry. If there was an atmosphere here, it was thin. Marco wondered why the STC had chosen such a barren world for their headquarters. Why choose an airless, lifeless rock, far from any source of light, heat, and energy? This was a frozen wasteland, the most inhospitable place Marco could imagine. But perhaps, he thought, that was why the STC had chosen this world--a world inaccessible, harsh, cruel, unforgiving, one that enemy lifeforms would overlook, perhaps purposefully avoid. This wasn't just a headquarters. It was a massive fortress.

The elevator moved significantly slower than a rocket. As Addy had suspected, it took a good hour before they reached the planet's surface. Here was a barren landscape, all dark rocks and dust, and it might have reminded Marco of Corpus, but the city seemed several times the size, its towers and barracks and hangars all lit. The elevator descended through an airlock and down a tube, finally coming to a stop underground. The doors opened, and the soldiers emerged.

They found themselves in an underground city, much like a space station itself, all winding halls and doorways and thousands of soldiers walking back and forth. Their new helmets' visors came with an augmented reality system that popped up luminous arrows to show them the way--a far cry from the crude technology back on Earth. But even with this virtual map, Marco and Addy got lost several times and had to stop and ask for directions.

Finally they found their way to a gymnasium. A hundred soldiers stood inside, all in black fatigues. An NCO stood before the soldiers, among the largest men Marco had ever seen, a hulking giant with a bald head, dark skin, and muscular arms. Marco counted three chevrons and two semicircles on the man's sleeves, denoting him a Gunnery Sergeant, two ranks above a regular sergeant like Singh had been. This warrior must have been fighting in the HDF for ten or twenty years to achieve this rank.

"Well, looks like we have a pair of party crashers!" the NCO said, turning toward Marco and Addy. "If I'm not mistaken, Corporal Marco Emery and Corporal Addy Linden have finally decided to grace us with their presence."

"Sorry, Commander!" Addy said. "We were busy killing about a million scum on Corpus."

"Addy, hush!" Marco whispered. He didn't feel like starting their first day here by antagonizing their drill sergeant.

"Only a million?" the NCO rumbled. "Just you wait until our invasion of Abaddon, little soldiers. You'll miss fighting only a million of the scum. Get into formation."

Marco and Addy hurried to form rank with the other soldiers. Glancing around him, Marco didn't see any privates. Everyone else was either a corporal or sergeant--experienced warriors.

"All right, boys and girls!" said the towering NCO. "My name is Gunnery Sergeant Bo Jones. I will be your worst nightmare for the next month. Some of you, like Corporal Linden here, might think yourselves hotshots. All of you have killed a million scum already. All of you have distinguished yourselves in battle. That's why they sent your asses to me in the STC, rather than let you rot down on Earth. But let me tell you: Up here in space, you are nothing special. You might think you've seen action during your short military careers. You ain't seen shit. There are horrors up here in space that'll curdle your balls and make your piss run red. Some pencil-pushing officer gave me the task of training you for an invasion of Abaddon. If you ask me, it's a waste of time. You're all scum fodder. But maybe, just maybe, one of you bastards will get lucky and fire a one-in-a-million shot and kill the scum emperor. For that chance, I'm going to train you hard. Welcome to the worst month of your lives."

An invasion of Abaddon.

Marco glanced at Addy. She looked back, eyes wide.

An invasion of the scum's homeworld.

Marco nearly fainted. Addy gave him a hesitant smile.

Their life as space corps warriors began.

CHAPTER FIVE

"Welcome," said Gunnery Sergeant Bo Jones, "to your new bodies."

A hundred STC trainees stared. Across the hangar, a hundred metal men stared back.

Addy leaned closer to Marco. "Fuck yeah," she whispered.

At first glance, Marco had mistaken the hundred figures ahead for robots. They were tall, bulky, and forged of black metal. Gears and cables and bolts thrust out from them, and rocket launchers rose on their shoulders. Their heads loomed, dark and hollow, peering with glass eyes. On closer inspection, Marco saw that the constructions were hollow. These weren't robots. They were suits. Suits that soldiers could climb into, like a hermit crab climbing into a shell.

"That's right," said Sergeant Jones, pacing in front of the suits. "These bad boys are the latest and greatest pieces of military technology the STC is wasting on your useless asses. Behold the Exoframe W78b Hardsuits, trademarked, all rights reserved, made by the blessed Chrysopoeia Corp. The scum have their exoskeletons, and you have your exoframes." The NCO kicked one of the towering metal suits. "These bastards are forged from steel and graphene, so they'll take a punch, or a bullet, or a scum claw to the balls. They're equipped with a grenade launcher, an air filtration system, gravity-adjusting boots, climate control, and your choice of AM or FM radio. Once inside your new skin, you'll jump higher, run faster, punch harder, and kill much, much more of the enemy. You *will* be the toughest sons and daughters of bitches this side of the galaxy. You *will* defeat the scum in these suits; they cost too much for you to die in. Does everyone understand me?"

"Yes, Commander!" they shouted.

"Where's the cup holder?" Addy asked to the sound of groans.

"Suit up!" said Sergeant Jones. "Today you become true killing machines. Literally."

A few soldiers ran toward the exoframes. Marco approached more cautiously. While others were already climbing in, Marco touched one of the exoframe's arms. The metal was cold. The suit loomed, a good foot taller than Marco. He realized that what he had mistaken for glass eyes were, in fact, flashlights mounted onto the helmet. He could see the symbol of Chrysopoeia Corp emblazoned in white across the chest, a snake consuming its own tail. Beside it appeared the symbol of the STC--the man and woman of the Pioneer Plaque--and finally the phoenix of the Human Defense Force.

Marco climbed into the suit. It felt like climbing into a man-shaped coffin. He fit his limbs into the proper cavities, and he found himself standing several inches taller than before, what with the suit's heavy boots. A memory returned to him of putting on his father's coat and hat many years ago. The photo still hung back home.

"Place your hands into the gauntlets," said Sergeant Jones. "Curl your fingers inward, then outward, three times, and your suit will seal itself."

Marco followed the instructions, and suddenly his suit changed--so rapidly his heart burst into a gallop. Slats of metal shifted and snapped into place. A breastplate slammed shut across his torso like a fridge door. A visor whooshed down from inside his helmet. He stood completely enclosed within the suit. He felt like a scum--a soft, gooey creature inside an exoskeleton.

"I am Iron Man!" Addy intoned from inside her suit. She began humming the riff to the Black Sabbath song.

"There are sensors across the inside of your exoframes that detect your movements and correspond accordingly," said Sergeant Jones. "Now take a step forward."

With a thud that shook the hangar, a hundred soldiers took a step forward. The suits were heavy but required no more effort to move than walking normally.

"Another step!" barked Jones.

They took another step. The suits hissed, clanked, thudded. Marco remembered driving the armored vehicle back at Fort Djemila. This was like operating an armored vehicle that fit perfectly around his body. Looking around him, Marco imagined he was seeing an army of robots. And perhaps he was--here were, in a sense, wearable robots.

Sergeant Jones stepped into his own exoframe, and its plates snapped shut. "Now follow me." His voice emerged from speakers in Marco's helmet. "You're going to need time to get used to your new skin."

They followed their drill sergeant across the hangar, down a corridor, and into an airlock. A pair of doors closed behind them. Another pair of doors opened ahead. The air gushed out, and they beheld the lifeless surface of the rogue planet.

"Remember!" said Jones. "There's only a paper-thin atmosphere here at Planet Nightwall. The surface will kill you in about thirty seconds with your suits off. There is a code word to open your suits, which I'm not sharing until we return indoors. In the meanwhile, do try not to shatter your helmets. Now march after me."

They marched out of the airlock, a hundred warriors in their exoframes, and onto the rocky black ground. The stars shone brilliantly above, barely any atmosphere to dim them, and a spiral arm of the Milky Way spread above. The lights of satellites, space stations, and starships blinked above among the stars.

For hours, they trained in their new skins.

They ran, following Jones--slowly at first, then running a full one hundred kilometers an hour. They leaped, soaring ten feet into the air. They climbed a sheer cliff, digging their metal fingers into the stone. They shattered boulders with their gauntlets. They rolled, somersaulted, crawled, and vaulted over canyons. At one point Jones instructed them to leap down a seven-meter cliff, which Marco felt so queasy about he nearly backed out. He had already broken his kneecap once in the army. He didn't relish breaking it again. Addy had to shove him over the cliff, and Marco fell with a shout, cursing her. He slammed down onto his metal knees, cracking the earth beneath him, ending up with bruises but no broken bones.

"The STC only has a few of these machines," said Sergeant Jones. "You will prove yourself worthy of these very expensive pieces of equipment. They are worth far more than you are. You will slay many scum with them. You will make me proud, or I will personally kick your metal asses."

After a few hours of agility, they began to fight.

They fired their guns at distant boulders, shattering the stones. They launched grenades toward a distant mountain. They fought hand to hand with their comrades, wrestling with great thuds of metal hitting metal. Marco found himself facing off against Addy, and the woman was vicious, swinging her metal fists, knocking her armored shoulders into him, and body checking him again and again, grinning all the while within her helmet. His suit protected him from the blows like a bulletproof vest protected you from a bullet; it kept you alive but hurt like hell.

"Addy, God!" he said when she slammed him down, then leaped onto him. "You weigh a ton--literally!"

"Ack, a talking scum!" she said and pounded his head against the ground. "Die, scum!"

His head rang. "God damn it, Addy." He kicked her off, and she flew several feet into the air, then slammed down hard onto the ground, cracking rocks.

By the time they returned into the airlock, Marco was exhausted, covered in bruises, and drenched in sweat. It wasn't that the suit was heavy; it felt no heavier than wearing clothes. It was the constant jumping, running, rolling, falling, and wrestling that left him weary to the bone.

That night, Sergeant Jones showed them to their new bunks. It was better than basic training, at least. Rather than tents in the desert, they had actual rooms with actual walls. And rather than share the room with an entire squad, each chamber included only three bunk beds. It would have seemed crowded and harsh for a prison cell, Marco thought. But after Ford Djemila, this small crowded chamber was a luxury. Marco even managed to nab a top bunk, despite Addy grabbing his leg and trying to yank him off. They shared the chamber with four soldiers who barely spoke a word of English. One was Chinese, two were African, the fourth Sri Lankan. Unlike Earth Territorial Command, which generally segregated its battalions by geographical location, the STC was truly mixed. Given that Sergeant Jones was American and spoke English, Marco was sure that most soldiers here were thankful for the translators installed into their helmets.

"Morning inspection at 5:00 a.m.!" Jones appeared at the doorway as the soldiers were changing out of their uniforms. "That gives you six hours to sleep. I suggest you use them." The drill sergeant left down the corridor, and they heard him repeat the words at another room.

Six hours. It was less than what Marco would sleep back home, but it was luxury compared to the two or three hours a night he had slept during basic. For six hours, Corporal Marco Emery, space warrior, slept like a bruised, battered log.

*****

The weeks stretched on, eighteen hours a day, six days a week of constant training.

They crawled through networks of tunnels, battling mock scum--robots of sharp steel--in mock hives. They once spent four days trapped in a labyrinth, seeking their robotic enemies in the darkness. They ran for days across the dark plains of the rogue planet, moving in complete darkness far from any base or city, firing their guns, drilling against hordes of holographic enemies. They climbed mountaintops--mountains three times the height of Everest. They plunged into canyons that delved deeper than the Mariana Trench. In their exoframes, they became like robots themselves, hearts of metal, fists of steel.

They spent one entire week in space, training inside a shadowy starship, blasting its cannons at asteroids and fighting one another in its twisting halls. They leaped from the ship in landing craft, again and again, plunging down toward the dark planet and slamming into the hard earth with a shower of stones. Another day, they leaped again and again from the starship, this time without landing craft, using instead massive parachutes that could barely catch the planet's thin atmosphere, that could barely cushion their fall. Jumping from space onto a planet, Marco decided, was the most terrifying experience in the cosmos. He relived it over and over in his dreams.

It was training beyond anything Marco had experienced on Earth. Here they weren't training to guard city streets, to fight the odd scum pod that landed on the road, to become cogs in a machine of millions. No. Here in space, they were training for invasion. They were training for true war. The equipment was more advanced, the beds and food better, and the weaponry put Earth's firepower to shame, but Marco found this training far more exhausting than boot camp had been. Day by day, it was chipping away at him. Often he could not distinguish between himself and the metal skin he wore.

He missed his friends. He missed joking with Elvis. Missed being near Lailani. Missed everything from Earth. There were rarely any smiles here in space. There was stone, darkness, fire, metal. Every day, he was thankful that at least Addy was here with him. He was going mad here, but perhaps she kept just a shred of his sanity still burning inside him.

He missed home. He missed it every day. As they ran, jumped, fought, he thought about his father, his library, his city. He wondered if he would ever see them again. Vancouver was gone. Humanity was preparing a massive assault against the scum.

When full war flared, what chance did Marco have of going home? And even should he survive an invasion of Abaddon, would there still be an Earth waiting for him, or would the second Cataclysm destroy what remained of his planet?

As the days of training went by, Marco noticed something.

Every day, there were more lights in the sky.

When he had first come to Nightwall, he had seen hundreds of vehicles orbiting the planet: hulking cruisers, fast and small starfighters, clunky cargo ships, and more. He had never seen more than a handful of ships together before, and seeing *hundreds* of them had spun his head.

But every day now, there were more.

When Sergeant Jones took them into space for their latest jump, he saw *thousands* of ships orbiting Nightwall and docking in her space stations. There were massive carriers that held hundreds of starfighters on their backs. There were warships lined with cannons large enough to climb into. There were cargo ships the size of skyscrapers. Among them all flitted countless smaller vessels--shuttles, starfighters, spies, bombers.

The attack on Abaddon is near, Marco thought. *Humanity is gathering all its strength for the assault. All our guns will fire together.*

He thought back to the greatest invasions in the history books. To D-Day. To Operation Barbarossa. To Napoleon's doomed assault on Russia. All those, it seemed to Marco, paled in comparison to what he saw brewing here.

They hit us on Corpus, so we destroyed their hive, he thought that night, lying on his bunk as the others slept around him. *We destroyed their hive, so they destroyed Vancouver. They destroyed Vancouver, so now we will assault with all our might.* He sighed. *I sure chose a great time to join the army.*

CHAPTER SIX

Kemi stood in the hangar, staring at the squad of L16 Firebirds.

She stood within the HDFS *Sagan*, a starfighter carrier the size of NYC's Freedom Tower. Here was one of the mightiest ships in humanity's arsenal, a legendary ship, a ship that had fought great battles and destroyed entire hives. Thousands of soldiers served within her halls, and fifty hangars lined her hull, each able to send forth a squad of starfighters. Today the *Sagan* orbited the rogue planet of Nightwall, but whatever world she approached best beware; here was a flying army, containing enough firepower to destroy civilizations.

Yet standing here in the hangar, Kemi was less impressed by the *Sagan* itself, more by the far smaller ships she carried. Here before her, fifteen L16 Firebird starfighters stood ready for battle.

Kemi had seen Firebirds before, of course. She had seen them fly over Toronto, patrolling the sky. She had even sat in one, the Firebird her brother had flown. But they could always take her breath away.

She approached one of the starfighters, hesitated, then raised her hand to touch its fuselage.

"The Chrysopoeia Corp L16 Fighting Firebird," she said. "Seventeen meters long, powered by twin nuclear engines.

Equipped with retractable wings with a span of twelve meters, enabling atmospheric flights. Highly maneuverable, supersonic, multi-role tactical fighter, proficient as a dogfighter and bomber. The bubble cockpit provides perfect visual display, along with a state-of-the-art computerized navigational and combat system. Armed with a G17 cannon capable of firing 20mm rounds, six heat-seeking Dirk missiles for close combat, a dozen long-range Nighthawk missiles, and a bay full of bombs to unleash hell on anyone below." She patted the hull. "It's a fine machine."

"You know your Firebirds, Ensign Abasi." Major Verish smiled at her, standing beside her.

"I grew up around them, sir," Kemi said. "My brother had a thousand posters and toys of the Firebirds--and eventually a real Firebird of his own."

"You've clocked over a hundred hours in the simulator by now," Verish said. "Are you ready to fly a real bird?"

She bit her lip. She was scared. The simulators were incredibly realistic, nearly indistinguishable from the real thing, but not to her heart, not to the tremor inside her.

"I crashed twice in my simulator," she said.

"Only on the first day," said Verish. "Most of my pilots are still crashing the damn things after a month." He climbed the ladder toward the cockpit. "This is a two-seater. I'll be right behind you."

Most Firebirds had only one seat, but Kemi saw the second seat lodged at the back of the cockpit. This was an L16B, a two-seater, often used in training. During real combat, she would fly the L16A with only one seat, but perhaps flying this starfighter now wouldn't be too bad. She gulped, climbed in after Major Verish, and took the front seat. She put on her helmet, then pulled the cockpit shut.

An array of controls spread out before her--buttons, switches, joysticks, touchpads. Kemi inhaled deeply.

Be like Lydia Litvyak, she told herself, as she had told herself during all her simulator flights. Born in 1921, Lydia Litvyak was the first female fighter pilot to shoot down an enemy plane. Born into a Jewish family, she had served in the Soviet air force during World War II, fighting the Nazis. She flew in sixty-six combat missions, shot down Nazi planes, and earned the rare title of "fighter ace." Since then, many women had become pilots. Today they formed half the pilots in the HDF fleet. But all that was thanks to dear Lydia, and Kemi held on to that woman's memory as the hangar doors began to open.

The air emptied out from the hangar, and Kemi pressed down on the throttle--too fast. The Firebird blasted forward and burst from the *Sagan*'s hangar with terrifying speed. Space opened up around her: the rogue planet below, a space station above, thousands of other ships around her. Or was the planet above her and the space station below? She was moving too fast, too fast, and this wasn't like the simulator at all, and she was going to crash, and--

Breathe. Breathe!

She inhaled deeply and pulled on the joystick, rising higher, then banked to the right. She found a spaceroad, a path lit by thousands of floating buoys, and flew among them. She was still moving slowly, but slow for a Firebird still meant hundreds of kilometers per hour, and the lights streamed at her sides.

"You're doing fine, Ensign," said Major Verish, sitting behind her. "Just keep moving down this path, then when you reach the end of the road, rise higher until you're flying five hundred kilometers higher up."

She nodded, maintaining her speed. Several other spaceroads spread around her, ribbons of light, and many jets flew along them. In orbits farther out, she could see hundreds of satellites. There was a system here. Some orbits for space stations, some for carriers and cruisers, others for satellites, each ship divided by class and distance from the planet. But it was all so dizzying, like trying to drive through bustling Manhattan during rush hour and a parade. Finally she reached the end of the spaceroad, where floating arrows of light pointed upward--an exit from this orbit. Kemi pulled back hard on the joystick, and the Firebird turned straight up, its tail toward the rogue planet. She flew until she had climbed five hundred kilometers.

"Excellent!" said Major Verish. "Now gradually increase speed. Bring us up to Mach 10. Keep the same trajectory."

She increased her speed, faster, faster still, rising to a dizzying three kilometers per second. She kept moving away from the planet, leaving the space stations and great carriers below.

"Watch out for those satellites," Verish said.

"Yes, sir, I see them."

They kept flying, and even at Mach 10--ten times the speed of sound--it was a while before they cleared the cluster of satellites.

I bet you never flew this fast, Lydia, she thought.

"All right, I think we found a nice spot of open space," said Verish, sounding so relaxed Kemi wouldn't be surprised if he kicked off his boots. "Now let's see you really fly. I've had a few of the boys send up some drones. Let's see you blast them apart."

Suddenly from below flew streaming, spinning, whizzing balls of light and metal and spinning blades.

Kemi winced. "Sir? You mean, use real weapons, and--"

"Unless you want those drones to tear our hull apart," said Verish.

Goddamn! Kemi thought.

The drones came flying toward her, each the size of a motorcycle--small targets. Blades flashed on their sides, and their lights flared. They looked very, very pissed off.

Kemi flew higher, banked, and rolled. The drones flew in pursuit. She counted five. *Damn it!* She increased her speed, but they flew faster. Lights flared out from one, and the Firebird rocked madly as something slammed into its tail.

"Better get rid of those drones," Verish said.

Biting her lip, Kemi tugged the joystick and swooped toward the planet. The drones followed, the lights blinding her. She kept plunging. More lights flashed out, blasting the Firebird, and the starfighter rocked again. The ring of satellites rushed up toward her, and below them hovered the lumbering warships.

Be like Lydia.

Kemi yanked on the controls, spinning around so fast she nearly passed out. She pulled her triggers, blasting up a stream of bullets.

She felt the cannon thrumming across the starfighter, heard the bullets expelled. A drone shattered and rained shards of metal.

Four other drones came flying down. She soared toward them and released a missile.

Metal exploded across space. More shards rained as another drone shattered. Kemi swerved hard, dodging the spray of shrapnel, and shot by the other three drones. They spun behind her, rising fast, firing at her ship. The Firebird jolted. For a moment, she lost control of the joystick and careened, then grabbed it again and spun in a wide angle, spraying bullets.

Two more drones shattered.

The last drone, the largest of the original five, raced toward her. Its blades spun. Kemi narrowed her eyes, fired a heat-seeking missile, then soared high and away. She flipped upside down in time to see the missile slam into the drone, and firelight filled the cockpit.

She breathed out shakily, floating for a moment upside down, the planet over her head.

"Sir!" she finally managed to say. "Each one of these missiles costs more than my father's Acura. And I just fired two."

"We have more money than pilots," Verish said from behind her, and she could hear the smile in his voice. "You did well."

She gulped. "Sir, those drones, could they have really hurt us? Really destroyed this starfighter?"

"They could have done some serious damage," the major said. "Good thing I know how to choose pilots. Now take us home, Ensign. Back into the *Sagan*."

She flew back nice and slow, though her heart still raced, and landed the plane back in the hangar. The bay doors closed, and they waited for the chamber to repressurize before climbing back out.

"How are the legs?" Verish asked.

"Shaky, sir," Kemi confessed. "Thank you for this. For flying with me." She hesitated, then added, "A month ago, all I wanted was to go home. To run from my fear. But . . ." She inhaled deeply. "Maybe this is better. Maybe this way I can face my enemies head-on. Maybe this way I can kill my demons instead of sweeping them under the rug. Two more weeks, sir? Until . . . well, you can't say, I know. But two more weeks, sir, and I'll be ready to kill them. To kill them all."

Yet that night, as Kemi lay in bed, the nightmares came back full force. She was lying again on the stone slab in the mines, strapped down with sticky tendrils as the centipedes rose above her. They were cutting her, stitching her together, forming a great centipede with many limbs, she and Marco and Lailani forming a single living, screaming organism. She tried to fly her starfighter, to kill the enemy, but she couldn't fit into her cockpit, and she kept laying translucent eggs, and she fell, fell, crashed down into a hive, vanishing until she became a great queen of arthropods. When she woke up, sweat covered her and dampened the sheets, and she could barely breathe.

She rose from bed and stared out the viewport at the stars.

They're out there, she thought. *The scum. Millions of them.*

She swallowed the lump in her throat.

"Kill them," she whispered. "Kill them all. Kill them all." Her tears flowed down her cheeks, and she kept repeating the words as a mantra. "Kill them all."

* * * * *

Einav Ben-Ari stood in a spacesuit on the cold, black surface of Nightwall's rogue planet. She stared down at the grave. Her fists clenched, and she hated that her eyes stung. She hated still being angry at him. Still letting him hurt her.

"You couldn't even be buried on Earth," she said. "You couldn't even give me that, could you?"

She stared at the epitaph on his gravestone. *Colonel Yoram Ben-Ari. Soldier. Husband. Father.*

"Soldier first," Ben-Ari said, lips curling bitterly. "Father last. But were you even that? Were you truly a husband, a father? Or nothing more than a soldier?"

Damn it. Now her tears were on her cheeks, and her helmet was fogging up.

Yes, she knew. He had always been a soldier, nothing more. His father had been nothing but a soldier too, as his father before him--a family of warriors, never putting down roots, not since the scum had destroyed their country fifty years ago, and even before that, the Ben-Aris had dedicated their lives to the wars among men. Once Ben-Ari had confronted him, had shouted, "You love the army more than me!" She still remembered how he had stared at her, how he had not denied it.

Ben-Ari looked away from the grave. She shouldn't have come here. If he had wanted her to visit, he could have chosen a burial on Earth. He hadn't even died here on Nightwall, had died out there in open space in some distant battle, had requested in his will a grave here. Not a grave among flowers and trees. Not a grave in a beautiful place of grass and birds. But here. In space. On a military base. A place where only soldiers could see him.

"Soldiers like me," Ben-Ari said. "Because that's all that I've known. All you ever let me know."

She thought back to her childhood. She had been only a toddler when her mother had died--not from a scum attack, not in battle, but of a bee sting. A fucking bee sting. She had been allergic, had died from a single bee, a shame her father could never forgive. How could he? His family had been dying in great battles for generations--fighting the scum, fighting terrorists, fighting Nazis, fighting the tsar. And his own wife--dead fighting a bee in the garden!

If some men might have left the military after the death of a wife, choosing to raise their daughter, Yoram Ben-Ari had done the opposite. He had dedicated even more time to his career, advancing quickly from captain to major, finally to colonel, a rank few soldiers achieved. He had dragged little Einav from base to base, letting his soldiers babysit her for hours on end. She had spent so much of her childhood in the company of gruff drill sergeants who let her play with bullet casings, decorate artillery shells, and ride on the cannons of tanks. All little Einav had ever wanted was a normal childhood. A house or apartment. A yard or balcony. A school. Not having to leave every few months.

And often her father left her.

For months at a time, he left.

He had never taken his daughter into space, on all his missions. He would go visit wondrous worlds. To negotiate peace with the Guramis, a race of sentient water-dwellers on a distant ocean world. To trade technology with the Silvans, a race of tree-climbers hundreds of light-years away. He would go on these wonderful adventures, see worlds of endless crystals, of trees that soared kilometers high, of underwater worlds of coral forests. And Einav would remain with one babysitter or another. And a month later she would see the photos, get a little gift, then move to another military base in some dusty corner of Earth.

Was it any wonder that, as a youth, Einav would sneak out to drink with solders, to sleep with soldiers in their bunks? That she had run away from her father several times, only for his sergeants to hunt her down and bring her back home, humiliated?

Yes. She had rebelled. Yet when the time had come, when she had turned eighteen, she had joined the military. She had gone to Officer Candidate School. She, a Ben-Ari, the last member of a long military dynasty--she would not be enlisted. No. That would be a shame her father would never forgive, worse by far than the shame of the bee. So Ben-Ari had done her duty. To her father. To her forefathers. To that old shadow box she carried with medals from wars long ago, medals her family had won with blood. She had earned a commission, become an officer, chosen a military career. She, the girl who had never known anything but war, anything but the army--she too had dedicated her life to the military. As an officer, she would remain in the HDF until she retired, would never know another job, another life. And someday, she knew, it would be her duty to marry a soldier, to give birth to future soldiers.

And that last thought made her sick.

"Because I can't be like you were, Father," she said to the grave. "I can't be that kind of parent. I can't bear to see another child live the life I did."

Bitter tears streamed down to her lips. Her father. The man idolized by his troops. The man studied at military academies. The man known on alien worlds as the grand ambassador, the bringer of Earth's gifts of technology and friendship. The man Einav Ben-Ari desperately missed, desperately hated, desperately loved. The man who had died far too young. The man who could have, perhaps, someday made peace with her as he had made peace with alien civilizations. The man who would now rest forever in these shadows of a distant world with no sun.

She turned around. She left the cemetery. She reentered one of the military bases that speckled this planet.

Drying her tears, Ben-Ari made her way to the base's cantina, where she found a vending machine. She bought a Coke, a bag of chips, and a sandwich full of mystery meat that probably predated the Cataclysm. The Coke came in a real glass bottle. Fancy.

She sat at a table with a view of a brick wall and a small television set showing a rerun of Chelsea vs. Barcelona from a couple of Euros ago. Santos scored a goal. Ben-Ari had just opened her bag of chips when a shadow fell, and she looked up to see Gunnery Sergeant Jones approaching her table.

"Mind if I watch the game with you, ma'am?" said the burly NCO. He held a box of french fries.

Ben-Ari gestured at the seat beside her. "Be my guest, but only if you share those fries with me. I think baby scum have gotten into my bag of chips, judging by how much air is in there."

The NCO offered her a fry. "If I may ask, ma'am: How's space treating you?"

On the television set, Alvarez shot on goal but hit the bar.

Ben-Ari smiled weakly. "Just because I'm a butter bar doesn't mean I'm completely clueless in space, you know."

Jones smiled too. "Meaning no disrespect, ma'am, butter bar or not." He glanced at the insignia on her shoulders--her butter bars, the mark of a junior officer. "It's just that . . . Space

Territorial Command can be tough on anyone when they first arrive, from private to general. It's cold up here. It's dark. It's fucking close to the goddamn scum."

"Everywhere is close to the scum these days, Sergeant," she said. "We've had our share of them on Earth too." She sighed. "To answer your question, yes, it's cold. It's dark. And I miss home. But this is the front line. This is where we muster for war. So this is where I'll fight."

Jones nodded. "Earth is worth fighting for. I had a son born just eight months ago, did you know? Never even met the little kid." He shook his head sadly. "But that's who I'm fighting for. My wife and little one. A chance to end this war, go home, and finally be a family."

He showed her a photo of a smiling baby. Ben-Ari stared at it for a long time.

"He's beautiful," she said softly.

"Where are you from on Earth, ma'am?" Jones said. "If you don't mind me asking, that is. I don't mean to pry."

She turned her head and stared out a window across the mess at the stars. "I'm from nowhere," she said. "Nowhere but this place. The HDF. The war. Sometimes I think that if this war ends, I won't know where to go, that . . ."

She paused. Why was she telling him all this? She barely knew Jones. He would be assigned to her new platoon, she knew. He would be her platoon sergeant. He would fight with her, be her second-in-command, her confidant and closest ally, the way

Singh had been her sergeant back with the Dragons. But still, she barely knew this warrior. Why was she spilling her secrets to him?

It was this damn place, she decided. This loneliness. This cold darkness. Her father's grave outside. Ben-Ari had rarely made friends even back on Earth. It was hard to make friends when you were a lieutenant, when every soldier around you was either a subordinate or a commanding officer, when you had to keep your professional distance from your soldiers, even from your sergeants. The curse of the butter bar. And it was even harder here in space. Here at Nightwall, among hundreds of thousands of soldiers, Ben-Ari had never felt more alone. Perhaps, in Jones, she saw something akin to a friend.

Another gift you've given me, Father, she thought. *No childhood friends. Nothing but emptiness.*

Sergeant Jones sensed the awkward silence, it seemed. He pulled a deck of cards from his pocket.

"Do butter bars ever play cards with us NCOs?" he said, smiling. "Or is that sort of like a princess playing hopscotch with her butler?"

"I'm no princess," Ben-Ari said. "Gin rummy?"

Jones nodded. "I'll deal."

He dealt. She cut the deck. They played. They played again. And slowly, Ben-Ari's anger faded, and she was smiling, even laughing. In a few weeks, she knew, the war would flare. They would fly to battle, to death, to devastation in space. But for now, for a few moments, space was a little less cold.

CHAPTER SEVEN

A month after landing at Nightwall, Marco and Addy completed their training--and were summoned at once, still sweaty and winded and reeling, to report to Space Station One.

"Space Station One?" Addy said, wiping her forehead. "Us?"

Marco walked beside her. They were hurrying down one of the massive tunnels that snaked beneath the surface of the rogue planet. Both wore their new pins on their lapels, showing the sigil of the STC. Both wore new STC service uniforms, rather than the combat fatigues they had worn in training. Their trousers and blazers were navy blue, the brass buttons polished, and beaked caps topped their heads. It was the nicest set of clothes Marco had ever worn. He felt like he was walking toward a wedding . . . or a funeral.

"What's Space Station One?" Marco said.

Addy raised an eyebrow. "Um, only the most important space station in the galaxy, Poet. That's where the generals work. It's like the Pentagon of space. It's like the Castle Grayskull of the army. It's like the Autobots' headquarters in the mountain with all the Dinobots buried underneath. Why the hell do they want *us* there? And why didn't they give us time to even have one fucking beer first?"

Marco wasn't sure. They had completed their training only today, officially becoming Space Territorial Command warriors. He had expected at least a night of relaxation: a couple of beers, a movie in the lounge, a good meal, a proper night's sleep. Even after completing basic training on Earth, a far humbler achievement, they had partied for a night. But moments ago, the urgent summons had arrived.

Corporal Marco Emery. Corporal Addy Linden. Report at once to Room 103, Level 7, Space Station One. Service uniforms required.

"Do you reckon they want to interrogate us again?" Marco said as they walked through the labyrinthine tunnels.

"They probably want to court-martial you for that time you clogged up the toilet," Addy said.

"That wasn't me!" Marco bristled.

"Yeah, yeah." Addy patted his head. "And I don't need my gas mask after they serve you cheese in the mess."

"I need my gas mask whenever you take your boots off in the bunks," he said. "That's worse than scum miasma."

"Good, maybe I'll poison you with my feet tonight." Addy nodded. "I'll finally be rid of you."

Marco groaned, but this felt good. This was like the old days, like how they'd bicker back home in the library. This was a little bit of comfort, a bit of banter to hold back the fear. And Marco saw that Addy was afraid too, saw the twitching fingers, the nervous biting of her lip, the way she tugged her hair.

They found their way to a space elevator, this one connected to Space Station One, a different station than the one they had first docked at. They spent a nervous hour in the round, transparent elevator cab, climbing hundreds of kilometers up into space. During the ascent, Marco kept looking around him, trying to count the number of starships orbiting the rogue planet. There were thousands here now, maybe tens of thousands. He had never imagined that humanity had so many. A massive army was mustering here, one to dwarf the fleets from the days of the Cataclysm.

This army could have fed millions of poor children, Marco thought. *It could have housed every homeless person on Earth. It could have rebuilt the world, a world still in the Cataclysm's shadow.* And it seemed to Marco that there were two tragedies to this war. There was the tragedy of lives lost. And there was the tragedy of lives left to languish.

They reached Space Station One and navigated its corridors. Marco had never seen so many officers in one place before. Officers were rare in every other base he had been to, but here they were everywhere. And not just young lieutenants like Ben-Ari either, but many older officers with gray hair, stars instead of bars on their shoulders.

They found their way to the seventh level, then to room 103. They entered to see a war room with fifty other soldiers already here, all in blue service uniforms. Only two faces were familiar to Marco. He recognized Gunnery Sergeant Jones, the man who had trained him for the past month. And he recognized his old platoon leader, Lieutenant Einav Ben-Ari, whom he hadn't seen since arriving at Nightwall. She too, it seemed, had completed her integration into the space corps, judging by her new uniform and the pin on her lapel. The others were all sergeants and staff sergeants, seasoned warriors.

Marco was of average size, but he felt like a child here. Aside from Ben-Ari, everyone here was massive. They all seemed to tower a foot taller than Marco. They all had bulging muscles. He didn't see any soldiers here as awkward as Caveman or Jackass, nor as small as Lailani. Everyone here seemed like . . . well, *superheroes* was the word that sprang to mind. It was as if he'd wandered into a room full of Captain Americas and Wonder Women, great heroes and amazons. Marco felt woefully small and young here, a mere scrawny librarian in a chamber full of superhuman G.I. Joes.

Marco and Addy saluted the lieutenant. "Ma'am," Marco said. "Reporting for duty." He looked around him, still unsure what this was all about.

"All right, we're all here," said Ben-Ari, looking at the group. "Welcome to your new unit. Welcome to Spearhead Platoon. Every one of you was handpicked for this elite unit. You will be taking part in a highly classified, highly dangerous, and highly important mission. Every one of you is here because you exemplify qualities the HDF is looking for in this mission."

Marco glanced at his fellow soldiers, then back at Ben-Ari. "Ma'am," he said, "Corporal Linden and I weren't briefed. What mission are we to undertake?"

"You will learn when the time is right, Corporal," said Lieutenant Ben-Ari.

"Will we be part of the invasion of Abaddon, ma'am?" Addy said. "Everyone's saying there will be an invasion, and--"

"Soldiers, silence!" rumbled Sergeant Jones. "You will receive more information when we see fit to share it. For now your task is to be brutally motivated to kick scum ass. That's all you need to know. And if you stray out of line, it'll be me kicking your asses."

Ben-Ari stared across the platoon. "We don't have much time to train together. We will split into three squads. Each squad will be commanded by a staff sergeant. Each squad commander will report to Gunnery Sergeant Jones, who will report to me. The next few days will not be easy. You will train hard together. You will train harder than you've ever trained. You will get to know your comrades' strengths--and weaknesses, if you can find them. Once our mission arrives, it will be critical that we can work together as a team. Do not take this responsibility lightly."

Marco glanced around him, but the other soldiers simply stared ahead, silently accepting their fate. Nausea filled Marco. What mission? What danger? Why was Ben-Ari revealing nothing? And why the hell was he chosen to serve in this group of superhero commandos?

"Staff Sergeant Bellet!" Ben-Ari said. "Step forward. You will be commanding Squad One."

One of the soldiers stepped toward the lieutenant. She sported a mohawk, tattoos across her hands and neck, and a smirk. "Yes, ma'am!"

"I'll read the names of your soldiers," said Ben-Ari, and she went on to read fifteen names--Marco and Addy among them. Both stepped forward to form rank behind Sergeant Bellet. Two more staff sergeants were called next, both beefy men with jaws like slabs of stone. Each took command of a squad. It reminded Marco of his platoon back at basic: three squads, one officer, one platoon sergeant. But everyone here was a rank or two higher.

No privates allowed, he thought. *Only experienced warriors.* Even as corporals, no longer green privates, he and Addy were the lowest-ranking soldiers here.

"Now follow me," Ben-Ari said. "Our training begins."

They walked through the space station and entered a locker room. They changed into black combat fatigues, then entered a gymnasium where they donned virtual reality helmets. For hours they trained through various simulations. They ran across a dry, alien landscape, the sun beating down on them, leaping over canyons, battling thousands of scum. They crawled through tunnels, firing at the nightmarish creatures. They delved into deep caves, battling towering monstrosities, each thirty meters tall. These were just simulations, of course. Just games, just images in their virtual reality helmets. But Marco could barely tell reality from dreams these days. It all seemed too real, even the stench the helmets produced whenever he fired into the creatures, shattering them, and as he fought, he found himself screaming, howling in fury and terror, and by the time the day ended, he was panting, tears on his cheeks.

I can't do this, he thought when he finally removed his helmet. He fell to his knees on the gym floor. *I can't fight again. I can't keep seeing this death.*

"On your feet, Emery!" Sergeant Bellet shouted, and Marco reluctantly stood up. They all shuffled out of the gym, sweaty, winded, and into the showers. Marco stood for a long time under the hot streams of water, staring blankly at the wall ahead of him. Addy was talking to him, but he couldn't hear. He was back in the simulation. He was back in the mines of Corpus. He was back at Fort Djemila. He was back in the snow on the day his mother had died. The hot water burned him. He couldn't feel it.

That night, the soldiers stretched out on their bunks, each squad sharing one room full of fifteen beds. Everyone fell asleep at once, but Marco left the chamber. He walked down the corridor until he reached Ben-Ari's bunk, a room she slept in by herself.

He hesitated for a moment. His eyes stung. The screams still filled his eyes.

He knocked on the door.

"Corporal Emery!" he said. "Reporting!"

After a moment of silence--"Come in."

He opened the door and saluted. He was surprised to see that Lieutenant Ben-Ari wasn't in uniform. She wore gray sweatpants and a white T-shirt. Pajamas. Her hair wasn't in a ponytail but flowed across her shoulders. It was strange to see her this way. As a person. A woman. Not just an officer. He was struck by how young she looked, only in her early twenties. In any other reality--just a girl.

"Corporal?" she said.

He closed the door behind him. Her bunk was small, containing just a bed, a desk, a chair.

Marco couldn't stop his damn eyes from stinging.

"Ma'am," he said, "I've come to request a transfer. I've come to ask to leave your new platoon. I don't belong in the Spearhead. Please, ma'am, allow me to transfer to another unit. A noncombat unit. I can work in the archives. I can guard. I can mop floors. I can clean latrines. I just can't fight anymore. I can't."

She looked at him in silence. "Marco, come. Sit with me." They sat together on the bed, and she continued in a soft voice. "I need you for this, Marco. I need my best soldier."

"I'm not your best soldier, ma'am," he said. "I'm not a warrior. Maybe I can be a good soldier doing something else, but--"

"You fought well in Corpus. In Djemila. You survived!"

He nodded, and now he couldn't stop his eyes from dampening. "I survived and everyone else died, and I can still hear them screaming. I can't see more death, ma'am. I can't. I can't. I feel so guilty that I'm still alive. I can't bear to even train for battle, let alone fight another battle. I think I have post-traumatic stress disorder. I think I need to see a psychiatrist, to get help. Please, ma'am. Let me leave."

He saw the pain that filled her eyes, saw the sadness in her smile. She placed a hand on his knee. "Marco, we all have PTSD. Every one of us. I do. Addy does. I bet half the people on Earth do. This is a brutal war that has broken us all. But we must remain strong. We must still fight."

"You won't even tell us what battle we're fighting," Marco said. "What our secret mission is."

"You will learn soon," she said. "I promise."

He rose to his feet. "I don't care what the mission is, ma'am. If you've appreciated my service up till now, grant me this request. Transfer me out of your platoon."

Her eyes hardened, and she stood up too. She stared at him steadily. "No," she said.

"No? Ma'am, I--"

"No," she repeated. "This isn't civilian life. You don't get to make your own choices here. None of us do. I need you, Corporal Emery. I need you perhaps more than anyone else in the Spearhead Platoon. You are integral for this mission. Nobody can replace you. You will understand when the time comes. You may not leave. My answer is no. Now leave my chamber. Go sleep. Training resumes tomorrow. Dismissed."

He left the chamber, eyes burning, rage flaring inside him.

No. No.

He clenched his fists as he walked back to his chamber.

No. No!

How had he ever thought of Ben-Ari as his friend? As a wise, kind leader? How could she refuse him? How could she condemn him to this pain after he had revealed how broken he was?

No!

Tears burned on his cheeks. He paused for a moment outside the bunk to dry them, then took a deep, shaky breath. He stepped back inside. Everyone was already asleep, and Marco lay on his bunk, fists still clenched, and when he finally slept, he was back in training, running again across the desert, the sun burning him, his friends dying all around.

CHAPTER EIGHT

For two weeks, they trained with their virtual reality helmets.

For two weeks, Sergeant Bellet led Squad One onward through swarms of scum on a desert world. For two weeks, they plunged through tunnels into the depths of the underground. They battled virtual scum. They battled massive monsters the size of dragons in underground halls. In simulation after simulation, they died. Scum claws tore them apart. Miasma burned off their skin. Tunnels collapsed, crushing them. Centipede scientists tortured them. Day after day, in their simulated world, they suffered brutal injuries, only to remove their virtual reality helmets, pant and shiver and spit, then start again.

Still Ben-Ari said nothing of the purpose of their training.

They were to invade Abaddon, the homeworld of the scum. They knew that much. But so would millions of other troops. The platoon's role in the invasion remained a secret.

When two weeks ended, the order came to dress in their service uniforms, the fine blue garments with the brass buttons. Prim, proper, and polished, the platoon walked through Space Station One, following their lieutenant. Marco wasn't sure where they were heading, but at least it wouldn't be for training, not in these uniforms, for which he was grateful. The past two weeks had left a deep weariness inside him, a near catatonic state of emotions, a deadness inside. Every week in the military, it seemed, was worse than the one before.

As they passed by a viewport, Marco saw more ships than ever floating outside, countless vessels. The invasion of the scum's empire was near, maybe only hours away.

The entire platoon stepped into a round, carpeted chamber deep within the space station. They stood in silence. They waited. There were no windows here, no monitors, just a large round table in the center of the room. And mostly silence. Marco wanted to speak, to ask what was happening, but a nervous tension filled the air. He stood among the others. When he glanced at Addy, she raised her eyebrows, gave him the smallest of shrugs, and worded, "I dunno."

A signal beeped. Sergeant Jones touched his headpiece, then nodded, stepped toward the doorway, and cried out, "Attention!"

Across the room, all fifty soldiers pressed heels together and squared their shoulders. The door opened, and a tall, white-haired officer entered the room.

Marco couldn't help but widen his eyes. The old officer sported two phoenixes on each shoulder. A two-phoenix general! It was the second-highest rank in the military, junior only to the Commander-in-Chief. Marco had never seen a higher rank than colonel up close before. He had always imagined colonels ranking somewhere between Jesus and God. But a general made a colonel seem as lowly as a private. There were only a handful of two-phoenix generals in the entire Human Defense Force, Marco knew. If junior officers like Ben-Ari could command a platoon of fifty warriors, generals could command millions, *tens* of millions of troops, orchestrating entire wars. If the Queen of England herself had entered the room, Marco would not have felt more awe.

"Hello, everyone, and at ease," said the general. "After hearing so much about you, it's lovely to meet you all. My name is Admiral Evan Bryan."

They had all trained under the harshest discipline, but now Marco saw the eyes widen, heard the stifled gasps. Evan Bryan? It seemed impossible. A practical joke. Perhaps just a man with an identical name. Evan Bryan was the pilot who, fifty years ago, had flown the only starfighter to make it past the scum's defenses. The hero who had lobbed a nuclear weapon against Abaddon, killing millions of scum and ending the Cataclysm, ushering in the long War of Attrition. Evan Bryan's face adorned posters in half the bedrooms in the world, smiled from mugs, T-shirts, video games. Hollywood's best actors vied to play him in movies. Children and even adults collected his action figures, dressed up as him for Halloween, or played Evan Bryan Taskforce online. It was always the same face, taken from the same photograph, showing a smiling, handsome young man, twenty-one years old, a twinkle in his eye.

When Marco looked at the silvery-haired admiral, he saw the same twinkle, the same smile.

It's him, he realized. *The living legend--it's him. He's seventy-one years old now and an admiral, but here stands Evan Bryan, the hero of Earth. Here in our presence!*

"It's really him!" Addy whispered, eyes so wide they looked ready to fall from their sockets. "Ethan Brandon!"

"Evan Bryan," Marco whispered to her. "Shush!"

The admiral came to stand by the round table--right by Marco and Addy. Marco's head spun. He hadn't even realized that Evan Bryan was still alive, had always imagined that the hero had died years ago. He could scarcely believe this wasn't a dream. This man, standing only a few feet away, had flown a small, damaged starfighter--back from the days when Earth barely even had the technology to build proper starfighters--and nuked the scum homeworld. It was like standing by a Napoleon, by a Yuri Gagarin, by a Churchill.

"All right, all right," said Admiral Bryan. "Put your eyes back in your sockets, all of you, and pull your jaws off the floor. We summoned you here for serious business, not for you to gawk." Yet as he spoke, a crooked smile creased his face, and he actually made eye contact with Marco and gave a small wink.

An awkward chuckle passed across the room. The soldiers all relaxed, a few still rubbing their eyes. Only Lieutenant Ben-Ari and Gunnery Sergeant Jones didn't seem shocked. Both stared ahead with grave eyes.

"You're probably wondering why you're all here," said Admiral Bryan. "First a little background." He hit a control on the round table, and a hologram appeared above it, showing a familiar location: the moon Corpus orbiting the planet Indrani. "Two months ago, Captain Coleen Petty of the Erebus Brigade, flying aboard the HDFS *Miyari*, led an infantry company into the mining installation at Corpus, answering a distress call. On that moon, we encountered a hive of *scolopendra titania* where the aliens were conducting genetic experimentations on human captives. The *scolopendra titania* had created hybrids, fusing human and alien DNA, and producing more hybrids using a human-hybrid queen."

Marco shuddered to remember the queen he had seen in the mine, a creature formed from a woman's torso and a massive scum queen's abdomen. He still saw that creature most nights in his dreams. The creature he himself had killed. He still woke up drenched with cold sweat from those nightmares.

Admiral Bryan continued speaking. "Captain Petty fell on that planet, along with most of her company. Lieutenant Ben-Ari led the platoon that slew the alien queen, then slew the king of the hive on the gas giant nearby. With her fought Corporal Emery and Corporal Linden, who are here among us today." He gestured at Marco and Addy, and all eyes turned toward them. Addy beamed and puffed out her chest, but Marco didn't savor the attention. He didn't want to remember those days.

"Thank you, thank you, autographs later," Addy said, incurring a glare from Sergeant Jones.

"As you all know," said Admiral Bryan, "the enemy launched a terrifying retaliation. They destroyed Vancouver, killing half a million people, soldiers and civilians alike." His eyes hardened. "It was a massacre we will never forget. Since

Vancouver's destruction, the scum have only increased their hostility, launching smaller attacks on cities across the globe. The doctrine of mutually assured destruction, which has remained in place for fifty years, has ended. Since the fall of Vancouver, we have been mustering our forces. A fleet has gathered here at Nightwall. Other fleets gathered around our other outposts on the frontier. We prepare for an invasion of Abaddon itself."

The hologram over the table changed, now showing a tan, rocky planet, covered in craters and canyons and mountains. Marco didn't need to read the caption to recognize it. Here was Abaddon, homeworld of the scum.

"My friends," said Bryan, "this will be the largest invasion in the history of mankind. This will dwarf even the invasion of Normandy two hundred years ago. We're going to send everything we've got to this planet. Tens of thousands of starships. Tens of thousands of starfighters. Three million soldiers of the STC, and with them, millions of Earth soldiers who are coming to offer extra manpower. We're hitting the enemy with everything we've got, with every last bullet in our arsenal. Our purpose is one: To finally end this horrible war. To finally defeat the scum, once and for all."

An awed silence, followed by a low murmur, filled the room. Finally it was Addy who raised her hand.

"But sir!" she said. "Isn't the idea of mutually assured destruction that, well . . . if we completely destroy them, they completely destroy us? If we hit them with everything we've got, won't they just destroy every city on Earth, like they did to Vancouver?"

"They will certainly try," said Admiral Bryan. "Over the past several years, we've secretly been developing a new defense system for Earth, and we feel we're finally ready to activate it."

The hologram switched to show a vision of Earth. Thousands of rockets launched from the planet, raising thousands of satellites into orbit. The hologram zoomed in on one satellite, revealing it to be, in fact, a manned cannon. Three soldiers sat inside, and the gun stretched out toward space.

"We call this system the Iron Sphere," said Admiral Bryan. "As our attack on Abaddon commences, Iron Sphere will be activated. Thousands of gun turrets will circle Earth as satellites, providing complete coverage of all major cities. As soon as scum vessels approach . . ." The hologram showed a cannon firing, destroying a scum pod. "In all our tests, Iron Sphere has a ninety-eight percent success rate. We believe that we can stop nearly all the scum vessels sent to retaliate against us. We can now defend the Earth from space itself like never before. It gives us the security--and the time--we need to complete our mission."

Marco did calculations in his mind, then raised his hand. "Sir, there are five billion people living on Earth. If we can save ninety-eight percent of them, that means that . . ." He thought for a moment. "A hundred million will still die. That's two percent, isn't it? A hundred million. That's like two hundred Vancouvers, sir. That's worse than the Second World War."

They all stared around the room. Lieutenant Ben-Ari frowned at him, and in her eyes, he saw her warning: *Do not question the admiral.*

But Admiral Bryan did not seem to anger. Sadness filled his eyes. "That is the sacrifice we must make. That is the sacrifice that will always burden my shoulders. But I think too of the alternative. If we allow the *scolopendra titania* to continue their war against us, how many more generations will be terrorized? How many more cities will fall? I have seven grandchildren, two of them old enough to soon join the military, to fight in a horrible war. I do not want my great-grandchildren to suffer the same fate. I do not want billions of humans to keep living in fear, to wear gas masks, to live running from bomb shelter to bomb shelter. The enemy grows bolder. If they destroyed Vancouver, they will not hesitate to destroy more cities, perhaps with years in between each assault, throttling their terror just enough to hold our full retaliation at bay. We cannot allow this to continue. We must strike now. We must suffer horrible losses now. We must watch millions die now. And we must win this war."

"We will win," said Addy.

"We will win!" repeated others in the room.

Marco remained silent. Vancouver had been a major escalation, but this . . . this felt like the Cataclysm again. He wanted to speak out, to urge peace, but perhaps Admiral Bryan was right. Perhaps there could be no peace with the scum. Or perhaps . . . perhaps the man who had first nuked the scum was making this personal. Perhaps Bryan wanted to finally finish the job for his own glory, his own bloodlust. Marco didn't know. Too many conflicting feelings filled him now. And many of Bryan's words did ring true. If Marco ever had children, grandchildren, he didn't want them to suffer as he had suffered, to grow up in war, to join the army at eighteen.

Maybe Bryan is right. Maybe this is the only way to finally end this horror.

"Sir," he finally said, "why us? Why are we here?" He looked around the room at the fifty soldiers, most of them strangers. "What is our mission?"

"As I said earlier, I handpicked every one of you myself," said Admiral Bryan. "I chose soldiers who had fought in scum hives before. Who had delved deep underground to face their kings and queens. Each one of you has fought battles beyond what other soldiers have. Some of you fought on Corpus. Others fought in other hives. All of you have survived where thousands of other soldiers perished."

"You want us to enter another hive, sir," Marco said.

Admiral Bryan hit a button on the table controls, and the hologram switched back to the dry, rocky Abaddon. The images now showed thousands of tunnels burrowing deep into the dry planet.

"Within Abaddon," Bryan said, "in tunnels many kilometers deep, lurks the emperor of the *scolopendra titania.* We do not know what he looks like. No human has ever seen an image of a *scolopendra titania* emperor. But we know that the emperor controls all his drones, all the hives of scum across the galaxy, using a complex system of communication we don't yet fully understand. Every single centipede in the galaxy, we believe, is connected to this vast network--the network controlled by the emperor."

"A sort of internet for scum," said Addy. "Scumternet."

Admiral Bryan nodded. "And it has a single point of failure. There are many scum kings, one per hive, but only one scum emperor. If we can take out the emperor, the network will die. Scum hives across the galaxy will detach from the rest of their civilization. The scum empire will crumble. We believe that emperors are thousands of years old, that it might take thousands of years for the *scolopendra titania* to recover from the loss of their current leader. We're going to land millions of soldiers on the surface of Abaddon, and most will engage with fighting the enemy on the surface. But one team will delve on a commando mission deep underground--to find the emperor himself." Bryan swept his gaze across the platoon. "You were handpicked to form this team. You will kill the scum emperor. The hope of humanity rests on your shoulders."

A moment of tense silence filled the room.

"But no pressure, right?" Addy said.

"Watch it, Linden," warned Jones.

"We've code-named your mission Operation Odin's Spear," said Admiral Bryan, "and we've named your new platoon the Spearhead. Lieutenant Ben-Ari will lead you, as she led the platoon on Corpus, and Sergeant Jones will assist her. I myself will oversee the fleet from our flagship, the HDFS *Terra*, but I will remain in constant contact with Ben-Ari and Jones. You will at all times have access to all the intelligence of the HDF--as well as our support, our pride, and our prayers."

Prayers, Marco thought. Perhaps it came down to that now. It all seemed so surreal, just a dream, like that night with Addy--an impossibility. *I'm only a librarian. Not even a writer. How has it come to this? How am I here, tasked with saving the world?*

Admiral Bryan was watching him, Marco realized. The silvery-haired man spoke softly. "It's not easy being a hero. I learned that fifty years ago. I'm here to help you. You will do this."

"Sir," said Marco, "I'm afraid. I probably shouldn't admit this in front of the others, but yes, I'm afraid." He inhaled deeply. "But I will also fight. Because you're right, sir. This must be done. We must win. So I will give it all that I can."

"I'll give more!" Addy said.

The admiral nodded, and a spark of amusement filled his blue eyes.

"I'm sure you will, warriors," the admiral said, and when Marco glanced toward Ben-Ari, the lieutenant gave him the slightest of nods.

Thank you, Marco, her eyes said. *I'm proud of you.*

Marco looked back at the admiral. "Sir, a question if I may. When we fought on Corpus, the hive was massive. A labyrinth underground. We only found our way because Cadet Abasi had been connected to the scum network. She had spent time in their lab, tubes running into her veins. Once we freed her, she could still sense the hive. She led us on the right paths. That's how we found the queen. Sir, the tunnels on Abaddon itself must be far more complex. How will we find our way to the emperor?"

Admiral Bryan stared into Marco's eyes. "You will have a guide. There is one soldier in our army--one among millions--who can connect into the scum's imperial hive. Who can sense all their pheromones, read all their messages, travel all their paths. She will lead you through the tunnels of Abaddon." He turned toward the doorway, and his voice softened, seemed tinged with sadness. "Enter, friend."

Clad in navy blue, Lailani entered the room.

CHAPTER NINE

As soon as they returned to her bunk, Marco laughed, raised Lailani into the air, and embraced her.

"Lailani!" He placed her down. "Are you all right? Did they hurt you?"

The other Spearhead Platoon soldiers were in their own bunks, though Lailani was kept separate. Her chamber was small and austere, the floor carpeted, and a tall window afforded a view of the fleet gathering outside. The place looked far more comfortable than a typical army bunk, but Marco noticed the camera mounted by the ceiling, staring down at the room with a cold black eye.

"I'm fine," Lailani said. "They didn't hurt me. They mostly showed me images and asked questions. Hour after hour, somebody sat right here--" She pointed at a chair. "And he showed me pictures of bugs. Lots of different kinds, some centipedes, others strange creatures I can't name. And he asked me the strangest questions. If I had seen them before. What they smell like. What colors they are. They were always black or brown or yellow, but he kept insisting I felt for other colors. And . . ." She shuddered. "They did things to my brain."

Lailani turned around and lifted strands of her short hair. Marco could see a scar on her skull.

"My God," he whispered.

"I'm not sure what they did," Lailani said. "I suppose they were checking for bugs in there." She gave a wan smile.

"But . . . they healed you, right?" They sat on her bed together, and Marco held her hands. "They cured whatever was inside you, didn't they? The . . . the scum?"

"Kind of. I think." Lailani chewed her lip. "They ran lots of tests on me. They even plugged stuff into my brain while I slept to record my dreams. And they collected all sorts of cells--blood, bone, skin, even a few tiny brain cells. I just hope I'm still a genius!" She made a face, cheeks puffed out, eyes crossed, and tongue thrust out. "Anyway, they said I'm almost completely human."

"Almost?" Marco asked.

Lailani nodded. "See, they were worried that my father was a scum. As if a giant centipede boned a woman and she gave birth to me. But it turns out I didn't even have a father. Sort of like Jesus. Immaculate conception! The scientists think that the scum took human sperm but changed it just a tad. Altered the DNA just by one percent, then impregnated my mother with it, maybe using a human clone. I'm ninety-nine percent human and one percent alien."

"That's not bad," Marco said. "That's almost entirely human." He breathed a sigh of relief. He too had wondered if Lailani were half scum, had almost imagined some lewd scene of a centipede copulating with a woman. "But why did the scum do this?"

"Well, that one percent of me that's scum? That's mostly the part that lets me connect to the scum hive. To smell them. To hear their commands. To feel colors. See, the scum don't communicate like we do. They barely use sight or sound. They mostly use a sort of strange Spidey sense, something that's hard to describe. It's beyond human senses. The closest thing I can compare it to is sense of smell, but that's not a fair comparison. Our human sense of smell is so limited. But the scum can detect chemicals that convey massive amounts of information. They can manage huge networks across entire hives, across their entire empire, just using these chemicals they can detect. It's how they communicate. They can even communicate across star systems, sending their pheromones through a network of wormholes the width of several atoms. It's really like a giant, stinky internet they're all plugged into. When I was on the *Miyari*, when I went bad, it's because the scum hacked into me through that network. Sort of how a human hacker might seize control of a computer across the internet. And they were able to give me commands, to control my movements. The scientists think the scum have done this to many other humans already, creating drones across Earth and the fleet, ready to strike."

Marco shuddered. "So anyone can be a scum agent. Anyone can sabotage the fleet from within."

Lailani nodded. "Anyone! The HDF is going to start testing everyone. They developed a test--they used it on me--to see if any other humans have that one percent part of their brain be scum. Anyone who's missing one or both parents is a candidate."

"But is that part still there?" Marco asked. "Can the scum still hack you?"

Lailani tapped her skull. "Not anymore! They planted a chip in my brain to block out scum commands. I can even feel it when I lie down. It's right against the inside of my skull. It's very small, just the size of a fingernail, but it releases a sort of chemical that blocks external commands from getting in. They say they'll have to change it to a fresh one in a few years." She grimaced. "I'm not looking forward to more surgery. They had to cut my skull open." She shuddered. "Oh, but the good news? I can still reach out! I can connect to the hive myself. I can read them, but they can't read me."

Marco understood. "So you've become a double agent."

"Sort of," Lailani said. "We trained. A lot! They took me to an actual scum hive, Marco. A hive on an asteroid a light-year from here--an empty one, abandoned years ago. And they had me run drills. They had me connect to the scum network, all the way across space. I could sense it even from the asteroid, because the place still stank of the scum. And I was able to navigate through the hive as if a map were in my brain. Sort of how Kemi was able to do it back on Corpus. Except Kemi only knew one hive. I can access information about *all* hives. So they took me to a second hive, this one on a desert world with a few real scum still inside. And we ran the test there too. And again, I could connect to the scumternet--that's what I call it--and find my way through. But the aliens were unable to stop me, unable to control me. Sometimes the chip in my brain would sting so much! That's when I knew they were trying to hack into my brain again. But they couldn't. It made me feel dizzy and nauseated, but it soon passed. So guess what? I can hack into them, but they can't hack into me. I'm now the greatest weapon in the HDF, Admiral Bryan says. Even greater than a starfighter carrier, according to him."

Marco wasn't sure he liked the idea of Lailani turned into a weapon, of her being sent deep into scum hives.

"Lailani . . ." He tightened his grip on her hands. "You realize what they want to do, right? They call it Operation Odin's Spear. They want to send you into the biggest scum hive in the cosmos, the one on Abaddon itself. They want you to lead our platoon to the scum emperor."

"I know," Lailani said. "My God, Marco, they asked me so many questions about the emperor. What he looks like. What he's planning. But I don't know. He's cloaked. I can feel his presence deep inside Abaddon. If I reach out now, I can do it again! But there's a shadow always around him. I don't know what he looks like, his size, his mind. There's a giant firewall around him. But I think I can find his location. It's like finding a black hole. You follow the darkness."

"Follow the darkness," Marco said. "We seem to be good at that."

Lailani leaned her head against his shoulder. "I thought of you a lot. It helped me. When they made me look at bugs, I thought of you."

He couldn't help but grin. "So bugs remind you of me?"

"No, silly!" She poked him. "You made me feel better. I missed you."

"I missed you too," he said. "I was worried I'd never see you again." He wrapped his arms around her. "Glad to have you back, little one."

"I can tell." She patted his crotch. "Unless you sneaked me in a banana."

His cheeks flushed. To hide them, he kissed her. She pulled off her shirt, then tossed it over the camera on the wall. The rest of their clothes followed.

"Fuck, I missed you," she whispered as he lay atop her.

As they made love, Marco felt a twinge of guilt, and he thought back to that one desperate night with Addy, that night when they had both been so afraid, had both sought comfort in each other. They had vowed not to speak of that night again, had vowed to forget it had ever happened. As Lailani moaned beneath him, burying her hands in his hair, he forgot about Addy, forgot about the looming invasion, forgot about everything but Lailani.

"Love you," he whispered, lying by her side as they gazed out the window at the floating fleet.

"Ruv ya," she said, then frowned. "Hey, I covered the camera, but . . . you suppose all those starships outside got a view?"

Marco cringed. "Oh God. I hope not. It's bad enough having public showers."

"It's all right." She patted his backside. "You got a cute butt. Flaunt it if you got it!"

"Looks who's talking!" He gave her a squeeze, and she squealed.

They fell asleep in each other's arms, and nobody came to remove the shirt from the camera. For one night, Marco did not dream. For one night, with all the terror and grief, there was a little bit of joy.

* * * * *

The next morning, a summons arrived for Marco to report to the Dome--the massive, transparent globe that topped Space Station One, the very heart of Nightwall, indeed of all Space Territorial Command.

Still in Lailani's bunk, he stared at the summons in numb disbelief. The letters floated across his helmet's visor on the floor, beeping.

The Dome. It was like being asked to report to the White House Situation Room.

And they want me there.

Marco felt queasy.

He looked at Lailani. She still lay in bed beside him, looking up at him, and gods above, she was beautiful, and gods above, he didn't want to leave her, and by those damn gods, this couldn't be good.

"Is it because I spent the night with you, the greatest weapon in the HDF arsenal?" he asked.

"It's probably because I turned you into a scum," Lailani said. "Prepare to grow centipede legs any second."

"Very funny, Miss Ninety-Nine Percent Human." He pulled on his uniform--the service uniform, the navy blue one with the brass buttons. Somehow approaching the Dome in his worn-out black combat fatigues didn't seem wise. Hell, he felt like he needed a tuxedo for this task.

He left Lailani in the bunk and took the elevator up through the levels of Space Station One. The station was shaped like a mushroom: a huge disk growing atop a lengthy stalk. Atop the disk, like an eye, rose a bulb. Marco had to pass through several security checks, locked doors, pat downs, finger scans, and eye retina scans before being allowed through. He finally entered the Dome.

And a dome indeed it was, completely transparent. The disk--the top of the space station--was visible all around, a plateau of metal and light. Above spread the fleet, hovering among the stars.

A lone figure stood in the room, his back to Marco, staring out through the transparent globe at several floating warships. His hair was silvery, and two phoenixes shone on each of his shoulder straps.

Marco pressed his heels together and saluted. Struggling to keep his voice steady, he called out, "Corporal Marco Emery, reporting!"

Admiral Evan Bryan, the hero of the Cataclysm, the great commander of this fleet, turned toward him. The old man returned the salute.

"Hello, Marco. Come, stand here with me. Gaze with me at the stars."

Marco approached and the two men stood together, a nineteen-year-old corporal and a seventy-one-year-old admiral and living legend, watching the stars.

"Marco, have you heard of Operation Neptune? Sometimes known as D-Day?"

Marco nodded. "Of course, sir. The Normandy Landings. It was one of the greatest naval invasions in history."

"Back then, of course, we didn't know how to reach the stars. Even satellites were beyond our technology. It would be a few more years before Yuri Gagarin launched into space, before Neil Armstrong walked on the moon, before Pat Szabo walked on Mars. Back in those days, when humanity fought itself, building a warship to sail on the seas was a complicated, expensive endeavor. The greatest warships of the era were marvels of military might and technology, each one an achievement, each one a miracle of engineering and human spirit. The Allies had a billion people on their side, and every soldier and civilian did his or her part for the war. The great admirals of the day landed in Normandy with nearly seven thousand ships. Seven thousand! And with them flew over ten thousand airplanes, and they landed over a million warriors on the shores of France. Half our planet, young Marco, dedicated itself to saving the world from the other half, and they put all their resources into destroying the enemy. It was among mankind's noblest, yet bloodiest, hours."

"I've read many books about the Second World War, sir. It was the largest war humankind knew until the scum attacked."

"Our population grew rapidly after that war," said Admiral Bryan. "From two and a half billion during World War Two, we grew and grew. When the scum first attacked, ten billion of us lived on Earth. And six billion of us died. I was a young man then, not much older than you are now. I still remember the heat, the light, the tidal waves, the long nuclear winter. I remember the collapse of civilizations. But I remember too nobility. I remember us banding together, rising like a phoenix from the ashes." He touched the golden phoenix on his lapel, sigil of the Human Defense Force. "And now again every soldier and civilian is dedicated to the war effort, to defeating the enemy, to ushering in hope. We do not crave war. We do not crave bloodshed. We love life. We love freedom. And so we gather this fleet, and we prepare to fight. A hundred thousand starships will begin their flight tomorrow, Marco, from single-pilot Firebirds to warships the size of towns. Within their hulls, they will transport ten million marines. It is the greatest single army mankind has ever mustered--greater than D-Day, greater than the Mongol invasions, greater than Operation Barbarossa. We have named our invasion Operation Jupiter. Long before we named a planet Jupiter, he was a god of the sky, and we will invade through the sky the way the brave Allies sailed through the sea in Operation Neptune long ago. This is humanity's greatest and most perilous hour. It is this hour that we will overcome . . . or we will fall."

"Do you think we'll overcome, sir?" Marco asked.

Admiral Bryan looked at him, his gaze somber. "I don't know. Marco, it is likely that we will fail. It is likely that the Iron Sphere defense system will collapse under the scum's retaliation. It is likely that our fleet will shatter in Abaddon's orbit. It is likely that your platoon will perish underground. But I believe that we stand a chance. I believe that our courage, our strength, our determination is enough. Does that comfort you?"

"Sir," Marco said, "I asked Lieutenant Ben-Ari for a transfer. I told her that I didn't want this mission. She refused to let me leave, but now I see that there's no other way. There's no retreat. We must win. I don't know how strong I am, how brave I am. But I don't doubt my determination."

"That is the best quality a soldier can have," said Bryan. "Strength can falter. Courage can wane. But a determined soldier marches on." He gave Marco a sly look. "And apparently sneaks into a highly secure, sensitive chamber and tosses a shirt over a security camera."

Marco's cheeks flushed. He knew it. He knew that's why he was here! "I'm sorry, sir. I couldn't help myself. I accept full responsibility and whatever punishment you see fit, I--"

But Admiral Bryan was laughing. "It's all right, Marco! I think that in today's military, we forgot too much about mirth, about bending the rules now and then. Not something you expect to hear an admiral say, is it? No, Marco, you're not here to be disciplined. You're here because you remind me of myself fifty years ago." He looked out at the stars. "I never wanted to be a pilot. I never wanted to fight. But damn it, the scum had killed five billion of us. And so I flew out. I watched my friends die. I watched two hundred lights--toward the end, we only had two hundred starfighters--blink out around me. And I watched the devastation my bombs unleashed on Abaddon, the death of millions of scum. They told me they're only arthropods. That they feel no pain. That they have no emotions. But still, that act--the killing of millions--still weighs on me."

"They said you disappeared after the war," said Marco.

"I did. For many years, I worked in silence. I still spend most of my days here in the Dome, rather than walking among the troops. Few back on Earth even realize I'm still alive." He smiled wryly. "Perhaps you were among them."

"Most days, I'm surprised I myself am still alive, sir," Marco replied.

Bryan's eyes saddened, and he placed a hand on Marco's shoulder. "This will all be over soon, son. But first we must fly through Hell. You must keep Lailani strong. You must give her comfort, laughter, love. That's why we chose you for this mission. That's why Ben-Ari wouldn't let you go. Because we need Lailani, and she needs you. She loves you very much, Marco."

His eyes stung. He looked away, ashamed of his tears. "And I love her, sir. I'm so scared of losing her."

Bryan stared in silence for long moments at the stars. "The curse of the general is in the numbers. We deal in life and death. I am sentencing thousands, maybe millions to die in this invasion, in my effort to save billions. And perhaps I will save those billions, but every light that goes out will haunt me. I'm old, Marco. I'm old, and much grief and guilt already fill me, and I will accept more of this burden. Perhaps someday you will be as I am now. An old man, looking out into space, burdened with so much guilt. But what comforts me, Marco, what gives me that determination, is a dream for your children. For the generation after yours. This invasion means suffering for us but peace for them. Tomorrow, for the generation not yet born, we will fly. We will fight. And we must win."

CHAPTER TEN

The Spearhead Platoon--fifty warriors in black--stood in the departure gate of Space Station One, staring at a massive chunk of space debris floating toward them.

Marco cringed. "Commander, incoming!" He pointed.

Addy ducked. "There's a giant piece of garbage flying our way!"

The tall, beefy Sergeant Jones grumbled. "Very funny, soldiers. That piece of garbage is going to be your home for the rest of the war, so you better learn to love it. She's ugly, all right." He looked out the viewport. "Don't doubt that. But that's just why we want you in her."

Wincing, Marco looked back out the viewport. No. It wasn't a giant pile of junk after all. It was a starship--or at least, a rusty pile of bolts that functioned somewhat like a starship. The hull was craggy, rusted, dented. The design was just a big, irregular sphere. But Marco saw engines' exhaust pipes, a slat of metal that looked like a hangar door, and cannons that thrust out like spikes all around the hull. It reminded him of a mechanical sea urchin, puffed up and bristling. It didn't surprise Marco when he saw the letters painted with flaking paint onto the hull: HDFS *Urchin.*

"The HDFS *Urchin*?" Addy said. "Looks more like the HDFS *Shithouse*, if you ask me." She glanced at Jones. "Commander, any chance we could officially change her name to *Shithouse*?"

Lailani nodded. "I'm game. I want to fly to war in a *Shithouse*."

"You two will fly to war in the brig!" rumbled the NCO. "Silence! Show some respect for a vessel in humanity's fleet."

Marco looked away from the *Urchin* and gazed longingly at the rest of the fleet gathering outside the space station. There were all manner of ships mustering there. The smallest, the Firebird starfighters, were flying back and forth in squadrons, aerodynamic and winged, able to fly both in space and atmosphere. Larger bombers, the size of buses, were docked at stations, soldiers busy loading explosives into their hulls. Cargo hulls hovered, boxy and functional, carrying many tons of munitions, everything from bullets and bombs to battle rations. Medical ships were gathering here too, their white hulls painted with red crosses, crescents, and Stars of David, ready to heal the inevitable wounded of the war. Warships loomed, hundreds of feet long, their cannons large enough to flatten entire towns, vessels that carried thousands of warriors. There were ships for engineers, for military intelligence, for logistics, for all other noncombatants from computer programmers to janitors.

Largest of all loomed the starfighter carriers, starships the size of skyscrapers, carrying entire marine brigades and flights of Firebirds. The largest of the carriers, the HDFS *Terra*, was visible in the distance, silvery and glimmering, the flagship of the fleet. Admiral Evan Bryan, they said, was flying on the *Terra*, would be leading this army to war.

Any one of those other ships was in better condition than the *Urchin.*

"Sergeant Jones," Marco said, glancing around to make sure no other units were nearby. "We were told our platoon would undertake the most important mission in this war. So why do we get the worst ship?"

A voice spoke from behind them, and Marco turned to see Ben-Ari walking toward them.

"Precisely because we're so important," she said. The commander of the Spearhead Platoon wore black battle fatigues, like her troops, and heavy black boots. Her plasma rifle hung across her back, and her hair was pulled back into a ponytail. "The scum will attack our fleet. They will hit us hard. They won't bother wasting energy on a hunk of junk like the *Urchin.* This ship, soldiers, is the safest in this fleet."

Addy sighed. "So we're camouflaging ourselves as a latrine. Lovely. I'd rather die in battle than live in a toilet."

"Not me," Marco said. "In the army, the toilet is the only place you get to read."

He hoped he would find time to read and write on the *Urchin.* Abaddon was still many light-years away. It would take the fleet days to get there, even flying in hyperspace at many times the speed of light. Marco had been working on *Loggerhead* in every stolen moment since arriving at Nightwall, and he was more than halfway through the novel now.

He didn't know what fate awaited him on Abaddon. He wanted to complete his novel before he died, even if it died with him.

The *Urchin* reached the space station. It had no automatic docking system. It hovered fifty meters out, and the station sent out an expanding bridge to lock with its hatch. As the platoon walked down the bridge, Marco got a closer look at the *Urchin*'s hull. It wasn't only dented and scratched and rusty. Somebody had somehow managed to spray rude graffiti across it, mimicking the nude man and woman from the Pioneer Plaque, symbol of Space Territorial Command. Only these figures looked quite a bit . . . better endowed than the originals.

"Oh my," Marco said.

"They seem nice," Addy said, looking at the graffiti couple.

They entered the starship, and Sergeant Jones gave them the grand tour. On the inside, the ship wasn't in much better shape. It looked fifty years old at least, maybe older, a relic of the Cataclysm. But despite its age and poor conditions, Marco thought it comfortable and roomy enough. There was a small kitchen stocked with food, a mess hall, a lounge, a hangar with three large shuttles, an officer's quarters, and three large bunks with fifteen beds in each. There were also gun turrets, twelve of them bulging from the ship, with heavy cannons and crates full of shells.

"These are old cannons," Sergeant Jones said, tapping one. "The kind used back in the Cataclysm. Antiques. But they're damn effective, and they'll punch through even the biggest scum ship. You'll man these cannons in shifts, two soldiers in each turret. I don't want to ever see a cannon without a pair of gunners at the ready."

The last stop on their tour was the bridge, a semicircular room with a viewport that stretched across the curved outer wall, affording a view of the fleet, the space station, and the dark planet below.

A pilot sat at the controls, wearing a navy blue service uniform with bright cuff links. Her hair was smooth, platinum-colored, and cut to the length of her chin. She rose from her seat, turned toward the platoon, and regarded them with lavender eyes. She smiled.

"Hello, masters!" She gave a little bow. "I am Osiris, all-purpose android, built by Chrysopoeia Corp for HDF service. Happy to serve you!"

Addy's eyes widened. "Osiris! You're with us too? You were transferred here from the *Miyari*?"

The android's smile widened. "You must have met one of my sisters, serial number T2353ac, serving aboard the HDFS *Miyari*. I am serial number T1143fd, normally serving aboard the *Sagan*, today serving you aboard the *Urchin*. Pleased to meet you! Would you like to hear a joke?"

"Oh God no," Marco said.

"Don't worry, master, I am a more advanced model than the Osiris you met aboard the *Miyari*," said the new Osiris. "My humor algorithms have been greatly revamped and strengthened. Why did the brain cell walk from one side of the brain to the other? I don't know. It hasn't really crossed my mind. It's funny because I'm an android and don't have brain cells."

"Yes, I can see your humor has vastly improved," said Marco.

"Thank you, master!" The android beamed. "Would you like to hear another?"

"I think you better save the rest for later," Marco said.

"That's all right, master. My new databases contain over thirty thousand, two hundred and--"

"Osiris, why don't you fly us off the dock for now?" Ben-Ari interjected. "The rest of the fleet is taking formation."

Osiris turned toward the viewport, and her eyes widened. She rushed back to her seat at the controls. "Of course, ma'am."

Marco stood on the bridge, watching through the viewport as the *Urchin* detached from the space station. As it floated across space, the bucket of bolts creaked and clattered, sounding like some old knight in a rusty suit of armor. The rest of the fleet was arranging a massive formation in space, thruster engines gently guiding every vessel into position. The HDFS *Terra* took the lead, two thousand feet long. The warships arranged themselves in V-shapes behind, and around them hovered smaller battleships, and around those flew the even smaller Firebirds.

There were thousands of ships here, and thousands more would be joining them from other bases across the frontier.

"It's the largest army ever assembled in one place," Marco said softly, gazing out the viewport. "Larger than any invasion in human history."

"This is a war between worlds, old boy." Addy patted his back. "Maybe you'll write a book about it someday. That is, after you're done writing *Jarhead*."

"*Loggerhead*, Addy. *Loggerhead*."

If I live that long, Marco thought. *If any of us do. If humanity itself can survive this. In this war, we show the cosmos that we're here to stay . . . or our species falls.*

* * * * *

On the sixth of June, fifty years to the day the scum had first attacked the Earth, humanity's hope crossed the frontier into the depths of enemy territory.

The flagship, the HDFS *Terra*, crossed the border first. The silver starfighter carrier left that area of space humanity had claimed for itself, entering the vast darkness of the scum's empire. On her deck flew Admiral Evan Bryan, the first man to have dealt the scum a devastating blow, the man now leading the invasion to finish the work of his youth. On his ship served a full brigade, five thousand warriors, and upon her hull shone a great golden phoenix, symbol of the Human Defense Force, in many ways a symbol of Earth, of humanity rising from the ashes, strong and bright again.

For a few moments, the *Terra* flew alone. She was a large ship--the largest in the fleet--but in the depth of space, she seemed fragile, a tiny shard of metal and light floating into the abyss. Those watching from behind waited with bated breath, perhaps worried that the enemy should swarm from all sides, that the beacon of humanity should extinguish as fast as it had kindled.

When the *Terra* floated onward into the darkness, the other ships followed.

Hundreds. Then thousands. Then tens of thousands. Then the full might of the fleet: a hundred thousand ships, ranging from vast cruisers to single-man starfighters. They sailed among the stars, the ships of Earth, following their flagship to war.

There were bulky, fortified warships, their cannons the size of redwoods, great artillery vessels that could blast cities from orbit. There were hulking cargo ships, great boxes of metal, transporting munitions and myriads of marines. There were small, quick patrol ships, some no larger than city buses, circling the larger vessels, defending their charges from any enemy that should appear. There were the massive starfighter carriers, terrifying pieces of technology, each the size of Earth's tallest skyscrapers. Only a few of them flew here, but each was like a floating army, and in their hangars waited hundreds of Firebirds, all ready for war. Thousands of the single-pilot fighters constantly patrolled around the fleet, forming a sphere of defense like the Iron Sphere that now encircled Earth.

But Earth now floated far behind, invisible from this distance, her sun too distant to see. Earth would have to survive on her own, to stand strong, to resist any fire that should strike her. Here, hundreds of light-years away, flew the might of the planet. Here--all that humanity could accomplish, all her determination, her hope for life, her valor. The labor of a species. The sword of a civilization.

Marco stood by the viewport, watching the fleet around him. He wished he could have flown on the flagship, the mighty *Terra*. Maybe on the *Sagan*, the newest carrier in the fleet, carrying many of humanity's best pilots. Or perhaps on the heavy, terrifying battle cruisers, predators of space. Yet should the scum attack, those mighty ships would be their most coveted prize. Marco and his platoon, the Spearhead, were too valuable to fly on a ship that would draw scum like rotting meat draws flies.

Their ship, the *Urchin*, clunked and clattered along, coughing out smoke and leaving a trail of screws and bolts. Older than the Cataclysm, it seemed ready to collapse should Marco just lean against the wall. To the scum, it would appear as little more than space debris. The *Urchin* is what the faded painted letters on its hull called it. Within the ship, the platoon still called it the *Shithouse*.

"At least we're safe here," Addy said. "No scum would waste time destroying this hunk of junk." She pounded on the viewport. "Hey, you fucking scum! You hear me? We're coming to kill you!"

"Careful!" Marco winced as bolts fell from the ceiling. "Never pound anything here. You'll do the scum's work for them."

They stood on the bridge, a room that looked more like a warehouse, all cluttered with metal crates and pipes. The semicircular viewport afforded a view of the fleet and the stars. A few of the platoon's warriors were manning the gun turrets that rose around the hull. The others crowded together here, watching the invasion begin. Osiris--the new Osiris, identical in every way to the old one--sat at the controls, flying the ship.

Addy ignored Marco. She waved her fist at the viewport. "Yeah, I know you're out there, scum! I'm going to stick my foot up your asses!"

"Thoraxes, Addy," Marco said.

"Up your thoraxes!" She hefted her gun. "I got me a Fyre gun now, scum. I'm going to roast your hides."

The louder Addy boasted of her battle prowess, the more Marco knew she was afraid, trying to hide her fear, to drown it under bravado and humor. For many soldiers, this method worked. To combat the stress and terror, they joked, bragged, threatened the enemy with whatever creative punishments they could imagine.

Lailani, however, stood very still and very close to the viewport. Her face was blank, and she spoke in a soft voice.

"They're out there. They know we're coming. They are angry. They are so angry."

A tense silence fell across the bridge. Addy glanced around, face pale, then scoffed.

"Well, good," Addy said. "I like getting 'em angry. Makes 'em funner to kill."

Marco thought back to his training, to the endless hours in his virtual reality helmet, running across rocky terrain under the blinding sun, delving into the hives, battling creatures in underground caverns. He didn't think killing even the most enraged scum was fun. He didn't want to be here, didn't want to fight. But Admiral Bryan's words returned to him.

Lailani needs you. She loves you.

Marco stepped closer to Lailani. They stood side by side, close enough for their fingertips to touch, and stared together out at the fleet.

"You can feel them?" he said softly.

She winced. "So much. So much, Marco. It's like a room full of shouting people and blaring music and chainsaws and trucks and endless noise. Only completely silent. Just feelings."

He slipped his hand into hers. "I'm here with you, Lailani. When it gets too much, just focus on me. Come back into this world. You don't need to always be in the hive."

"But I'm always in it," she said. "And it's so strong here. It's bugs inside my skull. I can feel them inside."

"Then we'll kill them," Marco said. "We'll kill them all, like Addy said."

She squeezed his hand, and her eyes dampened. "I hate them. I hate this part of me. We will kill them."

The speakers on the ships crackled to life. From them emerged a familiar voice. The platoon all stood still, listening.

"Warriors, pilots, and all soldiers of humanity. It is with honor that I, Admiral Evan Bryan, lead you in this journey. We have embarked upon the great flight, the final crusade. The hopes and prayers of humanity everywhere, upon Earth and all her outposts, fly with you today. In the company of your brothers and sisters-in-arms, you will bring about the utter destruction of the scum menace, the elimination of that cruel empire's tyranny over the galaxy, and security for our species to thrive upon our Earth and the planets beyond.

"Your task will be hard. The enemy is plentiful and brutal. He will fight savagely.

"But we are no longer the frightened, shell-shocked species we were fifty years ago, back when the enemy first devastated our world, when they butchered billions of our people. Over the past fifty years, I have seen humanity grow stronger, grow bolder, rise from the ashes like a phoenix. I have seen the Human Defense Force grow from a ragtag group of partisans into a mighty military that can challenge any force in the galaxy. Today we fly to victory!

"As we fly toward Abaddon, toward destruction of the enemy's planet, our brave brothers and sisters back on Earth fight to defend our world. We expect the enemy to strike Earth. We expect them to strike with furious vengeance. But we expect

Earth to fight them well. We will fight them in space. We will fight them in the air. And should they reach the fair soil and sea of our planet, we will fight them there too, in field and forest and city and ocean. As we fly to an alien world, we do not forget the world we leave behind, the world we--even here, so far from home--cherish and fight to protect.

"For fifty years I have served in this military, and I have seen in its warriors the noblest spirit of humankind. You are strong. You are brave. You will overcome. You will win!

"Good luck, warriors of Earth, and may the stars forever shine upon you."

They all stood silent for a long moment, staring out at the fleet. Finally Addy whistled.

"Not a bad speech," she said. "Still, not quite as good as mine."

Across the fleet, hundreds of exhaust pipes began to glow blue. Osiris turned from the controls to face the platoon.

"The fleet is beginning its activation of warp drive, ma'am," she said to Lieutenant Ben-Ari. "Engaging azoth hyperspace engines."

Marco noticed that only the largest ships seemed to have hyperspace engines. The smaller vessels, such as the Firebirds and ambulance shuttles, were powered by simpler thruster and nuclear engines, incapable of faster-than-light travel. As he watched from the viewport, he saw those smaller vessels move in closer to the larger ships. Many of those larger ships moved out to form rings around the fleet. Marco inhaled sharply, realization dawning on him.

"We're all going to bend spacetime together," he said. "We're going to suck up the smaller ships into our warp like a boat's wake sucking up smaller boats behind it."

"Correct," said Osiris. "If you fly close enough to a ship bending spacetime, you can fly within its curve, sharing its warp. We're creating a massive tunnel through space." The android smiled. "I'm proud to say: Even the HDFS *Shithouse* is equipped with azoth engines and prepared to help the warp."

"Don't call it that," Lieutenant Ben-Ari said. "This ship has a real name."

"Sorry, ma'am," said the android. "I thought it would be funny. Do you want to hear another joke?"

Addy groaned. "Great. Does every unit of these androids tell groaners?"

"Whoever coded them must have had a sense of humor," Marco said. "Or a streak of sadism."

The engines brightened across the fleet, shining pale blue. With a sudden blinding flare, the fleet's flagship, the HDFS *Terra*, blasted off into hyperspace, vanishing in a streak of light that stretched into the distance. With it, it carried the forms of a hundred smaller ships sucked into its warp. An instant later several other ships followed, streaking forward, leaving trails of light, dragging with them the smaller ships. One by one, the ships of the fleet popped out of regular spacetime, entering the warped space that would allow them to travel faster than light.

"Warp drive in three," said Osiris, "two, one . . . Activated."

Marco blinked.

He was hovering outside the viewport, gazing at himself standing on a bridge ahead. He rubbed his eyes and shook his head, and he was back in the ship, but the chamber was too small, curving like a donut, and Lailani and Addy stood above him. The viewport was a kilometer away, so small he could barely see it, and his legs were a kilometer long. He cringed and shook his head wildly, struggling to focus. Finally the dizziness and strangeness faded. Once more, he existed in regular three dimensions, standing among his platoon on the bridge of the *Urchin.* The rest of the fleet was still flying around them, a hundred thousand vessels, but the stars now formed lines all around them. They were flying through a vast tunnel of light, moving many times faster than the speed of light. It was impossible, of course, to travel faster than light, but they were bending spacetime around them, bending the very laws of physics.

"Jump to hyperspace completed," said Osiris. "Estimated travel time to Abaddon: Seven days, three hours, and twelve minutes."

A hundred thousand ships, Marco thought, gazing around him. His head spun again, and it wasn't the warp drive this time.

Some in the platoon returned to their bunks or the mess, but Marco remained on the bridge, watching the fleet flying through the tunnel of light. He could see spacetime curved around them, forming a pathway like a giant wormhole. Spacetime itself, the actual fabric, was invisible, but Marco could see the starlight bending, even wisps of engine light. When some of the Firebird fighters strayed too close to the warp's edge, they seemed to stretch out, their wings to bend, until they flew back toward the larger warships.

"We're like the Israelites following Moses through the Red Sea," Marco said. "But instead of fleeing Pharaoh, we're flying toward him."

"And will kick his mummified ass," Addy said.

"Try to get some sleep, soldiers," Lieutenant Ben-Ari said, walking toward the doorway. "Osiris will guide the ship onward. Use the next few days to rest."

"I'll stay up for a bit here if it's all right," Marco said. "Goodnight, ma'am."

Addy yawned, scratched her backside, and wandered away too. "Sleepy time."

The bridge emptied of soldiers, leaving only Marco and Lailani alone with the android.

"We're flying in a spaceship," Marco said. "Among a hundred thousand spaceships. Bending spacetime, traveling many times the speed of light, heading hundreds of light years away from Earth, all while piloted by an android. It's not what I was expecting when I showed up at RASCOM and a doctor cupped my balls."

"You know what they say." Lailani gave him a wan smile. "Nobody expects the Spanish Inquisition."

"Or the Scummish Inquisition, in our case."

"Hey, don't offend my people!" Lailani gave his arm a playful bite. "Chomp. Confess! Confess!"

"You're only one percent scum," Marco said. "So be quiet, you one percenter. Occupy Lailani!"

She bit her lip, stood on her toes, and kissed him. "You can occupy me."

He placed his hands on the small of her back, and he kissed her, and he knew what he was fighting for. Not just for Earth. Not just for humanity. For her.

A light caught the corner of his eye.

He turned toward the viewport.

Still holding Lailani, he frowned and pointed toward the edge of spacetime's curve. "Lailani, do you see a purple glow?"

She paled. She gripped his hand. Suddenly she was trembling. "Marco, I . . ." She gripped her head with both hands and grimaced.

The fleet's ships began to change formations. An alarm blared.

With indigo light and flaring white flashes, the tube of spacetime tore open, and a cloud of scum ships swarmed in.

CHAPTER ELEVEN

Sirens blared.

"Scum attack!" rose a voice from the speakers. "All pilots to your Firebirds!"

The alarms rang through the HDFS *Sagan*, one of forty starfighter carriers in the fleet. Kemi ran down the corridor. Hundreds ran with her.

"All Firebird pilots, take flight and engage the enemy!"

Kemi kept running, heart pounding. Through a viewport, she saw scum vessels fill the sky, their ships organic and veined, wreathed in purple flame. One of the pods flew toward the *Sagan*, and the carrier shook and roared like a thousand metal beasts. Kemi fell against a wall, pushed herself off, and kept running.

She burst into Hangar 18 where her squadron--the Avalerions--was positioned. Fifteen Firebirds were there. The other pilots were already climbing into their starfighters. Kemi saw Major Verish, commander of the squadron, close the cockpit on his own starfighter. Kemi raced across the hangar, leaped into her Firebird, and yanked the cockpit shut as the hangar doors began to open.

Air streamed out from the hangar into space, and before her, she saw the inferno.

"My God," Kemi whispered.

The scum pods filled space. Thousands were flying there. Several pods slammed into a cruiser, shattering the ship, and the explosion tore apart smaller vessels nearby. As the ships collapsed, they fell out from hyperspace, smearing into elongated lines of gray and red before fading.

"All right, pilots, stay close to me, and here we go!" said Major Verish, flying his ship out from the hangar.

Kemi glanced at the photo she had pinned to her dashboard, showing a young Lydia Litvyak, the first female fighting ace.

Be with me, Lydia.

She flew out from the hangar with her squadron, entering a sea of enemies.

Scum pods flew toward her squadron and slammed into the Firebird starfighters.

Kemi screamed.

One of their starfighters exploded, and the pilot's scream died in her headphones. Fire raced across her cockpit. Her ship shook madly. The hull dented. Shrapnel slammed into her. Another starfighter shattered, showering flames and metal across space, and Kemi kept flying, and a scum slammed into her cockpit, clawing the silica, trying to break in, and she fell, she fell, and below her spun hundreds of ships, firing their cannons, and the scum were everywhere, pods crashing into hulls, cracking metal, spilling out centipedes.

"Avalerion Squad, rally!" rose Major Verish's voice. "Battle formations!"

Kemi couldn't see the others. She couldn't breathe. Scum were everywhere. She fired her machine gun, sending rounds into a pod, and it burst, and another pod skimmed across her tail, knocking her into a spin. Space whirled around her. She saw scum pods slam into a massive cruiser, a ship with thousands of marines inside. The ship cracked open, and the warriors spilled out, hundreds, then thousands of them, kicking, screaming silently, dying in the vacuum. Shrapnel pelted Kemi's starfighter, nicking her cockpit. The shattered cruiser dipped, nearly split in half, and vanished from hyperspace with a streak of light and cracking metal.

"Ensign Abasi!" Major Verish's voice emerged from her headphones, and she looked up, and there--she saw him and the surviving Avalerions. From fifteen Firebird starfighters, ten remained. She pulled her joystick, flying toward them. A scum pod flew toward her, and she fired her machine gun, riddling it with bullets, and it cracked open, spilling out lavender fumes and centipedes. She flew through them, cracking their bodies, and rejoined her squadron.

The Firebirds quickly took formation. Kemi had only been training for several weeks, barely knew what to do, and this all seemed too big for her, too dizzying. Hundreds of other starfighter formations flew around them, streaming across space. The scum were everywhere. Thousands of them, maybe tens of thousands, slamming their pods into the human fleet. A cargo ship collapsed, spilling out water, gasoline, and munitions that burst and destroyed smaller vessels. The curves of spacetime began to straighten out. The scum slammed into an azoth engine of a starfighter carrier, and turbines rolled through space, and suddenly the Firebirds were all falling, stretching, shrinking, and the stars wobbled and snapped into single dots. Kemi was flying in regular space again, and all around her, starships were reappearing in reality, some right by her, others thousands of kilometers away. All formations seemed to crumble, ships flew upside down, ships spun madly. Some were still in hyperspace, streaming overhead, appearing as lines of light.

And in the confusion, the scum were merciless.

The alien pods--small fighters the size of Firebirds--flew everywhere, taking fluid formations like schools of fish. Larger vessels flew there too, massive, red, pulsing, sticky ships like the disemboweled organs of giants, lurching and leaking through space, pumping out more fighters from valves and sphincters. There was no metal in their fleet, no plastic, no smooth lines or sharp angles. They constructed their vessels from their own biology, spewing and sweating and expelling membranes to form these veined structures, giant eggs and shells of flesh. Their ships spurted miasma and globs of searing acid, tearing into the hulls of human starships. They belched out purple flames to roast Firebirds. They birthed centipedes that flew through the vacuum, their claws shattering the cockpits of Firebirds and ripping out engines from star cruisers.

And around Kemi, Firebirds fell from the sky. They burned, twisted, careened through space. They tumbled like sparks from a flame, vanishing into the distance, spinning and petering out. At her side, centipedes slammed into a Firebird in her formation, ripping it apart.

Everything was silent.

In the vacuum, everything was so silent.

Perhaps more than the devastation, the death, the monsters . . . it was the silence that unnerved her. She was watching a silent film of oblivion.

A pilot spun through space, a claw in his chest, and thudded against Kemi's starfighter, then scraped across the hull and vanished. The sudden sound--thud, scrape, fingernails on the hull--tore her out of her reverie.

"Major Verish?" she spoke into her communicator. "Maj--"

She looked over to his Firebird. Verish was still flying beside her, his cockpit cracked open, a scum feasting on him. Slowly, almost gracefully, his starfighter rose higher, higher, and slammed into the belly of a cruiser above. Fire rained.

Kemi's heart sank.

This wasn't supposed to happen, she thought. *We're still light-years away from Abaddon. We're being destroyed before even reaching our destination.*

Another Firebird collapsed nearby. Dead warriors wheeled through space before her.

Kemi touched the black-and-white photograph of Lydia Litvyak on her dashboard. Lydia was her inspiration in this war, but Lydia had also died at age twenty-three, shot down while assaulting a formation of Nazi planes.

Kemi raised her chin.

If I die, I die. I die fighting. Like her.

"Squadron!" she said. "Rally here, battle formation! Let's kill those sons of bitches."

The others flew closer--eight Firebirds, all that remained of their squad of fifteen. A swarm of scum pods streamed toward them, a hundred or more.

The squadron fired their missiles.

The projectiles streamed forth, leaving trails of light, and tore into the scum swarm. Pods shattered. Centipedes spilled out, spinning, slamming into starfighters. One cockpit crashed open, and the pilot tumbled out into space, only for other centipedes to grab him and tear him apart.

Kemi took a deep breath.

Feel them. Feel the scum. Think like them.

She cringed. She never wanted to think like the aliens again. But if she were to survive today, she had to connect to their hive. Had to smell them. Like she had back on Corpus.

She bit her lip, and she let them in.

Smells, visions, cruelty, hatred filled her mind. The network spread before her, a labyrinth of light and shadow, racing with a million senses.

She was Kemi. She was alien. She was them.

Kemi fired again, spraying bullets, ripping open more pods.

"Come on, boys and girls, higher!" Kemi said. "Follow!"

She soared.

"You're flying too high!" said a pilot, voice crackling in her headphones. "You're flying right at them!"

"Trust me!" Kemi shouted. "Follow!"

She soared and the other pilots followed, storming toward a cloud of pods. She swerved left hard. The pods flew to the right. The Firebirds sprayed out bullets. Kemi dived, and the other Firebirds followed, and an instant later a swarm of pods streamed overhead, narrowly missing them. Kemi zipped forward, knowing where every pod would fly a second in advance, able to whip around them as other squadrons collapsed. Their missiles flew, tearing into the enemies. All around, squad after squad of Firebirds burned. Kemi led her pilots onward.

I know you. I can kill you. You cannot hurt me again.

"See that scum meatsack up there?" Kemi said. "Let's rip it open."

They soared higher, bullets knocking back pods. The meatsack hovered ahead: a massive scum ship the size of a warship, throbbing and pulsing, veins rippling across its surface. Kemi was reminded of the medical experiments she had seen back in the hive. This ship seemed grown from such organic material, and she cringed, wondering if human DNA--maybe even live humans--formed part of its construction. She felt the ship's hatred ooze from it. It was a living, stinking creature, a vessel of meat and consciousness.

"Fire!" she shouted.

Missiles flew from the squadron, streaked through space, and slammed into the enormous sack of meat above.

The bloated scum ship burst open.

Fleshy gobbets, yellow liquid, and shards of what looked like bone spilled out. Centipedes followed. Kemi pulled her trigger, firing another missile into the opening. An explosion filled the scum vessel with light and fire. Kemi banked hard, swooped, and rose through a rain of fleshy globs. She fired again, firing bullets into a cloud of pods.

"Hell yeah!" shouted one pilot in her squadron, voice emerging through her headphones.

Around her, the rest of the fleet was beginning to regroup too. Warships were firing their plasma cannons. The great starfighter carriers were blasting out photon beams. Many human ships were still distant, trying to fly closer, to reach the battle. Space itself seemed to burn, a vast arena of light and plasma and fire and shattering metal. Beyond, far in the distance, the stars shone on, Earth's sun lost among them.

CHAPTER TWELVE

The battle raged around him, a theater of light and flesh and metal and blood.

Marco stood in one of the *Urchin*'s gun turrets. It was a bulky metal pillbox that bulged from the ship's starboard, dented and chipped. A rusty cannon thrust out from it. Through a narrow viewport, Marco could see the scum ships everywhere.

"Die, assholes!" Addy's voice echoed through the ship. She stood in another turret, and Marco saw the shells fly from her cannon, slamming into a scum vessel.

Marco aimed his cannon, a gun the size of an oak tree. The *Urchin* lurched. He nearly fell. He gripped the gun, planted his boots steadily on the floor, and stared through the viewport. The ship swayed, and there--a scum meatbag in the distance, firing globs of slime at the human fleet.

There were no triggers on this cannon. It was an ancient design, and Marco had to yank a cord like kick-starting a lawn mower. The cord tightened. A shell the size of a baby blasted out from the cannon, streamed through space, and sank into the scum ship. It was like firing a bullet into a slab of jelly. For a moment it seemed like the meatbag had swallowed the shell. Then the explosion tore the scum ship apart, showering out chunks.

Marco breathed out in relief.

"Hell yeah!" Lailani said, standing at his side. The tiny soldier lifted another shell, wobbled under the weight, and carried it toward the cannon. They loaded the gun.

Light flared through the viewport. Marco turned to see scum pods flying toward them. The *Urchin* jolted as the pods slammed into the hull. Centipedes spilled out.

"Damn it!" Marco yanked the cord, firing the cannon again.

White light.

Flames.

Pounding pain.

He flew backward, slamming into Lailani, falling, falling, and the light washed over him, and his ears rang.

He couldn't breathe, and he thought he was dying, and his throat constricted, and the smoke was everywhere. Ringing. Ringing in his ears. His ears were full of screaming, clanging cotton. He blinked, rubbed his eyes, saw blood on his fingers. Lailani lay beside him, curled up, coughing.

He managed to push himself up, to kneel above her. He pulled on his gas mask, then grabbed Lailani's gas mask from her pack and slipped it over her face.

"Lailani!" he said, and he couldn't hear his voice.

She rose, shivering, and they lurched backward and stared at the cannon. It had shattered. Bits of scum lay strewn across the gun turret.

"Scum got into the cannon," Lailani said. "Fuckers blocked it. Like an old Looney Tunes where Elmer's rifle backfires after Bugs sticks his finger in the barrel." She pulled a piece of shrapnel out of her leg and yelped in pain.

"The air's leaking out," Marco said. "Come, back into the ship."

He pulled her out of the gun turret, back into the main hull of the *Urchin.* His ears still rang, and he was bleeding somewhere, wasn't sure where, but blood was on his hands, on his cheeks. He slammed the round door to the gun turret shut, sealing off the breach. The *Urchin* lurched again as more pods slammed into it, and he and Lailani fell down hard in the corridor, banging their hips.

He rummaged through his pack and found his military-issued bandages. He slapped one onto Lailani, then found his own wounds--gashes on his hands--and bandaged them too. For a moment they sat together, breathing heavily. The ship rattled whenever shells blasted out from the other turrets.

"You all right?" Marco asked Lailani.

She nodded. "Shaken, and the leg hurts like a son of a bitch, but I'm all right."

"Let's go help at another turret," Marco said. "We can load shells."

She nodded, and they were limping down the hall when they heard the crackling behind them.

They spun around and saw it there. A scum in the corridor, ten feet tall, rearing before them.

Damn.

Marco pawed for his Fyre rifle. It still hung across his back. He managed to spin it around, to grab a plasma pack from his belt, to load . . .

The scum lashed its claws, knocking his rifle aside. Marco leaped back, fell down. Lailani fired her gun, and her plasma flared out, but the scum shoved her down, and the blast missed, and Lailani hit her head hard on the floor.

The scum leaped toward Marco. His gun was trapped under him. He drew his knife and tossed it, hitting the creature's mandible. A claw lashed down, scraping across his shoulder, just missing his neck. Marco yanked mightily, pulled his gun free, and roared up fire.

The plasma washed across the scum, and its exoskeleton melted, dripping searing-hot globs onto Marco, burning his uniform and skin. He grimaced and brushed them off, his fingers sizzling. Lailani rose to her feet, her helmet tilted, and blasted more fire, finishing the job. The scum curled up, exoskeleton melted. The soft innards still lived, throbbing, bubbling, mewling pathetically, but without the exoskeleton it was no threat.

"Damn, they are ugly without their shells," Lailani said, staring at the wiggling pink goo.

"Pink slime," Marco said. "It's what Spam is made of, you know."

Lailani smacked her lips. "Mmm, it's full of scummy goodness!"

Another gun turret had shattered on the ship, killing the two gunners. Marco and Lailani grabbed spacesuits from the corridor, then entered the breached turret, plasma guns firing. Three scum were there, feasting on the dead. Marco and Lailani burned them, melting their shells.

The vacuum of space gaped open through a crack the size of a man. In their spacesuits, Marco fired the cannon while Lailani kept loading more shells. Scum vessels shattered before them. Through the gaping breach in the turret, Marco could see the battle: thousands of ships, human and scum, firing their weapons. The scum's meatbags, as large as warships, kept belching out purple globs that seared through metal hulls. The smaller pods were whipping around the battle, fighting squadrons of Firebirds. Missiles streaked through the battle, lighting the darkness.

Marco had never seen, never imagined anything like this, over a hundred thousand ships firing their guns together, a battle that spread out for thousands of kilometers across space, some of the ships so distant they were merely specks of light shooting luminous streamers.

The battle lasted for hours. They fired shell after shell, ripping through the scum. Across the sky, the fleet pounded the enemy, and the Firebirds flitted between the cruisers and carriers, taking out the pods one by one.

Finally Marco and Lailani shot a last shell, tearing through a scum meatbag, and the battle ended.

The scum swarm was gone, its last few centipedes flailing into the distance.

"Victory!" rose distant voices from their ship. "Victory!"

But as Marco gazed across the fleet, he knew: *This victory came at a terrible cost.*

The fleet had shattered. Several carriers, each of which had held thousands of soldiers and hundreds of starfighters, had been destroyed. They now floated as chunks of metal. Cargo ships had fallen apart, losing precious water, food, and ammunitions. Countless Firebirds and their pilots were gone. Warships listed, dead, cracked open and filled with a few last centipedes.

Aboard the *Urchin*, the Spearhead Platoon stepped onto the bridge and stared at what remained of the fleet. The voice of Admiral Bryan rose from the speakers, crackling, grainy, vanishing and reappearing.

". . . We don't yet know the losses, but estimate . . . thousands of ships lost. Casualties will be in the hundreds of thousands. Medical bays will be moving between ships, and . . ." For a moment, nothing but static. ". . . salvage teams will attempt to repair those ships that still float. We will be opening a communication wormhole to Earth. News to follow. All ships, regroup in your formations. Report to . . ."

The signal gave a last crackle, then died.

For several hours, Marco sat on the bridge, watching the salvage efforts. Small ships zipped back and forth, some of them medical ships bearing red crosses, crescents, and Stars of David, others ships of engineers and mechanics struggling to repair cracked hulls and damaged engines. There was no time for funerals, no space to store bodies. Thousands of coffins were sent into space, a burial in darkness.

Throughout the day, updates came in spurts through the speakers. They had left Nightwall with a hundred thousand vessels, about half of them single-pilot fighters, the rest ranging from small three-man ships to massive starfighter carriers.

They had lost a quarter of their fleet.

Over two million soldiers had perished.

"This was a battle on the scale of the Somme," Marco whispered. "On the scale of Stalingrad. This was worse than Vancouver. This was the worst massacre since the Cataclysm. Two million lives, just . . . gone."

The platoon stood together on the bridge, heads lowered. They had won the battle, but this victory felt an awful lot like defeat. And Abaddon, homeworld of the scum, was still many light-years away.

Two million, Marco thought, still reeling. *This wasn't just a battle. It was genocide.*

"Look!" Lailani said, pointing. "There, between those ships!"

They all stared. A small swirl of light formed between two cargo vessels, expanding, then shrinking to a dot ringed by a halo. Behind it, they could see a strand swirl into the darkness like the funnel of a maelstrom.

"They've opened a wormhole to Earth," Marco said, and even through the grief, he felt a sense of wonder. "A way to communicate faster than light. See how the HDFS *Terra* is pointing its radio dishes toward the wormhole? They're going to send and receive signals through it."

For a long time, there was silence. Finally the wormhole closed, and Admiral Bryan's voice emerged through the *Urchin*'s speakers. The general sounded grim.

"We've received news from Earth," rose his voice through the static. "In response to our invasion of their space, the scum have begun their assault on Earth. The Iron Sphere defense system is standing. As expected, it is achieving a ninety-eight percent success rate at blocking the scum attacks. But two percent of the pods have gone through, and their punishment has been devastating. The cities of Calcutta, Yekaterinburg, and Chongqing are gone. We do not know the number of casualties, but we expect them to be in the millions." The admiral paused, then spoke in a hard, deep voice. "We will continue our mission. We have suffered terrible losses, but our resolve still stands, stronger than ever. Our fleet is still mighty. In ten minutes we will return to hyperspace and continue to Abaddon. We will defeat the scum emperor. We will achieve nothing less than complete victory."

Lailani raised her hand high and held out two fingers. "Victory."

Addy followed her lead. "Victory."

Soon the entire Spearhead Platoon--the warriors tasked with killing the emperor himself--raised their fingers in salute. "Victory. Victory."

Marco repeated the word with them, but he couldn't summon the determination he saw shining in his comrades' eyes.

He knew that their journey had just begun, that many more terrors waited on the way. Many more lives lost.

Millions are dead, he thought. *And we're still far from Abaddon.*

The ships reactivated their azoth engines, forming a new funnel of curved spacetime. They flew on--limping, bloodied, battered, hurtling toward the enemy's world.

CHAPTER THIRTEEN

They plowed on through scum space, hour after hour, day after day, cannons firing, plasma blazing.

The scum attacked relentlessly, harrying their flanks. Rarely a moment went by without alarms blaring, without scum pods streaming into hyperspace, without the Firebirds rising to face the menace. The enemy did not mount another major offensive. With each assault, they sent only a few hundred vessels against them. But their sorties came without rest.

"It's like *The Old Man and the Sea*," Marco said, lying on his bunk in the *Urchin*. He gazed out the window at the battle outside, a hundred-odd scum pods engaging a wing of Firebirds.

"The who and the what now?" Addy said.

"It's an old book," Marco said, thinking of Jackass. They had once had a long conversation about Ernest Hemingway. It seemed another lifetime now. "An old fisherman catches a great fish, so large it can't fit in his boat. He pulls it behind his boat toward the shore. Along the way, little fish show up and nibble, tearing off bits and pieces of the fisherman's catch. By the time he reaches the shore, there's nothing but bones."

Addy tilted her head. "Are you saying you want to go fishing?"

"I'm saying we're the big fish dragging behind the boat," said Marco. "And the scum are biting away at us. They lost the major battle at the border. So now they'll nibble and nibble."

Addy rose from her bunk, stepped toward his bed, and bit his arm--hard.

"Ouch!" he said.

"Nibble," she said.

"Why does everyone keep biting me?" Marco shoved Addy away when she tried biting him again. "Get lost. You're not a minnow, you're a goddamn shark with those teeth of yours."

The speakers in their bunk crackled to life, and Lieutenant Ben-Ari's voice emerged. "All troops report at once to the bridge."

Marco glanced around the bunk, but the others all shrugged. They smoothed their uniforms, pulled on their boots, slung their Fyre rifles across their backs, and left the chamber. They gathered in formation on the bridge, the entire platoon. Lieutenant Ben-Ari stood there in her battle fatigues.

"How many of you," she said, "are familiar with the Guramis?"

"The gourmet?" Addy asked. "Like Spam sandwiches?"

"Guramis," Marco said. "I've heard of them, ma'am." The platoon turned to look at him. "A sentient alien species. If I recall correctly, they live on an ocean world, spending their lives underwater."

Ben-Ari nodded. "Very true. The Guramis are highly intelligent and have developed an advanced technological civilization on par with our own. In recent years, the scum empire has encroached on their territory. The two civilizations have been clashing in space, with the Guramis losing most battles. The Guramis just began venturing out into space a couple of centuries ago, around the same time humans did. And they've suffered horribly at the claws of the scum. Only months ago, the scum assaulted the Guramis' world, poisoning the water. Millions of Guramis died."

Addy licked her lips. "Are you sure they're not made of gourmet Spam?"

Marco elbowed her. "Shush, biter."

Ben-Ari continued. "Recently, we reached out to the Guramis, requesting their aid in fighting the scum. Until now, the Guramis have refused, fearing scum retaliation. We believe the time is right to approach the Guramis again. They grieve the loss of millions of their kind. They will want a chance to fight back. We can offer them that chance. Their fleet--at least, what remains after their long war--is smaller than ours, but their starships are mighty."

"Great," Addy said. "Spam-fish flying fishbowl starships. As if things couldn't get any weirder in our lives."

Sergeant Jones growled and stepped toward her. "Linden, watch it, or your life will involve cleaning latrines for the rest of the war." That finally got Addy to shut up.

"Admiral Bryan has sent his orders," Ben-Ari said. "Our platoon will visit the Guramis' homeworld and meet with their high council. We're to convince them to fight with us."

The platoon glanced at one another, then back at Ben-Ari.

"Ma'am," said Marco, "why us? We're not dignitaries. We're not high ranking. With all due respect, we're just grunts."

"Yeah!" said Addy. "Why is it always us, the same people in this huge army, who do all the big stuff?"

"Watch it, Linden!" Sergeant Jones warned.

Ben-Ari looked at her boots for a moment, then took a deep breath and raised her head. "You're right," she said. "We're just grunts. We're not high ranking, we're not dignitaries, but we *are* famous."

"For clearing out the Corpus mine, ma'am?" Marco said. "Surely we're not the only platoon that--"

"Because of my father," said Ben-Ari. She took another deep breath. "My father was the first human to make contact with the Guramis. They will speak to no other human . . . aside from his daughter and the soldiers she leads."

Marco understood. He had heard of the Ben-Ari family, of course. Most soldiers had. They were a famous military dynasty, a family that lived in the Human Defense Force. Their country had been destroyed. They had no ancestral home, no wealth, no land. Their only home had been the military for generations. Einav Ben-Ari was only a lieutenant, a junior officer, not a mighty colonel or general, but her family name preceded her. Marco had heard that Colonel Yoram Ben-Ari, Einav's father, had been an accomplished officer. He hadn't known that Ben-Ari Senior had also been an explorer and ambassador.

"We'll emerge from hyperspace in an hour and head toward the Guramis' world," said Ben-Ari. "Oh, and everyone--wear your spacesuits. The Guramis are a gilled, water-breathing species, and their planet has no solid surface, not even an ocean floor. We'll be scuba diving."

As they walked back toward their bunk, Addy nodded at Marco. "You were right," she said. "Just like *The Old Man and the Sea*. Fish everywhere!"

* * * * *

The HDFS *Urchin*--Ben-Ari sighed to think of how her soldiers called it the *Shithouse*--flew out of hyperspace and glided toward the watery world ahead.

"Well, Father," she said softly, gazing out the viewport. "I'm doing what I always hated you for." She smiled bitterly. "I'm going to all the places you left me for."

She did not like thinking of her childhood. She did not like dwelling on her anger. Throughout so much of her childhood and youth, she had suffered that horrible anger, endless rage, shouting, breaking things, running away, crying in the darkness. As an adult, she had learned to release that anger, to always remain calm. It served her as a soldier, as a leader--but mostly, it served her as a person, as a daughter.

"All my childhood," she whispered, "I just wanted a home, Father. A house. A yard. A dog. Stability. I wanted you to have a boring job working nine to five, and I wanted more than anything to know my place in the world. But you dragged me from one military base to another. From one rocky outpost to another. I grew up among soldiers. I grew up in the military. I grew up with guns instead of teddy bears, with sergeants instead of babysitters."

Another deep breath.

Let go of the anger, Einav. You're not that girl anymore. You're not the girl dragged from base to base, who ran away five times, who sought comfort in alcohol and the arms of rough boys. You're a confident, successful woman now, a leader of warriors. All that matters now is the mission. Not the past.

She watched the watery world of the Guramis draw closer. At first it was just a blue marble, not unlike Earth, cloaked in swirls of cloud. Yet as they drew closer, Ben-Ari saw no landforms. The world was composed entirely of water. There wasn't even an ocean floor there, just liquid all the way down. Some scientists believed there was a small, metallic core buried deep within this planet, barely larger than an asteroid, but for all intents and purposes, here was a massive, floating bubble of water.

Her platoon joined her on the bridge. The soldiers stood together, watching the planet approach. The *Urchin*--this clunky, rusty old cargo ship, chosen precisely because it seemed useless--flew closer until the ocean world filled the viewport. From the water below rose several alien vessels.

"They're a lot nicer than scum ships," Addy said. "They look like fishing lures! Ironic, considering the Guramis are fish, right?"

Ben-Ari sighed. The girl was always speaking out of turn, and if this were any other time, any other war, Ben-Ari would have confined Addy to the brig by now.

In a way, Addy was right. The alien vessels did look a little like glittering, spinning fishing lures. They were long and slender, and the sunlight gleamed against them. Green and blue fins spread out from their silver hulls, coated with scales that functioned as solar panels. As the alien ships flew closer--there were three of them--Ben-Ari could see transparent bulbs bulging out from their thin hulls like eyes. Blue water filled the cockpits, and creatures swam within, still too distant to see clearly.

"The way humans fill their ships with air," Ben-Ari said to her platoon, "the Guramis fill their ships with water. In many ways, we humans are like fish ourselves, but instead of swimming in a sea of water, we swim in a sea of gasses."

"Especially after Marco eats cheese," Addy said.

"Very funny, stinky feet," Marco said.

Ben-Ari groaned. "I will court-martial you both someday, you know."

Osiris turned from the controls toward them. "Ma'am, the Guramis send a message. They say that if our ship is not waterproof, they will offer transportation down to their city."

"Tell them we accept," said Ben-Ari. "I think the *Urchin* is rusty enough as it is."

"The *Urchin*?" said Addy. "What's the *Urchin*?"

"That's the ship we're on," Marco said.

"This piece of junk?" Addy raised an eyebrow. "I thought it was the *Shithouse*."

Marco groaned. "You didn't really think that was the *real* name, did you?"

"Well, it suits it!" Addy said. "And that's what everyone calls it."

"Emery, Linden, enough!" rumbled Sergeant Jones. The burly, bald NCO was fuming, fists clenched.

One of the Gurami vessels hovered up beside them. They orbited the watery planet, two hundred kilometers above the endless ocean. From a distance, the alien ship had seemed small and delicate, a glimmering jewel, so dainty and beautiful by the bulky and boxy *Urchin*. But up close, Ben-Ari saw that the silvery ship was massive, easily three times the *Urchin*'s size. It had a central pillar, silvery and smooth like mother-of-pearl. Its eight wings thrust out like flower petals, coated in scales that changed color as the sun hit them, alternating between lavender to blue to gold to turquoise.

"Did you know?" said Osiris from the controls. "The Guramis build their ships much like the scum do. They produce the material from their own bodies, similar to how clams on Earth can produce pearls. In fact, the entire ships are made of a material similar to pearls."

"Maybe Marco can buy me one," said Addy. "I'll wear it as a necklace."

Two shimmering fins stretched out from the alien ship, spinning and coiling around each other, lengthening and forming a tunnel. They snapped onto the *Urchin*'s round door, enclosing it.

"All right, platoon, follow me," Ben-Ari said. "We're all going. Osiris, you stay and man the fort."

"The fort, ma'am?" the android said. "Man it?"

"Android the ship," Addy suggested. "That means you stay and guard while we're gone fishing."

Osiris smiled and saluted. "Happy to comply! Have you heard the joke about the fisherman and the . . ."

The platoon hurried off the bridge. They walked through the ship, wearing their spacesuits, until they reached the exit door. The suits worked in space, and according to everything Ben-Ari had read, they would work underwater too. They weren't bulky, white spacesuits like those astronauts had worn in the old days when the astronaut Pat Szabo had first walked on Mars. Here were slick, form-hugging suits, black and deep blue, similar to diving suits used on Earth's oceans. Fitting, perhaps. Oxygen tanks hung across the soldiers' backs, and they wore their Fyre plasma guns too. The rifles were designed to work in water--Earth's navy used them too--and Ben-Ari figured the weapons would impress the Guramis.

They want to see that we're warriors, she thought. *That we can defeat the scum. And they want to see me, the daughter of the first human they ever knew.*

They opened the door. The Gurami tunnel, formed from the scaly fins, spread before them like a jet bridge. Air from the

Urchin's airlock filled the tunnel's vacuum. Once the platoon had entered the tunnel--it was a tight squeeze--they closed the *Urchin*'s airlock behind them. They now hung in a thin, translucent cylinder hundreds of kilometers above the planet. The material bent under their boots; it seemed as thin as paper. Ben-Ari winced. If the material tore, it would send them plunging down to their fiery deaths in the planet's atmosphere. They would be nothing but ashes and chunks of spacesuit by the time they reached the ocean.

At the end of the tunnel, where it connected to the Gurami ship, stood a shimmering doorway like mother-of-pearl. The doorway--it looked a bit like a seashell--pulled open.

Water flowed into the tunnel.

"Bath time!" Addy said. "Anyone bring a rubber ducky?"

"Good, maybe it'll wash the stink off your feet," Marco said.

"Just be careful around the cheese, Marco," Addy said. "We'll be able to see the bubbles."

"How mature, Addy." Marco rolled his eyes. "I forgot that they drafted seven-year-olds these days."

The water rose around their boots, then their knees, finally their chins. It was warm and soothing. The water level kept rising, soon halfway up Ben-Ari's helmet, and she fought the ridiculous feeling of panic as it rose above her nose. Her head was enclosed within a helmet. She could breathe fine in here. Still, it was a little disconcerting once the water rose over her head, filling the tunnel.

A melodious voice flowed from ahead, deep and beautiful.

"Enter, humans. Welcome."

Ben-Ari led the way, swimming into the alien starship.

She had grown up with her father's stories, but she had never joined him on his journeys. Einav Ben-Ari herself had never been beyond the solar system until this year, let alone inside an alien starcraft. She gazed around, struggling to hide her wonder from her platoon.

She floated in a vast, round, glittering chamber, a piece of the ocean risen into space. As a child, her mother had once taken her to an aquarium, and little Einav had marveled at the massive tanks full of seaweed, coral, rays, sharks, and colorful fish. This place put that old aquarium to shame. There were waves, actual waves here, probably produced synthetically to mimic the world below, the same way humans mimicked gravity on their starships. Plants the size of oaks grew here, swaying in the water. Among them floated wondrous organisms, so small that Ben-Ari could have caught them in her palm. Each seemed to have a different shape: some like jellyfish, others like spinning wheels, some finned, all spinning and gleaming with bioluminescence. They were, perhaps, this world's version of plankton.

"Hello, Gurami!" Addy said, waving at a tiny jellyfish. "We come in peace!"

"Um, Addy?" Marco said. "I think you're talking to their food." He pointed. "Look."

Ben-Ari looked too. An alien came swimming toward them, about twice the size of a human, consuming the smaller creatures as it advanced. Its actual body was small, but graceful fins rose from it, blue and purple and coiling like banners, forming most of its size. Three indigo trumpets thrust out from its head, forming three mouths, and four eyes blinked above them. Dozens of golden tendrils hung from the alien's underbelly like the stalks of jellyfish, trailing through the water. As a child, Ben-Ari had once owned a betta fish, a beautiful animal that had lived for two years in a fish bowl. This alien--a Gurami--reminded her of that old pet.

"Um, Marco," Addy whispered behind them. "Don't mention the tuna you had for lunch. Might have been a relative."

"Addy, shush!"

Ben-Ari glared at the two--they really did need time in the brig--and returned her eyes to the alien.

"Thank you, kind Gurami," she said, "for welcoming us aboard your vessel. My name is Lieutenant Einav Ben-Ari, daughter of Colonel Yoram Ben-Ari, a man who knew your world well. I come to you now with friendship and with important words for your leaders."

The Gurami bobbed in the water, its fins swaying. Several more of the aliens swam behind it. Ben-Ari noticed that there seemed to be three kinds of Guramis. Some had long purple-and-blue fins like curtains, another type was silvery and fat, while the third kind was smaller and plainer, their underbellies blobby and their backs lined with spikes.

Of course. Ben-Ari thought back to her father's stories. The Guramis had three genders. The fat silvery ones laid the eggs. The purple ones showed off their beautiful fins, with the loveliest member allowed to fertilize the eggs. The plain ones roosted on the eggs, their backs spiked to deter predators. Ben-Ari knew that some species in the cosmos had three, four, even five genders, but she had never seen them with her own eyes.

The Gurami seemed to nod, purple and blue fins flowing. The tendrils beneath its body swayed like curtains, and one of its mouths--shaped like a trumpet--trilled with a beautiful, melodious voice, raising bubbles. "We know of the great tragedy in your world, of the great cruelty of the enemy, of the great battle only several turns of the world ago. Come with us into the waterdepths. Time moves slowly in the sea but ever races in the great dryness above. Time is now our enemy. Come, now! Into the murk. Into the great Mother Sea."

The ship began to descend back toward the watery planet. Through the round windows, Ben-Ari could see the stars, then swirling clouds and blue skies. There was barely any tremble, barely any heat to their reentry. They descended through the cloudscapes, through rain, through rainbows, through swirling plains, layer after layer of clouds, and finally--with barely a jostle--into the water.

They dived through the ocean. Through the windows, Ben-Ari saw a sea of life. Algae grew from floating pods, leaves swaying. Countless creatures swam, some ring-shaped and glistening with beads of light, others elongated and graceful, some blobby and tentacled, others spiky and scaled, all beautiful. She had never seen so many colors, so much variety of life.

They kept descending until they reached an underwater city. There was no seabed in this world, no ground to raise structures on. Buildings floated here, round and silvery, full of windows. It was a city of huge bubbles, some small as houses, some a kilometer wide. Thousands of Guramis swam between them, fins streaming like banners of purple and blue and gold. There were vessels here too, long and silvery, spinning lazily as they moved between the bubbles like enormous dancing plankton. Artificial lights shone in bulbs that floated through the city. There was no permanent structure to this city. The buildings all bobbed, drifted, sometimes even bounced against each other.

The ship took the platoon to a large, shimmering globe that hovered in the city center. Here the platoon exited the starship, swam through the ocean, and entered the globe. The warm water was so salty and dense Ben-Ari barely had to move her limbs. She floated. The High Council of the Guramis swam within this globe, beautiful and ancient beings, their bodies adorned with necklaces of shimmering shards that changed color as they moved.

"Welcome, daughter of Earth," they sang through their trumpet mouths. "Welcome, daughter of the human we loved, the human who swam with us, who came from the great dryness above."

Ben-Ari spoke to them, as her father had years ago. She spoke of the great war against the scum. She spoke of the battle on the frontier where thousands of ships had burned, where they had defeated the scum. She spoke of a great invasion to end the war, to destroy the scum emperor, to shatter the evil empire that had been spreading across the galaxy. The Guramis listened carefully, bobbing, eyes flashing whenever she described a tragedy, such as the fall of Vancouver.

Finally they too spoke. "We are beings of peace," they said together. "We live for beauty, for music, for color, for light. But the dry centipedes are creatures of destruction, of hatred, of death. They slew many of our people, shattered many of our globes, and infected our Mother Sea with their poison. We fought them alone. Many of us died. But still we swim. They mistook us for meek, but we are fierce. They mistook us for cowards, but we are courageous. The enemy destroyed most of our ships, but we still have a fleet armed for war. We will send that fleet with you. Three hundred dryships shall fight in your war, daughter of Earth. They will slay many centipede pods."

Three hundred ships. It wasn't much. Not when facing an empire as massive as the scum's. But every little contribution helped. Ben-Ari nodded.

"Thank you, children of the water," she said. "We will fight together as siblings-in-arms. We will defeat the enemy."

The HDFS *Urchin* flew away from the watery world, and behind her flew three hundred "dryships"--the starships of the Guramis. They rose through space like massive, glimmering plankton, their scaled wings spinning and catching the starlight, their slender hulls bulging with glassy domes full of water.

They were beautiful, graceful ships, but they were more than that. And they proved their might within only moments.

As they were heading back toward the main fleet, a swarm of scum pods--fifteen of them--crackled out of hyperspace and streamed toward them.

The *Urchin* fired its guns, lobbing shells at the enemy. But the true wrath came from the Guramis' dryships. Slender cannons unfurled upon their tops like sprouting plants, organic and graceful. They bloomed open, flowerlike, and blasted out pulsing globs of energy. The pulses shattered the scum pods. Centipedes spilled out, only for the dryships to fire bolts of light, searing the creatures in space.

"Damn!" Addy said, watching from the *Urchin*'s bridge. "Fish can fight, man!"

Ben-Ari nodded. "They can fight. And our work is not done." She raised her chin and stared out at the stars. "We will find more allies on the way to Abaddon. This is the great hour for all free civilizations. All the galaxy will rise."

They rejoined the fleet, traveling through hyperspace for another few light-years. Then the *Urchin* emerged from the funnel again, flying toward another planet.

This time, they flew toward a rainforest world, a planet with no oceans but a vast network of rivers and trees that grew hundreds of meters tall. Ben-Ari and her platoon descended in a shuttle through mist. Among the trees, they found vast cities built of wood, rope, and crystal. A race of sentient aliens called the Silvans lived here. Their torsos were disk-shaped and coated with thick brown fur. Eight eyes blinked on one side of their bodies, while mouths and nostrils breathed on the other side. Six prehensile tails grew in a ring around their bodies, able to grab the branches, use tools, and build starships.

"They look like a cross between spiders, starfish, and monkeys," Addy said, which Ben-Ari had to agree with.

"We will help you," the Silvans said, speaking by clicking and clacking their teeth, which Ben-Ari's communicator translated into English. "The scum have infected many of our trees with rot and have overrun our moons. We will fight them."

The Silvans raised four hundred starships built of crystals and amber, and through gemstones the size of boulders, they could fire photon beams to sear open scum pods. Soon these ships from the jungle world, like the Guramis' ships full of water, flew with the human fleet.

At another world, they found a battle raging. It took a hundred Firebirds to descend to the planet and destroy the scum crawling across it. It was a beautiful, sunny world, its hills alive with singing flowers. A race of aliens lived here, shaped like living harps. Their vocal cords were outside their bodies, golden and thin, which they plucked with elongated fingers, communicating with music. Their fingers could also build tools, and they had built starships from gold and steel, full of many strings to pluck instead of buttons to press. Those harp-ships could blast forth deadly laser beams, and hundreds of them rose to fly with the fleet.

World after world, Ben-Ari raised the civilizations of the galaxy. All those who had suffered under the scum. A world where floating, living spheres of metal communicated using magnetic fields. A world of aliens composed of gassy clouds, portable souls who moved in suits of armor left over from an earlier stage of their evolution, like hermit crabs in abandoned shells. A world of aliens formed from intelligent beams of light, massless creatures who were able to control the minds of animals on their world, harnessing their physical bodies to build their starships, like ghosts possessing flesh. A world where swirls of liquid ink lived in bubbles, able to raise floating starships that could blast out electricity. A world with creatures not unlike Earth animals, with four limbs and a head, but who were microscopic, no larger than dust mites, yet able to raise floating cities the size of scum pods and fire nuclear weapons. A world of sentient plants, moving on roots, who flew ships which Addy described as giant flowerpots. A species of intelligent moss that coated asteroids, able to hurl their stony vessels at enemies.

Some worlds could only send a handful of starships. Some could send fleets of hundreds. But all joined the fight. All hated the scum. Dozens of species, the civilizations of this small corner of the Milky Way, of this vast cosmic arena, rose together.

They all knew my father, Ben-Ari thought, flying in the *Urchin. They will all fight for his memory. And for peace in this galaxy.*

Humanity had flown here with a hundred thousand starships, had lost a quarter along the way. Now thousands of new starships joined them. Starships of crystal, of metal, of stone, of light. Starships from across the galaxy.

Humanity still led this fight. Humanity still formed the bulk of this fleet. But for the first time in this war, humanity did not fight alone.

The Alliance of Free Civilizations flew on, moving closer every day to Abaddon, to evil, to the greatest battle of their time.

CHAPTER FOURTEEN

He sat in the engine room of the *Urchin*, and he wrote in his notebook: "The End."

For long moments, Marco stared at the notebook.

The End.

He had always imagined that, when he finished writing *Loggerhead*, he would cry, or maybe dance, or maybe just sleep for hours. Instead, he just sat, staring, not knowing how to feel.

"Well," he said. "It's done."

Lailani had been curled up in a nearby nook by a window, watching the stars. She rose and padded toward him, barefoot, wearing her fatigue pants and a white tank top. She stood behind him, leaned her chin on his shoulder, and looked at the notebook with him.

"The end," she read from the page. "You finished your book!"

He nodded. "The last few chapters only took a couple of weeks. Lots of time here on the *Shithouse* as we fly to battle. Also, the novel is told via the letters of a mentally challenged man, so I wanted to leave in lots of spelling and grammatical errors. Made it faster to write."

"A man who's writing letters to a turtle," Lailani said. "I remember. He was in a car crash."

"The reader doesn't know that at first," Marco said. "I guess I shouldn't have spoiled the book for you. At first we just see the letters of a homeless, mentally challenged man who places his letters in a bottle, then tosses them into the sea, addressing them to a loggerhead turtle. But later, when a woman visits him on thc beach, claiming to be his daughter, we learn about the car crash that broke him, how he used to be a doctor, and . . . Well, now I'm really spoiling it." He closed the notebook and placed his hand on the binding. "It feels so strange to finally be done. To have finally completed this book I've been thinking about for years."

Lailani grinned. "Can I read it?"

She reached for the notebook, but Marco pulled it away. "I don't know. I'm still not sure I got it right."

"Oh, I'll love it anyway." She hopped around him. "I feel like I'm almost a coauthor, what with watching you write it so often."

Marco thought for a moment, looking out the window. "You know, there's a good chance that we're not coming home."

Lailani tilted her head. "Way to sour the mood, Emery."

He looked down at his notebook. "I'm happy that I completed this novel. But I worry that I'll die in this war, that nobody will ever read it, that it'll die with me."

"Then somebody at least should read it," Lailani said, reaching for the notebook. "Give it here!"

She took the notebook from him, and he handed over six other notebooks--the entire novel. She curled up in the nook again by the window, and she opened the first notebook.

As the fleet streamed outside, Lailani read. Sometimes she gasped. Other times she laughed. For a long while, she simply lay curled up, reading silently. Halfway through, tears filled her eyes, dampening the notebook. That night, as Marco slept, Lailani stayed up late, reading, and she kept reading the next day, notebook after notebook, even reading during their meals in the mess.

Finally, in the evening, she approached Marco. He was sitting in the engine room again, back in the same nook, watching the stars. She hopped into the nook with him, pulled her knees to her chin, and hugged her legs.

"I finished reading," she said.

Marco was suddenly afraid that she had hated it. Or worse--that she had found something of him, of his soul, in the novel, and that it disturbed her, even disgusted her.

"Thank you for reading," he simply said, voice soft, dreading the worst.

Lailani tightened her lips, tilted her head, and thought for a moment. She looked into his eyes. "Marco, it's beautiful. It's so sad, and . . . and just sad, mainly. But a sort of bittersweet, beautiful kind of sad, like rain in a distant field when you're all alone. I wish I were good with words like you so that I could describe how I feel." She shuffled closer to him, wrapped her arms around him, and kissed his cheek. "Thank you for writing it.

The whole world, the whole galaxy, needs to read this book." She tapped her chin. "Well, maybe not the scum. Not sure they're quite the literary types."

"Thank you for reading," he said again, and now these were words of relief, of true gratitude, of love.

She leaned her head against him. "We just need to make it back home now. To make sure the novel is published. So no dying on Abaddon, all right? Deal?"

"Deal," he said.

She stretched out her legs, pressing her feet against the edge of the nook, and they looked out at the stars together.

"Marco, when we go home to Earth, can I live with you?"

"You want to move in together?" He smiled.

She nodded. "I do. I don't have a home on Earth. I was homeless before the army. Maybe I can live in your apartment, above the library, the place you told me about. I'll work for room and board. But mainly I think it can be nice to live together."

Marco wrapped his arms around her and kissed her cheek. When he had first met Lailani, she had joined the army to die in battle--a sort of grand, heroic suicide attempt, following her failed attempt when slashing her wrists. Hearing her speak of a future meant more to him than her praise for his book.

"When we're back on Earth, you'll live with me. In my home in Canada. Addy and my dad live there too."

"Will they mind me being there?" Lailani said.

"Addy loves you, and my dad will too," Marco said.

"And someday, when your book makes you rich and famous, you can buy us a giant big house," Lailani said. "I'm just kidding, you know. I don't need a big house. Even a little apartment is fine, if it's near some trees and water. And if you're there with me. And if you write more books for me to read."

He mussed her hair. "Any more conditions?"

"Just one," she said. "That once we're in Canada, we never speak of this. Of the army. Of the scum. Of what happened in the mines. We can speak of our friends that we lost. But only to remember the good times, the times Elvis sang, and how Beast talked about Russia, and how Caveman loved flowers. But not about how they died. Not about the bad things. Promise me that."

"I promise," he said.

Lailani chewed her lip. "Maybe Lieutenant Ben-Ari can live with us too. She's homeless too, you know. She grew up on military bases. And Sergeant Stumpy too. We can pick him up from Nightwall on the way back."

"I think that it's getting rather crowded in our apartment," Marco said.

"I like it crowded," Lailani said. "The worst thing in the world is loneliness."

They held each other, watching the stars in silence for long moments. Marco noticed that tears were flowing down Lailani's cheeks.

"Lailani," he said. "What's wrong?"

Her tears dampened his shirt. "I'm happy," she whispered, voice shaking. "I'm happy like this with you. I don't want this to end. I don't want us to reach Abaddon. I don't want us to fight. I just want to stay like this, with you holding me."

"Soon this war will be over," he said. "And we'll spend our days in the library, talking about books. And we'll walk in the park and along the beach, and we won't be afraid anymore, because there will be no more monsters. The world will be good again, and we'll be happy. Happy to just live together, to remember our friends, to grow old together. And once we're there, once we're in that world, I'll never let you go."

"Promise?"

"Promise."

"I'll fight for that." Lailani wiped her eyes. "When I first joined the army, I had nothing to fight for. Only hatred of the scum. Of myself. But I'll fight for that, Marco. To grow old with you. To see people read your book. For this moment when we sat together watching the stars." She stuck her tongue out at him. "Also, we'll make adorable mixed-race babies."

Marco nodded. "Yep. Apartment definitely getting crowded."

Lailani closed her eyes, and they sat together as the fleet streamed through space. Toward fire. Toward death. Toward a hope for a better tomorrow.

* * * * *

"No, Addy, look," Marco said. "The dragon moves diagonally, like this."

Addy sat, biting her lip, squinting at the counter squares board. "Is this the dragon?" She lifted a piece.

Marco groaned. "Addy! That's a griffin. And that's *my* griffin. Remember, you're the white pieces."

"I want to be black," she said, reaching for one of his knights.

"Hands off!" He slapped her hand away. "Addy, take this seriously please. Counter squares is serious business."

They were sitting in the *Urchin*'s lounge, a cluttered chamber above the engine room. The floor rattled as they flew through hyperspace, making the pieces vibrate on the board. A few other soldiers sat in the chamber, some playing cards, others gazing out the viewports at the rest of the fleet.

Addy finally lifted one of her pieces--a white cannon--and moved it a few squares forward, only for Marco to capture it with his elephant.

"Fuck this shit!" Addy shouted, leaping to her feet. "This game is fucking stupid."

"I wasn't very good at first either," Marco said. "But it's hardly stupid. It's an ancient game of skill, strategy, and--"

"Want to play hockey, nerd?" Addy said. "Because I'll kick your ass. All those times you were playing this even nerdier version of chess as a kid, I was on the ice." She rolled up her sleeve, showing off her tattoo of a blue maple leaf, logo of her favorite team. "*This* is a game."

"Well, until Ben-Ari decides to install an ice rink on the *Urchin*, counter squares is what we have," Marco said. "Your turn. Just give it one more try."

Addy groaned, sat back down, and spat. She moved her wyvern three squares forward, capturing Marco's fortress. "There! I killed you."

Marco responded by advancing his catapult, capturing her wyvern.

Addy stared at the board for a second. Then she stood up and pointed her rifle at the board.

"Whoa, whoa!" soldiers across the lounge said, leaping toward Addy and pulling her back.

"I'm going to blow a hole through this goddamn fucking board!" Addy was screaming. "Come on, Marco. Let's settle this with a good old fistfight."

Marco shook his head sadly. "All brawn, no brains, that one."

A few soldiers dragged Addy off to cool down. Marco sighed and reset the counter squares board. All his life, he had suffered Addy's temper. Even before she had moved into his home, he had experienced her rage at school. He still remembered that day in first grade when she had wrestled him at recess. She had been so fierce they had rolled across the yard, then onto the rusted old metal hatch of a bomb shelter. The hatch had crashed open, and Addy and Marco had fallen six feet onto a hard concrete floor. The hatch had then shut above them, raining rust, sealing them in the dark chamber. Only by a miracle had they not broken any bones. But even after the shock of the fall, Addy--in a rage over some minor slight--had continued to wrestle Marco right there in the bomb shelter. It had taken an hour for her to calm down, another hour of calling for help before a teacher had found them there and pulled them out.

He was so lost in thought he barely noticed Gunnery Sergeant Jones approach. The huge man--he stood halfway between six and seven feet, and he must have weighed nearly three hundred pounds--sat down at the table in front of Marco, taking Addy's seat. The chair creaked. Marco looked up at the Spearhead Platoon's second-in-command, and his heart twisted, expecting trouble. Jones had a giant bald head, mahogany skin, and a cheek scarred from an old battle. He looked every inch a warrior, capable of snapping even Addy in two with his bare hands.

"So you think you're good at counter squares?" the NCO said.

"Better than Addy, at least, Commander," Marco said.

Jones gave a small smile. "Let's play." He moved a pawn. "Your move."

Marco moved a pawn of his own. Jones responded by bringing out his dragon early--a classic Crane Gambit. Marco responded with the typical defense, moving his fortress out to block the attack. But Jones didn't respond with the usual second move of the gambit, instead opting to bring out another pawn, then another, then finally advance with both his cannons. Marco frowned at the board. This was more opposition than he had faced from Addy, no doubt. After a few moments of playing, Marco lost his dragon, his wyvern, and his elephant. By the time Jones had trapped his griffin, it was all over.

"The boys and I used to play all the time," Jones said. "Back when we served on Titan. Play again?"

They played two more times, Jones winning those games too, though Marco put up a strong defense in the third game and nearly forced a draw.

"You see," said Jones, "many people make a classic mistake with counter squares. They think that to win the game, you need a long-term plan, executed masterfully step-by-step."

"That's what I try to do," Marco said.

"I know," said Jones. "And I was able to quickly see your plan each time and thwart it. Meanwhile, you were trying to see if I had a plan, but you couldn't figure it out, correct?"

"Correct," Marco said. "I thought you were attempting a Crane maneuver at first, but you changed it."

"Winning counter squares isn't about having a complicated plan," Jones said. "It's about playing by basic principles. Controlling the center of the board. Creating strong defenses. Bringing out offensive pieces when the moment is right. With every move I make, I ask myself: Does this strengthen my position on the board? Does this adhere to the basic principles of the game? I don't try to think more than two or three moves ahead. I just try to strengthen my position with every move and gradually advance toward final victory."

Marco understood. "So you improvise."

"In a sense," said Jones. "But only because I can judge every new board and decide if it's in my favor." The NCO looked out the viewport at the fleet. "War is like that too, as I see it. Admirals and generals come up with end goals, but if their plans are too rigid, they will fail. The best soldiers improvise in the field, just trying to strengthen their position with every move."

"Even life is like that," Marco said. "Life has a way of messing up your plans." He thought of his plan to work in the archives back on Earth, to live a life with Kemi. "You try to make the best of each day as you find it. Which isn't always easy. Not on the bad days. Days when you lose people."

Jones nodded. "It's easy to win at life when everything goes right. When things fall apart, when loved ones die, when the world burns, when it seems like there's no path to victory--that's when we must look carefully at our board, make one move at a time, and just keep fighting."

Marco wondered how many friends, how many loved ones, Sergeant Jones had lost. Marco thought about the friends he had left behind. Of Beast, Elvis, Jackass, Caveman, Sheriff. Of his commanders, his mentors--Corporal Webb, Corporal Diaz, Sergeant Singh. Every day, Marco missed them, wished they could be flying here too. Every day, as the fleet drew closer to Abaddon, it was harder to find hope, to believe there could be victory.

And every day, the fear grew that he would lose others. Lailani. Addy.

That night, Marco lay awake in his bunk for a long time. The others in his squad slept around him, fifteen warriors in the shadows. Tomorrow Marco expected to spend long hours at the cannon, firing at any scum who approached. Scum sorties had been attacking every day, chipping away at the fleet. But no sleep found Marco. As they drew nearer to Abaddon, his dread grew. In the rattling of the floorboards and humming of the engines, Marco had begun to hear a voice, deep, rumbling, but the words were too muffled to understand. In his dreams, though, that voice spoke clearly to him--the voice of the scum emperor, welcoming him into his lair, sawing Marco open and stitching him into a new creature. Marco could barely sleep more than an hour straight most nights.

A shadow rose before him.

Claws stretched out.

Marco lay in bed, unable to move, just to stare. He tried to kick. He tried to reach for the gun under his pillow. His arms were paralyzed. He wanted to scream. *Scum on the ship, scum on the ship!* His lips wouldn't move.

"Poet?" The scum jabbed his shoulder. "Poet, you asleep?"

His mind reconnected with his body. Marco could breathe again. It was only Addy standing above him, wearing her pajamas.

"Addy, fucking hell, I thought you were a scum. What are you doing--" He frowned and fell silent. There were tears on her cheeks.

She sat down on the bed beside him, then lay down. "Marco, I'm sorry I got angry at you before," she said. "With your stupid game."

"It's all right," he said.

She touched his arm. "And I'm sorry about all the other times too. How I'd tease you a lot back home. How I'd wrestle with you. How I was a huge pain in the ass."

"You definitely kept my life interesting," Marco said.

Addy buried her face against his chest. "I'm scared, Marco. I'm scared that I'll lose this war like I lost the game. I'm scared that I'll lose you. I'm not even scared of dying. I'm scared of living, Marco. Of living on without you, without Lailani, without Ben-Ari, without those we lost already."

"Me too," Marco said quietly.

Addy looked at him with damp eyes. "I know we're not supposed to talk about it. I know we're supposed to forget it ever happened. But I liked having sex with you. I usually just had sex with big tough guys, and you're my friend. You're my *best* friend. And that's why it was good. And I'll remember it. Even if you're with Lailani, even if people die. It's something good that happened. Never think otherwise. I really love you. Even when I'm a pain in the ass."

"We're going to survive this," Marco said. "Both of us. We'll go back home together when this is all over. We'll live above the library, and I'll play counter squares with Dad, and you'll play hockey. Sometimes I'll even watch the games with you, and we'll eat wings and drink beer. We'll talk about the war sometimes, but only the good memories, the funny parts, like when we pissed into milk cartons in the tent, or when we smuggled candy out of the vending machine. And we'll laugh and be happy, and in a few years, we'll realize that all the good times outweighed the bad.

There will be no more war at home. No more gas masks or bomb shelters. No more kids going into the army. There will be books, family, friends, laughter, love." He kissed her cheek. "Because I love you too, you stinky pain in the butt."

"I like that," Addy said. "I'll think about that when we fight the scum. About home." She closed her eyes, still lying beside him. "Can I sleep here tonight? Lailani won't see, and I won't do anything naughty to you, no matter how much you want it."

"Only if you don't snore," Marco said.

"Promise."

She slept, and finally Marco could sleep too, and with Addy's warm body beside his, he did not dream.

CHAPTER FIFTEEN

"Hey, de la Rosa," Addy said, pulling on her uniform. "Why do you have that rainbow tattoo on your arm?"

They were in the locker room of the *Urchin*, and Lailani was drying her hair in front of a mirror, wearing a white tank top, her tattoos exposed.

"Never heard of pride?" Lailani said.

Addy tried to brush her hair, but the blond locks were a thick, knotted mess. She grimaced as she pulled her brush through them. Fuck it, she should just cut her hair short like Lailani's.

"Yeah, I heard of it," Addy said. "But I thought you're banging Marco."

Lailani shrugged and pulled on her uniform's button-down shirt. "So? I like him. Even though he's a boy. He's not like most boys. He's softer, kinder, wiser. And I like his book. Hey, I can play on the opposite team too." She glanced at Addy's own tattoo. "What's that blue leaf?"

"The *best* team!" Addy said. "The Maple Leafs!"

Lailani raised her eyebrows. "Football? Do Santos or Alvarez play for them?"

"Santos and Alvarez play *soccer*," Addy said. "I'm not some European who gets the names confused. And no, the Maple Leafs are a hockey team. The best damn team in the whole world." She raised her chin. "I was doing great in their tryouts. I could have joined the team if not for this goddamn army."

Lailani's eyes widened. "Wow, I bet the Leafs won the cup a bunch of times!"

Addy grumbled. "Well . . . sort of. A while ago."

Lailani nodded. "I see. So it's been a couple of years since they won. It happens." She tilted her head. "How long since their last win?"

Addy mumbled under her breath.

"What's that?" Lailani said.

"A hundred and seventy-nine years!" Addy said. "All right? Happy?"

Lailani gasped. "The best hockey team in the world hasn't won the cup since--"

"Shut it!" Addy said.

Lailani stuck her tongue out at her. "I'm going to stick with football."

Addy groaned. God damn it. She wanted to hate this girl, but she couldn't help but like Lailani.

She's like me, Addy thought. *She's strong. Not physically, maybe. But she's got balls of steel.*

Addy thought of that night they had first arrived at Nightwall, treated like prisoners, interrogated, torn away from their friends. She thought of how she and Marco had been so afraid, so lonely, how in their dizzying fear they had made love--raw, sweaty, half in a dream. She didn't like speaking to Marco about it. It still felt wrong to her, but she never regretted that night, how she had grown closer to him, to her best friend.

Since then, being near Lailani had felt odd to Addy. She wasn't jealous. That couldn't be it. She liked Lailani, and she was happy that Marco had found happiness with her. And yet, whenever she saw Marco and Lailani together, whenever she thought of them making love, Addy felt a strange pang, just a little bit rejected, a little bit sad.

It's not because I love Marco, Addy thought. *Not like that, not like a woman loves a man, despite that one night. It's because he's always been my best friend, and maybe I'm losing him just a little.*

Of course, Addy herself once had a boyfriend. She had left Steve when boarding the rocket to RASCOM; he had been due to be drafted just a few days later. She hadn't seen or heard from the big lump since. Addy doubted she would for another five years, not until their service was over. At least if they both survived that long, which was looking unlikely.

Our whole hockey team joined the army, Addy thought. *The whole team is gone. Some of us probably dead.*

And suddenly rage filled Addy.

She raged against the scum who had caused this war.

She raged against her politicians and generals who had found no path to peace.

She raged against the loss of Elvis, of Beast, of all the friends she had left behind.

And raged against herself, the fear inside her that would not leave.

She raged against this whole damn cosmos.

"Addy, you all right?" Lailani said, and now her voice was soft.

Addy nodded, realizing that her eyes were damp. "I was just thinking of home. Hockey games. Hot dogs and beer. The people I left behind." She rubbed her eyes. "I'm happy for you and Marco, Lailani. Honestly. I feel a bit like a third wheel, but I'm happy."

Lailani laughed. "Not a third wheel. A third musketeer. That's us now. You, me, and Marco, and nobody can break this trio."

Addy hugged her. She towered over Lailani; the top of Lailani's head didn't even reach her chin. But she could think of no finer soldier to fight alongside.

"More like the three stooges," Addy said, and Lailani laughed.

"Now come on, let's find Marco," Lailani said. "We'll let him be Curly."

"Good!" Addy said. "So I can be Moe and beat him up."

They left the locker room as the *Urchin* flew onward through the darkness.

* * * * *

They had chicken wings on the *Urchin*.

Actual chicken wings!

They weren't taken from real chickens, of course. They had been grown in a lab somewhere on the frontier, flash frozen, and forgotten ages ago in the *Urchin*'s pantry. Lailani knew that many soldiers, especially officers, turned up their noses at lab-grown meat, preferring the real thing from real animals, even if those cuts had to be delivered all the way from Earth. But to Lailani, as she stood staring at the wings warming up in the microwave, this seemed like heaven.

When the microwave dinged, Lailani removed the plate and placed it on the table in the small, cluttered kitchen of the *Urchin*. She sat, staring at the wings. Five plump, steaming chicken wings, coated with barbecue sauce. For a long time, she didn't eat. Instead, she remembered.

She was a child again, an orphan wandering the streets of Manila, the most crowded metropolis in the world, a city where half the population of twenty-two million was homeless, many of them starving. With eleven million other homeless, hungry souls, Lailani would crawl alongside train tracks, begging for scraps from passengers as the carts trundled by. She would join hundreds as they climbed mountainous landfills, swarming toward the dump trucks when they arrived, leaping into the trash, rummaging, seeking anything that wasn't too rotten to eat. Candy wrappers with some crumbs still clinging to them. Bones with some skin and fat. Peels of fruits and vegetables. Anything to stave off that hunger, a battle against flies, rot, disease, and millions of other starving souls fighting for every scrap.

Lailani's mother had sold her body to the Western men who flocked here. Several times a day, her mother could make a handful of pesos, letting some aging, white-haired, overweight Western man claim her skinny, thirteen-year-old body. But even her mother had not survived long, had died so young that Lailani could barely remember her. And so Lailani, herself thirteen now, survived alone. Stealing what scraps she could. Rummaging. Going hungry most nights.

Many of the girls her age were prostitutes. There were always Western men here in Manila. Thousands, tens of thousands of them, entire communities of them. Some came as tourists, seeking not landmarks but flesh. Others lived in apartments along the beaches, their dollars from home worth a fortune in the east. Some had fallen in love with their whores, had married them. Some men took their girls back west; it was the dream of most prostitutes. But Lailani refused to fall into that trap, as she refused to fall for *hintan*, the drug that claimed so many of the girls. Prostitution, she knew, led to hintan, the only way to dull that pain. Hintan led to madness, to a slow death. Her mother had died such a slow death.

No. She, Lailani, when she chose to die--it would be quick.

It was one sweltering summer day when Lailani dared leave the train tracks and landfills, when she dared roam through the bustling streets by the water. Millions of people lived here, crammed together into the densest place on the planet. They had no permanent homes. They lived in shacks built from scrap metal and tarp. Countless of those huts spread out in massive shantytowns, pressed together, destroyed every year by the hurricanes or a scum attack, only to be rebuilt from the scraps. There were no streets between them. There were only rivers of water floating with debris. Often the streams were so thick with trash one couldn't even see the water, only a film of plastic and wrappers and wood and cloth and rotten food and human waste. Lailani waded through it.

Huts of corrugated metal, rotten plywood, and tarp roofs rose alongside her, people peering between slats of wood. They weren't true homes, just rickety shelters the homeless cobbled together, kilometer after kilometer of them, a sprawling shantytown of hunger and disease. There were no schools here, no libraries, no hospitals, no hope--just a daily struggle to survive, millions of people crammed into the labyrinth, scrounging for food, for a handful of pesos, for another day in Hell. Here was her home, the only reality Lailani had ever known.

But farther out, as Lailani kept walking, she could see the skyscrapers of Makati, the glittering center of Manila. Skyscrapers. Real skyscrapers like they had in Hong Kong, in Tokyo, in Singapore, in those glittering cities beyond the water, so close to here yet unreachable to her.

But Makati was reachable.

Makati was only a few kilometers away.

And so that hot day, Lailani walked. She walked through water that was chin-deep, wading through rot and filth and shit. She walked along cluttered streets bustling with thousands of colorful jeepneys, the rickety and garish cabs of the Philippines, as ubiquitous as yellow taxis in New York. She walked through markets where vendors sold spices, knockoff watches, exotic animals, stolen electronics, and shoes stitched with logos like *Nyke* and *Ribook*. Jumbles of electrical wires crackled and buzzed overhead. Rot dripped down decaying concrete walls, roofs crumbled, and rust covered the metal sheets of makeshift walls. But the farther Lailani walked, the nicer the city became. Soon she saw houses--real houses, actual houses with barred windows and tiled roofs, not just shacks in a shantytown. Tall fences enclosed them, and armed guards stood outside the gates, scowling at her. Farther into the city rose apartment buildings, thirty stories tall, and Lailani could see families on the balconies, families who wore real clothes, not just rags, who ate real food, not just trash. Children who had parents. Parents who had jobs. People who knew how to read and write. Who had a future. Who had hope.

Tears flooded Lailani's eyes as she walked toward the skyscrapers of Makati, this pocket of wealth in this hive of poverty.

She had spent her life, all her thirteen years, only a couple of hours away from here, but she had never come to this place before. She gaped. She saw shopping malls, actual shopping malls like in the stories, glittering buildings surrounded by palm trees. She saw families walking dogs and driving foreign cars, not just riding mopeds or bikes. She saw many foreigners--soldiers, diplomats, priests, businessmen from Japan and China and even as far as America. Some of them frowned at her--this barefoot youth in rags. Her kind was expected to stay in the shantytowns, the train tracks, the landfills, not mingle with the city's elite. But Lailani was too hungry, too tired, too angry to care. She was dying, she knew. She would die from hunger, or suicide, or a scum attack, or disease, from a descent into hintan. She doubted she would live to be fourteen, and so she walked here, ignoring the upturned noses.

She approached a restaurant with a neon sign, showing a red and yellow chicken winking at passersby. Lailani couldn't read the sign, but she knew this logo, had seen its wrappers in the landfills. The Happy Chicken Joy Wings restaurant, a favorite of the city's middle class. An armed guard stood at the front of the restaurant, and when he aimed his assault rifle at her, Lailani fled to the back alley. Here, behind the restaurant, she found a large trash bin and several stray cats.

She waited until the rusty back door opened, until a worker in a yellow and red uniform emerged to toss a garbage bag into the bin. Once the worker was gone, Lailani climbed into the bin, tore open the garbage bag, and beheld a treasure--a treasure such as the city slums never offered.

There were cups of cola, some drops still at the bottom. There were greasy napkins and plastic cutlery. And mostly there were bones. Thousands of chicken wing bones, many with bits of meat still attached.

Lailani lifted the entire garbage bag from the bin and dragged it into a deeper, darker alley. She worked for a long time, picking bits of meat, fat, and skin off the bones and placing them on a cobblestone. She feasted.

That night, she was sick.

She vomited again and again, shivering with fever. All next day, she could only lie curled up.

But the following day, she returned to that bin, and she pulled off the bits of meat from the chicken wing bones. And she found an old woman in a nearby shop who had a little portable stove, and the old woman agreed to fry up the meat in exchange for half the meal. Some of the meat, Lailani realized, sat inside the restaurant garbage for hours, sometimes even days, before being tossed outside into the alley. By then it was rotten, but frying could kill the disease, and when Lailani ate the meal that second time, she kept it down.

She returned to the alley a third time. She stole a third bag of bones. Again the old woman fried them for her in exchange for half the meal.

Lailani began to return to this alleyway every day, and to other alleyways behind other Happy Chicken Joy Wings across the city. Every morning, she trudged through the shantytowns, collected the bones, had the old woman fry them and place meals into plastic bags, then walked back. She traveled through the slums, carrying ten, sometimes twenty plastic bags full of fried bits of chicken meat collected from the bones in the trash. She sold them to the poor, those who had a few spare pesos earned from begging, prostitution, stealing, or odd manual jobs when they could find them. Sometimes, at the end of such a day, Lailani even earned enough pesos to buy a cup of coffee and a bread roll.

Some days, even with the meat fried up, she got sick. Some days, she saw the children she sold the bags of meat to grow ill, vomit. Maybe some of them died. Yet what choice did Lailani have? It was eat bad meat or starve to death. And so she fed them. Her mother had chosen one way to survive for a few years; Lailani chose another. Pag pag girl, they called her in the slums. Pag pag, the name of the food she sold, fried pieces of skin, fat, and morsels collected off bones in trash bins. Pag pag, full of disease and filth, the difference between life and death.

And Lailani knew as the days stretched on, from illness to illness, that she was only staving off death for a while. Another few months. Maybe another year if she were lucky. When she turned fifteen, she was amazed to have lived that long. She was amazed that the human body and soul could survive so many days of pain. By the time she was sixteen, they found her in an alleyway after three days of vomiting, her wrists slit with a shard of broken glass.

When she was eighteen, she boarded a rocket, landed in RASCOM, shaved her head, and became a soldier.

Now the old, scrawny urchin sat in a starship named the *Urchin*. Now the pag pag girl was a corporal, a seasoned warrior. Now she sat before a plate of real chicken wings--not bones, not scraps from the trash, but real wings with juicy, plump meat--and tears kept streaming down her cheeks.

She could have easily avoided the military, Lailani knew. She could have hidden away in the slums. But she had told the army she had an American father. She didn't know who her father was. Her mother had never told her. But she had said he was American, and they had believed her, had let her serve in the Western Command with Americans and Canadians and Brits. The wealthy half of the world, the Makati of the globe. She had joined to die in this war, but she had found friends here. She had found love. She had found Addy, Ben-Ari, and Marco. She had found these real chicken wings that her tears kept splashing.

And now, as the *Urchin* flew toward war, toward a devastating battle where millions perhaps would die, Lailani just wanted to live.

She lifted one wing, like lifting a holy artifact. She ate. She ate them all, leaving no scrap of skin or fat, and when she tossed the bones into the trash, she let out a sob.

She returned to her bunk, where she found Marco, Addy, and some of the others playing a game of poker.

"Yo, de la Rosa!" Addy said. "You want in?"

Lailani nodded. She sat between them, and Marco dealt her a hand. They played cards--walls around them, a roof over their heads, food in their bellies, flying to war.

As Marco and Addy were arguing about the rules, Lailani looked out the viewport. She could see thousands of other ships, millions of soldiers aboard them. The greatest battle in the history of humanity awaited them, only days away.

Lailani often doubted her faith. It was hard to believe after seeing the cruelty of the cosmos. Yet she had taken to wearing a small cross in the military, and now she prayed silently.

Please, God. Let us all go home. Let us survive this war. I've been dead all my life. Let me finally live.

They flew on into the darkness.

CHAPTER SIXTEEN

Tens of thousands of starships streamed through hyperspace, charging the last few light-years toward the homeworld of the scum.

Marco stood with his platoon on the bridge of the *Urchin*, staring through the viewport, ready for war.

This is it, Marco thought. *In a few moments we'll be at Abaddon. The planet of the scum. The great battle of our generation. In a few moments the gates of Hell will open, and we'll face the greatest victory or the worst defeat in human history.*

Around him, the others were nervous, he saw. A few soldiers gulped. One was mouthing silent prayers. Most just stared ahead, eyes hard, hands clutching their guns. Waiting for the blood, for the screams, for the terror.

We're strong, Marco told himself. *We can do this. We can win.*

Through the viewport, he could see much of the fleet. Most of the starships were human vessels, ranging from massive starfighter carriers to small Firebirds that zipped back and forth in battle formations, defending their larger brethren. Thousands of cargo ships, huge metal boxes, carried millions of human marines from both Earth and Space Territorial Commands. In this battle, both corps would fight side by side. Not just warriors were here but also medics and doctors and nurses, priests and clerics and monks, cooks and janitors, mechanics and engineers, computer programmers, pilots and navigators, warehouse workers, intelligence officers, singers and comedians to entertain the troops, and countless other professionals the military relied on. Millions of people. It was impossible for Marco to grasp the sheer size of this army. Here before him--the Human Defense Force, the largest organization in human history. Here was a flying nation dedicated to one purpose: victory.

And among the human ships flew thousands of other vessels, the starships gathered from across the galaxy. The aquatic Guramis in their elongated, silvery ships with scaly wings, their hulls full of water. The forest-dwelling Silvans, furry disks with a ring of tails, who flew in vessels made from crystal and amber. A dozen other species flying in great spheres, in serpentine tubes, in blobs of shimmering light like mobile suns, in pulsing balls of metal that spun madly like pulsars, and some ships that were barely more than flecks of lightning and shadows against the stars.

The day was here.

They were about to reach Abaddon.

Lieutenant Ben-Ari walked to the head of the bridge and faced the platoon, her back to the viewport.

"You have all trained for this," she said. "You have all fought in simulations of Abaddon. You have all fought in scum colonies across the galaxy. You're ready for this. Once we arrive, we expect opposition in space. We expect a battle with a scum fleet. But we will break through. We will enter our exoframes, and we will jump down to the planet in our landing craft. Once there, de la Rosa, you will lead the way. Can you feel the hive?"

Lailani nodded, fists clenched. "A little. It's hard to sense it from hyperspace. But it's there. He's there. The emperor." She winced. "I can feel him, hear him calling me, even now. He knows we're here. He is angry. He is cruel." She sucked in air. "I can find him. I can lead you to him. We will kill him."

Marco looked at her. She looked back. He gave her the smallest of nods and smiled. The hint of a smile touched her lips too.

I'm with you, Marco told her, and he didn't need to speak.

I know, Lailani replied without words.

"I've known some of you since basic training," Ben-Ari said. "I've met others only a couple of months ago. But I want you to know this: I am proud of every one of you. I believe in every soldier here. I am honored to fight among you. I believe that this is the best platoon in the military. Our enemy is determined. He is ruthless. He is strong. But *we will defeat him.*" She raised two fingers. "For victory."

The rest of the platoon raised two fingers too, forming Vs. "For victory!" they cried.

Osiris sat at the controls, facing the viewport. The android turned her head toward them. "Arrival in ten minutes."

Ben-Ari nodded. "Fireteams, go man the gun turrets. The fleet will emerge three hundred thousand kilometers away from Abaddon. That's as close to a planetary body as we can get in hyperspace. We expect that scum fleets will defend that entire distance. We'll have to fight for every one of those kilometers. I want everyone in their exoframes. We might be breached, we might be boarded, and we must be ready to fight hand-to-claw aboard the *Urchin* if it comes to that. When we're ready to invade the planet, I'll give the order, and we'll race into the landing craft. Understood?"

"Yes, ma'am!" they replied.

"Now go. Into your exoframes and to the cannons!"

The platoon raced toward the warehouse where they kept the Exoframe W78b Hardsuits. They climbed into the hulking wearable robots. When Marco flexed his fingers, the metallic plates slammed shut around his limbs and torso, and the helmet closed around his head. He was now encased in metal, a passenger inside a bulky robot. Sensors within the suit picked up every movement of his muscles. As he walked, the suit's legs moved in tandem. He was six inches taller this way, far heavier, and many times stronger. In this suit, he was a superman. He could run fast enough to chase a car, could lift that car over his head. His Fyre plasma gun snapped into place at his side. He raced through the ship, his suit whooshing and clanking. The others ran with him.

Marco and Lailani leaped into one gun turret, a pillbox that thrust out from the hull of the *Urchin*, affording a view of the fleet. Several other gun turrets rose across the ship, cannons thrusting out like spikes on a sea urchin.

Osiris's voice emerged from the speakers in the platoon's helmets.

"Thirty seconds until we leave hyperspace," the android said. "Twenty-nine. Twenty-eight. Twenty-seven. We have time for a joke, I think--"

"No jokes!" Ben-Ari said.

"Sorry, ma'am! Twenty-three, twenty-two . . ."

Marco inhaled deeply and steeled himself. He looked over at Lailani. Through the helmet of her exoframe, she met his gaze. She nodded and raised two fingers gloved in metal.

"Victory," she said.

"Seventeen," rose the android's voice. "Sixteen . . ."

Through the viewport, Marco could see the blue azoth engines across the fleet turning off. The curving starlight began to straighten.

"Thirteen. Twelve . . ."

The streams of light outside gathered into smudges. Nausea rose in Marco. He felt as if he were floating outside the gun turret.

"Eight. Seven . . ."

The world seemed too small, minuscule. His consciousness lived in the emptiness. There were infinite dimensions, not just three, and suddenly he was very young, lying in bed at home, afraid of ghosts in the closet, and he was very old, ancient, alone in another bed. Time and space all swirled inside him and around him. He watched himself from afar.

"Three," said Osiris, and he saw her face in his mind. "Two. One. Emerging into normal spacetime."

With a long whooshing sound, they dived out of hyperspace and into the solar system of the scum.

In the distance--a yellow planet.

With fire and endless malice, the fury of countless enemy ships charged toward them.

* * * * *

Marco stared, frozen.

Death.

He stared at death.

He had seen war, had been born into war. Throughout his childhood, he had run from the scum, leaping into bomb shelters, fleeing the monsters. He had fought in battles, had faced armies of aliens. In Fort Djemila. In the mines of Corpus. On the border of the empire. He had known terror, had seen friends fall, had seen evil rise from the abyss.

But he had never seen anything like this.

Staring through the viewport, Marco couldn't move, couldn't breathe. Tears filled his eyes.

"Death," he whispered.

He had thought humanity's fleet, with its hundred thousand starships, large and powerful. They were, he now realized, nothing but a toy army. Before him in space, hiding Abaddon behind them, rose true power. True cruelty. Before this enemy, he knew, there could be no victory. There could be no hope. Only pain. Only death.

Streaming through the darkness toward them came the enemy--a million scum ships, covering space.

Many were small, no larger than the Firebirds, globs of hardened flesh wreathed in purple fire. Thousands were larger, as large as humanity's greatest starfighter carriers. Some were larger still, flying scum hives the size of mountains, pustules opening on their surface to spurt out yellow pus.

Through his helmet's communicator, he heard Addy scream. "Die, bastards!"

From the cannon next to his, only a few meters away along the hull of the *Urchin*, a shell blasted out toward the enemy.

Thousands of other ships in the Alliance joined Addy. The firepower of humanity and her allies flamed forth.

With both hands, Marco pulled his cannon's cord.

There was no need to aim. Wherever he fired, he would hit an enemy. With an ear-shattering explosion, the shell blasted out into space. Myriads of other weapons fired from the Alliance's fleet. The great warships blasted shells. The thousands of Firebirds flew forth, firing both bullets and missiles. The alien Alliance ships fired their weapons too: laser beams, lightning bolts, metal rounds, streams of plasma, and crystal shards. Before the massive bombardments, thousands of scum ships fell. Pods shattered. Several of the larger, bloated ships--they looked like floating organs--broke open, spilling out yellow liquid and thousands of centipedes. Flames raced across the shards of pods great and small and consumed the scum who hurtled through the darkness.

But countless more enemy ships still charged toward the Alliance. All the dead scum--thousands of dead--were barely noticeable in this horrible swarm.

The weapons of the enemy fired.

Sizzling globs of acid streamed forth. Tiny pods the size of human heads raced forth, moving at many times the speed of sound, ringed in fire. With sound and fury and flame, the weapons slammed into the Alliance fleet.

The cosmos seemed to shatter.

Firebirds tore apart. Transport vessels cracked open, spilling out marines. A starfighter carrier listed and slammed into a cargo hull, and both ships exploded, taking down a hundred nearby Firebirds. A Gurami ship tore open, spilling water and finned aliens.

"Incoming!" Lailani shouted, pointed, and--

Fire.

Searing metal.

The *Urchin* rocked madly. Pods slammed into her, denting the hull, spilling out centipedes. The scum raced across the ship, wrapped around the cannons, and slammed their claws against the hull.

"Fuck!" Lailani said. "Marco, help me, the Gatling guns!"

They left the cannon, leaped up ladders, and grabbed the controls for the .50-caliber machine guns that rose above the main cannon. They pulled the triggers, and bullets streamed out, cutting into the scum that crawled over the ship. More pods came racing forward. Marco leaped back down, grabbed a shell, and loaded it into the cannon. Lailani hopped down beside him and yanked the cannon's cord like kick-starting a chainsaw. The shell flew and slammed into an enemy vessel the size of a school bus.

Fire, shards of ships, and corpses filled space.

Marco and Lailani fired shell after shell. Across the *Urchin*, the other fireteams were firing their own cannons. Throughout the sky, across thousands of kilometers, the battle raged. The warships blasted massive cannons. Tens of thousands of Firebirds streamed through space, firing missiles. Pods swarmed everywhere like clouds of insects, shattering, burning, firing, crashing into Alliance ships.

Not only the humans fought here, but their alien allies too. Two balls of spinning metal, each the size of a building, rolled forth, tearing into the scum meatsacks. A Silvan ship, built of crystals and amber, shot beams of light but shattered as scum landed onto it, ripping out its crystals. Gurami vessels sprouted flowery cannons, firing laser beams. Ghostly ships, composed of pure energy, spun madly, burning scum pods.

Yet everywhere, even these mighty aliens were falling. Their strange corpses--furred, scaled, metallic, liquid, gaseous, some just waves of light--floated through space among the human bodies. The dead thumped against ship hulls, got sucked into engines, and burned in cannon fire. Thousands of centipedes floated through space, expelled from shattered pods, still alive and feeding upon the dead.

"HDFS *Urchin*!" rose a voice through the speakers. Marco recognized Admiral Bryan's voice speaking from the HDFS *Terra*. "You're too exposed out there. Bring yourself into our wake! We'll protect you."

"Happy to comply!" rose Osiris's voice.

"Keep those cannons firing!" Now it was Ben-Ari speaking. "We're carving a path toward you, *Terra*."

The *Urchin* turned in the sky and began flying toward the far larger HDFS *Terra*, the flagship of the fleet. Marco understood.

We're the most valuable platoon here, he thought. *We're the team tasked with killing the scum emperor. They don't want us aboard the main ships--those are prime targets for scum--but they want us near enough for some protection. We'll be like a true sea urchin swimming between whales.*

They fired shell after shell, tearing into the scum, but the enemy kept flying in from all sides. A pod slammed into the hull of the *Urchin*. The ship jolted and moaned in protest. Another pod crashed into the ship's stern, and through the gun turret's viewport, Marco saw fire blazing from their engines.

"One engine down!" Osiris cried through the speakers.

"Get us closer to the *Terra*!" said Ben-Ari. "Gunners, keep those shells flying."

They lurched forward, swaying, dipping. Hundreds of scum pods came flying toward them. The shells weren't enough. Another pod slammed into the ship. Another. Bullets flew as a squadron of Firebirds raced toward the *Urchin*, knocking back scum. A second Firebird squadron swooped from above, raining missiles. But the scum were too many. Pods tore into the single-pilot starfighters, shattering them. Hot metal shards flew and peppered the *Urchin.* A pilot tumbled through space and thumped into the hull. A pulsing blob, a giant scum ship, came wobbling toward them, and Marco fired another shell, ripping into it.

A glob of sizzling pus slammed into the gun turret where Marco and Lailani were standing, and the viewport shattered. The acid spilled into the chamber, and the air shrieked out into space. If it weren't for their exoframes, they'd have suffocated.

"We're breached!" Marco said.

"Scum!" Lailani shouted, pointing.

The centipedes scuttled through the crack in the viewport, entering the *Urchin.*

"Bugs on board!" rose Addy's voice from deeper in the ship.

"They're everywhere!" cried another soldier.

"Keep us flying, Osiris!" Ben-Ari shouted. "Get us to the *Terra*! Soldiers, kill those scum!"

A centipede reared before Marco, claws gleaming. He fired his rifle, drenching it with plasma. Two more scum widened the crack in the hull, raced in, and leaped forward. One slammed into Lailani, knocking the gun from her hands. Another hit Marco, and he fired, missed. With hydraulic hisses, he swung his metal arm and drove his gauntleted fist into the scum. The exoskeleton dented. He swung again, again. Claws drove into his exoframe, nicking the metal, cracking a gear. The scum's head leered before his helmet, mandibles clattering. The alien's mouth opened, revealing a dozen clacking claws within. Those claws reached toward Marco's visor, ready to shatter the hard fused silica. Marco tried to shove the creature off, could not, even with the added strength of his exoframe. More bugs kept crawling through the cracked hull, and more pods came racing toward them.

Marco steeled himself.

A pod slammed into the *Urchin*, and the ship jolted, raising him and the scum into the air.

Not wasting an instant, Marco grabbed the creature and swung it across his shoulder. The centipede hit the ground, and Marco raised his gun and bathed it with white-hot plasma. The alien curled up, exoskeleton melting, wailing pathetically. Lailani was busy firing her gun at other scum who were invading through the breach. When one alien dodged her plasma and leaped toward her, a swing of her robotic arm cracked its exoskeleton and severed a claw. Marco finished the job with his Fyre.

"Scum on the bridge!" rose Osiris's voice through the speakers. "Require assistance!"

"Damn," Marco said. "Lailani, can you handle the cannon?"

She nodded. "Got it. Go help Osiris."

Marco ran through the lurching ship.

He ran through the corridor in his exoframe, his metal boots thudding against the floor. Another breach was open here, and scum were crawling in from a pod that clung to the *Urchin*'s hull. Marco sprayed them with plasma. As he raced past the breach, he could see the battle outside. A fresh squadron of

Firebirds was escorting the *Urchin* on its flight toward the starfighter carriers. Beyond them, the battle spread out for many kilometers, thousands of Alliance ships and scum pods firing their weapons, slamming together, burning, killing. Planet Abaddon was still a distant sphere, countless pods defending it.

He reached the bridge. Osiris was standing in the corner, firing a plasma rifle at a group of scum that were crawling toward her. Marco sprayed out his plasma with hers. A few of the scum turned toward him. One of the creatures made it past the inferno and slammed into him, claws cracking the metal of his exoframe. Blood spurted from Marco's leg. He fell down hard, managed to slam the scum onto the floor, then pounded down his metal fists, again and again, crushing the alien, breaking its shell, and he wanted to hurt it. He wanted these creatures to suffer. For what they had done to his mother. To his country. To his friends. For Elvis, Jackass, Beast, the rest of them. For how they had tortured Kemi. He was still beating the alien's lifeless corpse for long moments when Osiris touched his shoulder.

"Master?"

He took a shuddering breath and rose to his feet, metal fists dripping yellow blood.

"I'm fine," he said. "They're gone."

But he wasn't fine. Because the scum had done more than hurt him. They had invaded him, had changed him from the inside, just as surely as they had infected Kemi and Lailani. They had turned him into a man he didn't know.

Other warriors of the platoon burst onto the bridge, wearing their exoframes, their fists dripping scum innards. Marco no longer heard the aliens' screeches. For now, it seemed the *Urchin* was clear of invaders.

Marco looked out the viewport and could see the *Terra* ahead, along with several smaller--yet still large enough to dwarf the *Urchin*--human warships. They were all firing their cannons at the enemy as Firebirds circled them. A squad of Firebirds was flying alongside the *Urchin* now, and one of the starfighters came to hover in front of the viewport, so close that Marco could see the pilot inside.

His heart skipped a beat.

He frowned.

For a second, he made eye contact with the Firebird's pilot.

"Kemi?" he whispered.

CHAPTER SEVENTEEN

"Marco?"

They were both wearing helmets. She was inside a Firebird. He was inside the *Urchin*, wearing an exoframe. But she made eye contact with him, even through viewport and visor. She knew it was him.

Marco.

His eyes widened as he stared at her from across the distance. His jaw unhinged.

Kemi's Firebird squadron had received orders to defend the *Urchin*, to accompany her to whatever meager protection the warships offered in their wake. She had never imagined she'd be protecting Marco.

Flying by the ship's bridge, she hit her controls, doing a scan of local exoframe routers. She saw his name pop up in the nearby network: Corporal Marco Emery. She hit his name, and she spoke into her mic.

"Marco?"

He waved at her from the bridge, and his voice emerged from her headphones. "Kemi! What the hell are you doing here? How did they let you fly a Firebird?"

"Because they're crazy!" Kemi replied. "Marco, your ship sustained a lot of damage. It's breached in several places. We'll keep flying around you, but keep those cannons firing. The scum--whoa!"

She hung up on him. A group of scum pods were racing toward her.

Kemi sneered and fired her Firebird's machine gun.

The bullets sprayed out, popping the scum pods as if they were rotten pumpkins. The centipedes spilled out, and Kemi fired her plasma cannon, melting the creatures.

She glanced back at the *Urchin.* The bulky, dented ship--by God, it was ugly, more of a floating bucket of rust than an actual starship--had made it into the shelter between the larger warships. Her orders had been clear: Defend the *Urchin* at all cost. Its warriors had to reach Abaddon.

And Marco among them.

Kemi was relieved that he was still alive, but terror filled her too. The top brass wanted Marco on the planet for something. He was wearing an exoframe, an expensive piece of machinery, worth as much as an entire Firebird. They didn't give exoframes to anyone, just the elite commando soldiers, which Marco--bless his heart--certainly wasn't.

They're sending him into danger, she thought. This had something to do with Corpus. It had to. The army knew he had experience fighting in scum hives, killing their queens and kings. Kemi shivered. *They want him to enter the hive of Abaddon.*

And Kemi knew: this was a death sentence.

But she had no time to consider it further. The battle raged full force. Admiral Bryan's voice emerged from her speakers.

"All Alliance ships! Form a spearhead behind the *Terra.* We're charging toward the planet. Engage all enemies in your way, but do not be drawn aside for skirmishes. Your only target is reaching Abaddon. Fly forth, free civilizations of the Milky Way! To Abaddon and to victory!"

The HDFS *Terra*--the greatest warship humanity had ever built--blasted its thruster engines, roaring out fire, and charged through the scum. Its cannons fired. Its prow ripped through pods. Thousands of warships flew behind it, forming a massive triangle in space, firing all their weapons. Thousands of smaller vessels followed, both human and alien, firing all their guns. They stormed toward the planet ahead, moving at thousands of kilometers per hour.

"Firebirds, surround the spearhead," came the order.

"Avalerion Squadron, follow," rose the voice of Kemi's new squad commander, replacing Major Verish.

Kemi glanced back at the *Urchin*--this dented box Marco flew in, its hull stained with ash and scum blood. For now, she had to part from him.

Goodbye, Marco, she thought. *Stay alive, damn you. Stay alive down there.*

She pulled her joystick, rising higher with her squadron until they flew above the vast surface of the HDFS *Terra.*

Abaddon was closer now, a desert planet coated with mountains, craters, and canyons, a world many times the size of Earth. The scum had evolved in this planet's caves and burrows, had spawned from this rock to spread across the galaxy, a disease passing from world to world. Only one man--Evan Bryan, who now commanded the starship that flew beneath Kemi--had ever reached this planet, had ever hit the scum on their own soil. Bryan had piloted only a single, small starfighter that day fifty years ago, an early Firebird model that was downright primitive compared to what Kemi now flew.

Today we'll hit them with the firepower of an entire fleet, she thought.

But the scum fleet was determined to defend their home. More and more pods came rising from the planet, streaming toward the Allies. Thousands of scum ships, ranging from vessels the size of Firebirds to wobbling blobs the size of starfighter carriers, hit the Alliance from all sides, spewing fire and sizzling globs. Every moment, another Alliance ship shattered. Alien vessels collapsed, some spilling out water, others exploding into crystal shards. Firebirds fell, one by one, a rain of fire. A carrier burned, listed, and slammed into a warship.

But the fleet charged onward. Plasma blasts, shells, lasers, bullets--they tore a path through the scum, and the ships--thousands of ships--barreled on through the swarm toward the rocky planet.

Kemi's starfighter rose and fell, zipped left and right, and she felt caught on a storming sea. There was no sound in space.

She couldn't hear the starships shrieking, couldn't hear the dying screaming, couldn't hear the explosions or the raging flames. All was a silent painting of fire, of falling starships like burning autumn leaves, like rising sparks from flame. All was a great show of light and fury and death and molten metal and honor. She flew onward. She flew like her brother had flown on his doomed mission. She flew for humanity. For Marco. For freedom. But she also flew for the fear inside her, those nightmares of the mines, of the evil she had seen.

And she felt them. The *scolopendra titania*. She could not hear in space, but she could sense their thoughts, their thrumming hive, the network of the centipedes, all connected like the roots of many trees forming a single organism. They had connected her to this network in the hives of Corpus, and she still could tap into it, see the branches of consciousness forming across the battle, invisible lines running from pod to pod, back to the planet below. To him. To the emperor. She could foresee all their movements. They flew toward her, and she dodged, knowing in advance their direction. They fired at her ship, and she skirted the attacks, fired back at them, shattered them, for she knew where they would aim before they shot. A Firebird dived at her side, slamming into the *Terra*. Another Firebird exploded. One by one, her squadron's starfighters perished, but Kemi flew onward.

You cannot kill me, she thought. *I'm one of you. I know you. I'm you, and I'm vengeance. You made me into this weapon.*

The other Firebirds rallied around her, squadron after squadron, falling in the flames, more replacing them. Warship after warship collapsed, but others flew forth. And before them--the scum perished.

Hundreds of pods. Thousands. Tens of thousands. They burned. Space blazed with countless flaring scum ships like a galaxy of crumbling stars.

"To Abaddon!" rose a cry through her speakers--the voice of Admiral Bryan, leading the fleet.

"To Abaddon!" Kemi cried.

"To Abaddon!" rose the voices of her squad pilots.

And through the flame and poison of the scum swarm, through the death of millions, through shattering metal and sacrifice, they charged toward the planet.

Thousands of Alliance ships fell. Millions of soldiers perished. A great death, a great sacrifice, a genocide here in space, the single largest battle in human history. They flew through it. They charged onward. Kilometer by kilometer, death by death. They made their way through.

They reached the orbit of the scum's world.

They had left home with a hundred thousand ships, with ten million troops. They arrived at Abaddon with perhaps a few thousand vessels, with perhaps a million lives.

But they reached the planet.

And through the speakers, emerging into every cockpit and bridge across the fleet, rose the voice of Admiral Bryan.

"Bomb them. Destroy them."

And with a thousand thin strands, the missiles flew forth.

Fire and dust and heat flowed across Kemi's cockpit, and she fired all the last missiles in her arsenal, and she saw nothing but white light.

* * * * *

"Bomb them," said the voice in the speakers, the voice of Admiral Bryan, the man who had punished the scum fifty years ago. "Destroy them."

Marco and Lailani stood in one of the *Urchin*'s gun turrets. Outside the viewport, covering their field of vision, spread the rocky surface of Abaddon.

Marco and Lailani looked at each other. They understood.

Lailani lifted the white shell, the one painted with a red-and-blue molecule. She loaded it into the cannon. Here wasn't just a typical bomb filled with regular explosives. This was an erisitrol tetranitrate bomb, the most powerful explosive known to humanity, nicknamed the Eris bomb. It wasn't a nuclear weapon, but it came damn close.

Marco grabbed the cannon's cord. He looked at Lailani.

"Together," he said.

She grabbed the cord with him. They yanked it back together.

The cannon fired. The Eris warhead flew.

Thousands of bombs flew with it from across the fleet.

For a moment, silence. A pause in the battle.

Then white light flowed across space, and the world of Abaddon trembled.

"Fire again," came the command.

They fired again.

The bombing of Abaddon continued for hours. Marco and Lailani kept loading shell after shell, blasting the planet's surface, tearing down mountains. Mushroom clouds rose one by one, forming collapsing forests. As the warships fired, the Firebirds kept flying around them, picking out the last scum pods still attacking the fleet. More human ships fell. Barely any alien allies remained. And still the Alliance bombed.

As Marco kept firing, as the blasts kept raising mushroom clouds on the planet, a sickness began to grow in his stomach.

"We're exterminating an entire species," he said, and the words tasted foul. "I'm not sure I like this."

"They're bugs, Marco." Lailani loaded another Eris shell into the cannon.

"And they're intelligent," Marco said. "As intelligent as humans. We defeated their fleet. Should we really carry out genocide against them?"

"Marco." Lailani's eyes flashed, and she shoved the shell into the gun, then gripped his arms. "Listen to me, Marco. I felt them. I know them. I'm one of them in many ways. Their emperor spoke to me. A million of their voices screamed inside me. They are pure evil. Every last one of them--cruelty distilled. They are demons. All they care about is killing."

"Killing," Marco said and nodded. He exhaled shakily. "Maybe we've all become like them."

Lailani's eyes were hard. "Don't go soft on me, Marco. I don't need this. Not now, not as we're about to win this war." She sighed. "Besides, our bombing isn't exterminating them. We're killing only a handful of them." She looked down at the planet being bombarded by the fleet, and she winced. "I can feel them crying out, trying to reach past the chip in my mind, to control me, to plug me into their hive. They're hiding underground. A few of them died near the surface, but only a few. They're in their hives, protected from our bombs. Waiting for us. And he's among them, Marco." Her voice dropped to a strained whisper, and her face paled. "The emperor. He knows me. He knows my name."

Marco tightened his lips and fired another shell. "Then we'll kill him. You're right, Lailani. There's no use showing mercy now. I don't have to like what I'm doing. And I don't. But you're right. This must be done, and we must kill him. For Earth. For the future of our species."

"And for our adorable mixed-race babies," Lailani said, finally giving him a smile. "And for all the puppies we're going to adopt."

The shelling continued hour by hour. As the scum's fleet shrank, the human fleet surrounded the planet, blasting it from all sides. Finally Marco and Lailani had to sleep, letting a second fireteam operate their cannon. Seven hours later, they woke up to see the fleet still bombing the planet. They resumed their work at the cannon. A cargo ship flew up toward the *Urchin*, and a team rolled in crates full of more shells. The bombing continued, pounding crater after crater into the planet below.

For hours, the fleet bombed.

They slept again.

They woke to a third day of shelling Abaddon.

"Bloody hell," Addy said that third day, sitting in the mess hall with half the platoon. The other half was still at the cannons. "I never imagined the HDF even had so many bombs."

Marco sat at the table with her, Lailani, and twenty other warriors. Chicken wings steamed on plates, and empty bones rattled in bowls. Marco glanced out the viewport toward the planet below. Thousands of shells were flying from the fleet down toward the planet, streaking like comets and exploding below.

"We're using every last bomb we've got, it seems," Marco said. "Years and years, decades' worth of bombs, trillions of dollars' worth of bombs, stocked up for this war. Admiral Bryan means business."

"Admiral Bryan is a badass." Addy nodded.

Marco began to wonder, however. He stared down at the explosions rocking the planet. Admiral Evan Bryan, back when he had been only a young pilot, had nuked this very world, slaying many scum. On Earth, he had been hailed as a hero. He had, after all, deterred the scum from continuing their genocidal attacks against Earth, ushering in the horrible--yet preferable by far--War of Attrition. A hero? Yes, Marco had often thought so. Like most boys, he had hung a poster of the smiling Captain Evan Bryan on his bedroom wall. Yet watching the bombardment continue, he wondered whether Bryan was less a hero, more of an exterminator--a man consumed with rage, with lust for vengeance, with a burning desire to extinguish a species. Marco didn't wish to exterminate the entire alien race of the scum, even after all they had done, only to stop them from attacking Earth. Was Bryan interested in victory . . . or in genocide?

"I wonder how badly Earth is suffering," Lailani said. "We haven't heard news in days."

Addy cringed. "Maybe that's bad. Maybe they don't want to tell us because Earth's getting the shit kicked out of it."

"Last we heard," Lailani said, "three entire Earth cities had been wiped out. And that was days ago. The scum might be hitting Earth as hard as we're hitting Abaddon." She shoved her tray away. "War is so fucking stupid."

"War stinks," Addy said.

"Just like your feet," Marco said.

"Only because my feet kick your ass," Addy said, to which Marco had no comeback.

"Soldiers!" The voice boomed through the mess, and they all turned to see Gunnery Sergeant Bo Jones standing at the doorway. The towering bald man was dressed in his battle fatigues, sleeves rolled up to reveal coiling tattoos. "Get into your exoframes and head to the shuttle hangar."

Addy leaped up from her chair. "We're blasting down now, Commander?"

"Soon enough," said Jones. "Exoframes, and move it! You'll finish your meals in the scum emperor's dining hall."

"Mmm, all the slugs we can eat!" Addy said, racing toward the door. The other soldiers followed.

As Marco stepped into his exoframe, his heart pounded, and he couldn't keep his fingers from shaking.

This is it, he thought. *The invasion. It's here.*

He thought back to his old dream, to standing on a desolate planet, the scum scuttling toward him. If Lailani was right, even after three days of bombardments, the scum were still alive, waiting safely in their underground hives.

After three days of shelling, the guns of humanity fell silent.

No more hellfire rained down upon Abaddon.

A distant observer would be forgiven for believing that peace had come. Down on the planet, the dust settled upon a pocked surface.

No more scum pods flew. The creatures all lurked below, waiting. Marco didn't need Lailani to tell him that this time. He could feel them himself, millions of them, creeping in their burrows. Here would not be a hive like on Corpus, only a few kilometers long. Here waited hives the size of a planet.

The platoon gathered in the hangar, all in their exoframes. Three shuttles awaited them, bulky landing craft, big armored boxes with propellers and turbines.

"Ma'am?" Addy raised her hand. "You know, the thought struck me. When we get hives of ants back home, we just pump them full of poison. Remind me why we have to land on the planet? Can't we just gas the fuckers from up here? Anthrax, mustard gas, Marco's old underwear?"

"Try your socks," Marco said. "Deadlier than Agent Orange."

Lieutenant Ben-Ari stared at them. "We've tried that before. On many hives. The scum are the toughest bastards in the cosmos. They can breathe anthrax like it's potpourri. Even if we could develop a bug or molecule that's poisonous to them, they can hold their breath for years, and their armor can withstand anything we splash onto it. And if they do sense danger, they just dig deeper. Only one thing works with the scum." She patted her rifle. "Shooting them."

Addy sighed. "And I reckon an army of ten million Osiris warriors is too expensive?"

Ben-Ari smiled wryly. "Much too expensive. Osiris costs more than the starship she's flying." The lieutenant turned toward Lailani. "Now, de la Rosa, this is a large planet--many times the size of Earth. Are you sure we're flying over the right place?"

In her exoframe, Lailani was no longer small and weak; she was a machine of metal and fury. Yet behind her visor, her face was pale, and dark bags hung under her eyes. She looked out the viewport, and the desert surface of Abaddon reflected on her visor, all craters and canyons and dry death.

"Yes." Lailani nodded. "I can feel him calling out to me. He's right below us. We just need to fly straight down." She wrapped her metal glove around her gun. "Let's end this. Once and for all, let's end this nightmare."

Marco stepped toward her. He placed a gauntlet on her shoulder. "We will end this."

Ben-Ari nodded. "All right, soldiers! Operation Odin's Spear is about to commence. Into your shuttles! It's time to shoot some bugs."

The Spearhead Platoon's three squads stepped toward their designated shuttles. Sergeant Bellet led the first squad. Tall, tattooed, and sporting a platinum mohawk within her helmet, she entered one shuttle. Her soldiers--including Marco, Addy, and Lailani--followed. Lieutenant Ben-Ari, commander of the platoon, entered the same shuttle. Meanwhile, Gunnery Sergeant Jones--the platoon's second-in-command--entered the second squad's shuttle. Marco was surprised to see Osiris join the third squad in their shuttle. Evidently, even the costly android would be invading today. Across the rest of the fleet, Marco knew, hundreds of thousands of marines were entering their own shuttles.

Inside the shuttle, Marco found rows of seats with metal shoulder bars. It reminded him of an amusement park ride. The soldiers sat down, and the bars snapped into place across their torsos, securing them into their seats. They looked to the world like massive, metal robots, their human faces barely visible behind their visors in the shadows of the shuttle.

For long moments, they waited. Silent.

Then a voice crackled to life from the speakers--the voice of Admiral Evan Bryan.

"Fifty years ago, the scum devastated our planet, murdering billions. Our fathers, mothers, children, siblings--they fell to the enemy. For many years, we languished in darkness, beaten, bloodied. But we rose to our knees, then to our feet, then back into the sky. Today, fifty years after that first terrible attack, we near the day of our victory. We flew from Nightwall with a hundred thousand ships and ten million brave soldiers." A long pause. "On our journey here, we've lost all but five thousand ships and half a million souls. We will forever grieve for our fallen comrades. We will forever honor their sacrifice. Those of us who remain--we are strong, we are courageous, and we are ready for victory. In a few moments you--half a million of Earth's finest--will deploy to the enemy homeworld of Abaddon. There you will fight the scum in their burrows. You will defeat them in their own homes. And you will slay their emperor. The battle will be long and difficult. Our enemy is powerful. Do not underestimate him. The scum will fight viciously. But they will fail. They will die. Earth and her allies will strike hard today. We will have victory! Good luck, warriors of Earth, and may God, the stars, and the cosmos bless you."

The hangar doors began to open. The shuttle had only a small, rectangular viewport, but through it Marco could see Abaddon's surface a few hundred kilometers away. From where he sat, he couldn't see the other shuttles nor the rest of the fleet. It felt like facing that rocky arena alone.

You're down there, Marco thought. *The emperor. You who've been infecting my mind with your visions. You who hurt Lailani, who ordered her to kill my friends. You who sent your warriors to murder my mother.* He clenched his fists, sudden rage flaring through him. *You whom I will kill.*

"Hold on to your asses!" Sergeant Jones said.

The shuttle began to move toward the hangar's open doors.

"Here we fucking go!" Addy shouted. "No fear!"

"No fear!" the soldiers replied.

"Victory!" Marco cried out, surprised at himself, his pulse pounding in his ears.

"Victory!" they all called in reply.

With roaring engines, the shuttle burst out from the *Urchin*'s hangar and plunged down toward the planet. Thousands of other shuttles streamed down with them. The invasion of Abaddon began.

CHAPTER EIGHTEEN

Like a shower of comets, thirty thousand shuttles rained down toward the desert planet.

Marco clung to his seat, teeth rattling. His head kept banging against the back of his helmet, and he clenched his jaw. Around him, his comrades sat, fists grabbing the handlebars. The shuttle shook madly. The sound was deafening. They plunged down, down through space, and fire blazed outside the viewport. The shuttle walls heated. Sweat drenched Marco. The shuttle screamed, an almost human sound, as it plunged through the outer layers of atmosphere, screeching, shaking, tearing through the sky of Abaddon.

With a flash, the flames vanished. Through the viewport, Marco saw yellow, endless sky and a cracked desert below.

The shuttle shook with every kilometer descended--and they were descending several per second. Marco banged against his metal suit. He forced himself to take quick, short breaths. Through the viewport, he could see the other shuttles, myriads of them spreading into the horizon, and the desert tilted. Mountains rose, taller than any on Earth, and canyons cracked the land, and mesas thrust up like teeth, a painting all in tan, yellow, and sickly brown. The sun beat down, blinding and white. The shuttle became sweltering, a searing oven.

"He's near," Lailani said, speaking through her communicator. "Right below us. I can feel him pulsing. Calling to me. Waiting in the darkness." She gasped and let out a cry. "He knows! He--Careful!"

For a moment the shuttle's flight steadied, and silence fell.

Marco stared outside.

On the surface of the planet, great volcanoes yawned open like bursting sores.

With blasts of smoke, yellow lava shot upward.

The streams of molten rock flared up, great geysers, rising many kilometers into the air. One jet washed over a shuttle nearby, pulverizing it. Across the sky, more geysers tore into other shuttles, cracking the metal, burning the soldiers within.

"Dodge them!" Ben-Ari cried to the shuttle's pilot, a soldier named Hocking.

"Got it!" Sergeant Hocking replied, tugging the controls on the shuttle. The propellers roared, and they swerved in the sky. A pillar of yellow lava soared beside them. The heat baked the side of the shuttle. Droplets hit the hull, tearing through the metal, and air whistled. The windshield shattered, and the shuttle swerved again. Another pillar of lava rose, foul, acidic, stinking. It bathed the side of the shuttle, and drops flew inside. One glob hit a soldier at Marco's side, eating through his armor. Droplets hit Marco's boot, searing the metal, and he grunted and kicked them off.

"Hocking, get us out of their path!" Ben-Ari shouted.

"Goddamn scum vomit!" Addy cried, ripping off a panel of her suit, the pus eating through it.

"Another one incoming!" shouted a man.

The shuttle tilted. Marco looked out the shattered windshield. He saw the geyser rising toward them.

Fuck.

He ripped off his seat's handlebars and leaped across the shuttle. The spray drove in, washing over seats, tearing into soldiers. Men and women screamed. The searing liquid hit a soldier's helmet, shattering the glass, eating the face within. The shuttle spun madly, out of control, rising, falling, tumbling.

"Hocking!" Ben-Ari cried, but Marco saw that the pilot was dead. As the shuttle spun, he caught glimpses of the others. Shuttle after shuttle was exploding in the sky, falling, leaving trails of smoke, and crashing onto the planet.

Marco gripped a crack in the wall. He pulled himself toward the cockpit, yanked the dead pilot out of her seat, and grabbed the controls.

"Marco, do you know how to fly?" Ben-Ari shouted.

"No, but he played lots of space video games as a kid!" Addy shouted, her arm burnt. "Maybe that'll help."

There were two joysticks here. Marco grabbed one in each hand, pulling them randomly, struggling to steady the shuttle. One of the joysticks seemed to control left and right movements, the other up and down, though Marco wasn't sure which was which. They lurched through the sky. A blast of lava rose toward them--

or whatever this foul material was--and Marco tugged one of the joysticks, hoping it was the right one. They banked sharply, dodging the stream.

"Marco, to your left!" Addy shouted.

Marco looked. Another shuttle was there, only feet away from them. He pulled hard to the right, and suddenly they were plunging nose down, and soldiers flew from their seats, and air roared through the cracks. Marco tried to steady their flight, to pull up their prow. He managed to yank up sharply, then dive to the right. The joysticks threatened to rip free from his hands. A jet sprayed toward them, and Marco tried to dodge it, missed most of it, but the blast caught their tail. One of their turbines tore free, spun through the sky, and suddenly they were spinning too. A geyser washed across a shuttle nearby, and its propellers tore off, and its door blasted outward and flew and slammed into Marco's cockpit. His propellers followed, and the two vessels slammed together, and the cockpit shattered and stabbed Marco's exoframe with a thousand hot shards. A soldier screamed behind him and flew out the breached hull, only to be sucked into another shuttle's engines, causing the vessel to explode two seconds later.

Marco's shuttle was tumbling, barely held together. Only one of their engines still worked. His suit damaged, his cockpit falling apart, he grabbed the controls, tried to steady their flight. Balls of fire rained around them--the other shuttles. The ground rushed up toward them. Marco yanked back hard on both joysticks, and their nose rose, and they skimmed over the ground.

Come on, land, land, land--

Boulders rose ahead from the ground like teeth. They tore into the shuttle. The vessel rose into the air, spun, slammed down hard upside down, and they were careening. Another soldier flew out from the hull, only for the shuttle to run him over. Sparks and blood showered. They tore grooves through the earth, racing, burning, knocking another shuttle aside, slamming through boulders before finally slowing, slowing, spinning, slower, slower . . . then coming to a stop.

Shuttles crashed down around them.

Flames crackled.

They lay on the surface of Abaddon, upside down, their shuttle smashed.

Soldiers groaned. A few were still fastened to their seats, heads dangling upside down.

"Marco," Addy said, "you obviously didn't play *nearly* enough video games."

Marco struggled out from his seat and began to help soldiers out from theirs. Some were injured even with their exoframes. One man's leg was bent, the bone shattered within its metal frame. Another woman was burnt. The yellow lava had melted her armor's joints and seared the skin. A third soldier hung dead from his seat, neck snapped during the crash. The survivors climbed out from the ravaged shuttle onto the cracked, beige surface of Abaddon.

The desert landscape spread before them into all horizons. Tan mountains rose in the distance. The land was rocky and cracked. Here was a desert of boulders, canyons, and mesas like giant discarded blocks. It was almost like being back at Fort Djemila--a lifeless, monochrome wasteland. Abaddon's gravity seemed heavier than Earth's. Marco could feel this at once, and he was thankful for his exoframe that provided extra strength to his legs. Most of the troops in this war weren't wearing the expensive exoframes, just their standard battle fatigues. Walking here would feel like walking with a forty-pound weight on your shoulders.

Yet even those soldiers were the lucky ones. Across the desert, countless warriors lay dead. Thousands of shuttles had crashed and burned. Corpses lay in piles of smashed and molten metal. Only ten feet away, Marco saw a corpse hanging out the shattered window of a shuttle. Below the shoulders, there was nothing but a long, dripping red mess like a bloodied rag with some hair and teeth. A few corpses lay burning in the sand. Not all the fallen were human. A Gurami floundered on the sand, suffocating without water to breathe. A human corporal was pouring water from his canteen onto the fish, to little effect. One of the Silvans, a furry disk with six tails, was dragging itself up a hillside, seeking its brethren in a shattered vessel built of crystals and amber.

"It wasn't supposed to go this way," Marco said, staring at the devastation.

"No shit, Shirley," Addy said.

"You mean Sherlock," Marco said.

"It's Shirley," Addy insisted. "Like Shirley Temple. She took no shit from nobody."

Yet some shuttles had made it down. Others were still descending, and the volcanoes on the planet's surface were still spurting up streams of yellow fluid. With every geyser, the ground shook and Marco nearly fell. Only half the shuttles were making it down. Their warriors emerged and arranged themselves into their squads and platoons. It was an impressive force, thousands of warriors gathering in the desert. But it was such a small fraction of the warriors they had left Nightwall with that Marco's belly knotted.

"Spearhead Platoon, rally here!" Ben-Ari said, emerging from the shuttle.

They gathered around their lieutenant, organizing into their three squads. The tattooed Sergeant Bellet, never losing her smirk, led Marco's squad. He stood behind her, Addy and Lailani at his sides. The others all formed rank in the desert nearby. The Spearhead Platoon had left Nightwall with fifty soldiers; they were down to forty now. Across the desert, other platoons were gathering around their own lieutenants, then grouping into their companies and battalions.

"De la Rosa," Ben-Ari said. "Can you still connect to--"

Lailani screamed.

Marco grabbed his gun. The desert began to crack open.

"Scum!" he shouted.

From countless cracks and holes across the desert, the enemy emerged.

"Fire!" Ben-Ari shouted.

The platoon needed no encouragement. They arranged themselves into fireteams, stood in a circle, and fired their guns.

Plasma bolts blasted out, slamming into scum. Marco switched his gun to automatic and spurted out a flaming turret, turning his Fyre rifle into a flamethrower. The scum screamed and burned. Thousands were advancing from all sides. For every scum that died, ten more emerged from underground. Across the desert, soldiers crumbled before them. Centipedes ripped into men and women, tearing flesh off bones. Soldiers fell, eviscerated. A man cried out for his mother. A woman wept as scum fed on her severed legs.

"Platoon, make your way to shuttlecraft 56A!" Ben-Ari shouted, pointing. "With me!"

Marco saw it there, maybe five hundred meters away. A heavy shuttlecraft, much larger than the one they had crashed. Soldiers tugged down a massive ramped doorway on the craft, and Marco saw armored vehicles inside.

Sand tigers, Marco thought, remembering them from basic. *Our rides.*

"Come on, squad!" Sergeant Bellet howled, firing her gun. "Stop scratching your balls and make for those sand tigers!"

They ran in two rows, spraying out plasma in all directions. Their metal boots cracked the earth. Scum died all around. Some of the centipedes leaped through the plasma, claws flashing. A soldier ahead of Marco screamed, claws tearing through his exoframe. Another scum leaped at Marco, and he swung his arm, knocking it down, and Addy stepped on it, crushing its exoskeleton. With their exoframes on, they were no longer just frail humans. They were as strong, fast, and heavy as the scum themselves. Their plasma kept tearing the creatures down.

They fought their way for every step. Another soldier fell. All across the desert, more shuttles were struggling to land, only for bursts of acid to tear into them. Those shuttles that did reach the ground faced the scum leaping from cracks and burrows. Firebirds screamed overhead, unable to bomb the scum without also hitting the soldiers. Attack choppers hovered, trying to pick out the scum one by one--agonizing work. Entire companies fell, overflowing with centipedes. As Marco ran, he saw a canyon crack open nearby, and the ground swallowed a platoon. The fifty warriors fell, screaming, into a pit of scum below.

We should never have come here, Marco thought. *We can't do this. We can't defeat them on their own soil. We were fools.*

He looked up, seeking the HDFS *Terra* in the sky. Yet it was too far to see, especially in this searing sunlight. Marco thought back to Admiral Bryan's words--both his speech to the troops and his private words to Marco. He tightened his lips.

Fifty years ago, Bryan did not despair. I won't despair now.

He fought through the scum, gun firing, fists swinging. Their claws slammed into his armor, denting it, cutting him, but he ran on. It was only five hundred yards, but it felt longer than his great run at the end of basic training.

Finally, winded and bleeding, the platoon reached the shuttle that was unloading the sand tigers. The armored vehicles stood in the desert on their chained caterpillar tracks, heavy machines that weighed sixty tons each, topped with .50-cal Stinger machine guns. They were thick, ugly, warty beasts of gears, chains, and heavy metal the color of sand, almost as big as tanks. Here were no slick, state-of-the-art machines of the STC. These were the rude, crude brutes Earth Territorial Command had brought with it. Marco had fought in a sand tiger at Djemila, had seen these heavy tracks crack open scum. Each vehicle was large enough to transport an entire squad. Spearhead Platoon would need three.

As scum approached from all sides, dying in helicopter fire, Sergeant Bellet pulled down the back door of one sand tiger. When opened, it formed a ramp. Their squad raced in. On the inside, the sand tiger was surprisingly small; a huge portion of its girth was the thickness of its walls. There were two benches here among boxes of supplies and ammunition. A narrow passageway led to the driver's seat, while a ladder rose to the gun turret.

"Commander," Marco said, "Lailani and I operated one of these gun turrets in the Battle of Djemila."

Sergeant Bellet nodded. She pointed to the ladder. "Get up there, both of you, and kill the scum."

It was a tight squeeze in their exoframes, but Marco and Lailani managed to scale the ladder and emerge into the turret. It was open to the air, only a low metal ring around them. The stinger rose like a scorpion's tail. As they had back in Djemila, Marco grabbed the machine gun while Lailani grabbed the wheel that aimed it.

"I can feel him," Lailani said, speaking into every helmet in the platoon. "The scum emperor. His anger is like the volcanoes. We almost landed right over him, but the crash took us a few kilometers off course. There, beyond those mountains." She grimaced. "He knows we're coming. He's not happy."

Scum were beginning to climb the sand tiger. Marco fired the machine gun, tearing them off.

"We're right with you, de la Rosa," rose Ben-Ari's voice, coming from another armored vehicle. "Lead the way."

Down below, Addy was at the driver's seat, and the sand tiger began to crawl forth. At their sides, hundreds of other sand tigers were emerging from shuttlecrafts and rolling across the desert. Exoframes were heavy and strong; sand tigers were heavier and stronger. The caterpillar tracks crushed the bugs under sixty tons of metal.

The remains of the Human Defense Force rolled forth. Hundreds of sand tigers. Then thousands. Scum cracked beneath them. Their machine guns fired, sending chunks of scum exoskeleton flying. More shuttles kept flying down through the gauntlet, some of them crashing, others landing to deliver troops and vehicles. Soon a battalion of Behemoth Mark IV tanks joined the fray, metal beasts twice the size of the sand tigers. Their cannons fired, tearing into swarms of scum. Clouds of dust and sand rose everywhere. Firebirds roared overhead, firing their own machine guns, tearing into the myriads of scum that were still emerging from cracks and swarming toward the army.

Marco wasn't sure how many soldiers were making it down onto the planet, but one thing he knew: for every human warrior, there were thousands of scum on this world, too many for even their artillery, air force, and armor to defeat.

We need to kill the emperor beyond those mountains, he thought. *It's the only way to finally defeat the scum.*

"We're getting closer," Lailani said, her voice carrying through their communication system to the rest of the platoon--and, Marco assumed, to Admiral Bryan who flew above in the *Terra.* "He's getting louder. He's calling to me. He--" She gripped the sides of her helmet. "I can't stand it. I can't. I can hear him. I can see what he's showing me. What he will do to us. How he will deform us."

"Hang in there, de la Rosa." Ben-Ari's voice emerged from the speakers now. "You're doing great. I'm proud of you. Keep leading us there. He won't hurt you with us here."

Lailani pointed. "That way. Addy, turn left just a bit. Between those two peaks. Do you see them?"

"I see them," Addy said, driving the vehicle.

"Past those peaks, there's a hive," said Lailani. "It runs deep. Much deeper than Corpus. His evil is rising from there, everywhere, seeping through the air. So much buzzing! All of them. Millions of them screaming inside my skull." Tears filled her eyes. "They're all chattering together. They're so evil."

Marco kept firing the machine gun, killing the scum on the desert ahead. "We're going to silence them, Lailani. All of them. Just hang in there. You're doing great."

The thousands of tanks and sand tigers charged forth, raising storms of dust, plowing through the enemy. They broke through one kilometer, then another. Vehicles fell every few meters. Cracks opened in the surface, and tanks tumbled into pits of scum. Some of the more brazen centipedes leaped onto sand tigers, slew the gunners, and slithered into the vehicles to consume the soldiers within. The husks of vehicles remained behind in the desert. But the others charged onward, firing their guns, cutting through, claiming another kilometer. Hundreds, soon thousands of Firebirds flew above, adding their firepower to the convoy.

All were following Marco's sand tiger. All were following Lailani.

You joined the army to die a heroine, Marco thought. *But you're going to live, Lailani. You're going to live as a heroine.*

"Hanging in there?" he said.

Lailani looked ashen, but she nodded. "I think so. The chip is blocking most of it. We--" She screamed and clutched her helmet. "Marco!"

"Lailani, wh--"

The desert cracked open ahead.

A creature burst out, large as a whale.

"Fuck!" Addy screamed below.

For an instant, Marco could only stare, heart still, breath gone.

It was an insect--an insect to dwarf their armored vehicle. It looked like something halfway between crab and beetle, all body armor and claws and antennae. It must have stood a hundred feet tall. Several more cracks opened in the desert, and more of the gargantuan creatures emerged, bellowing in rage, insects the size of warships.

"Kill them!" Addy screamed.

"No shit, Addy!" Marco said. "I thought we'd ride them!" He fired his machine gun.

Bullets slammed into a rearing insect, doing it no harm. Across the desert, the other vehicles were firing their own machine guns, but even the massive .50 cal bullets--large enough to rip human bodies apart--ricocheted off the giant insects' exoskeletons.

A tank fired its cannon. A shell flew and slammed into one of the insects, denting its armor. Enraged, the creature grabbed the tank with claws like tree roots, lifted it overhead, and hurled it across the desert. The tank--all one hundred tons of it--slammed into a sand tiger, crushing the armored vehicle. More tanks were firing. The insects grabbed more vehicles, lifted them, and tossed them back onto the convoy.

"We need grenades!" Marco shouted down into his sand tiger.

Sergeant Bellet hopped up into the gun turret with him and Lailani. It was just large enough for the three of them.

"Here!" She handed him one grenade, another to Lailani. "Use these. I--Fuck! Linden, steer!"

One of the giant insects came swooping toward them, bellowing. Addy pulled the steering wheel hard to the right, and the sand tiger stormed forward, swaying in the sand. Exoframes came with folding grenade launchers on their shoulders. Marco activated his, and the gun unfurled with a series of clicks. He loaded a grenade. He aimed. He fired.

The grenade flew and slammed into the massive insect. Lailani and Bellet's grenades followed a second later.

Three explosions rocked the enormous beetle. Its armor cracked open, exposing its innards. Marco grabbed the machine gun and fired, hitting that opening. The bullets pierced the soft flesh, and the insect screamed and fell, narrowly missing them. The desert shook.

"Addy, left!" Marco shouted. Another one of the beetles was leaping toward them. He fired another grenade, hit it, and followed the blast with bullets. Addy steered out of the way.

"I can't see a damn thing!" she shouted. "Too much dust!"

More of the creatures kept emerging from the sand, attacking the convoy. Firebirds streamed overhead, firing missiles into the insects. One of the beetles spat a glob of saliva skyward, hitting a starfighter. The Firebird crashed down into a tank. Both vehicles burned.

"Almost there!" Lailani said, pointing. "It's getting stronger. Almost there! Just past those ridges!"

The sand tiger charged, raising clouds of dust, as behind it stormed the thousands of other vehicles. Their guns cut their path through the enemies. They reached a rocky passageway between the two peaks, and the vehicles raced up the slope, and--

From the mountainsides, creatures leaped down.

They were huge scorpions the color of the stone, each the size of a battleship.

One scorpion tail slammed into a tank, shattering it, punching through the metal. A Firebird swooped, and a scorpion leaped and grabbed the jet in its jaws. Addy kept driving, and Marco fired another grenade, and a scorpion raced toward them.

"Addy!" Marco shouted, firing his machine gun, and Lailani and Bellet hurled grenades, and--

The claws grabbed them.

The giant scorpion lifted their sand tiger into the air, then hurled it across the desert.

The massive vehicle, all sixty tons of it, tumbled through the sky like a toy. Lailani fell out of the gun turret. Clinging on with one hand, Marco grabbed her. They flipped through the air, and the soldiers inside shouted, and they came flying down toward the desert floor. The sand tiger was above Marco. The desert below.

He cringed and shoved off the sand tiger, pulling Lailani with him.

They slammed into the desert, the metal of their exoframes denting and sparking against stone. The sand tiger slammed down at their side, missing them by inches, and crushed Sergeant Bellet in the gun turret. Blood leaked.

Marco rose, his metal suit creaking. Half the plates were dented, the rest hanging loose, and a crack halved his helmet. He helped Lailani rise. Their sand tiger lay upside down beside them, soldiers struggling to emerge from within. A scum scuttled toward them, and Marco fired a plasma blast, killing the creature. In the distance, tanks and jets were still battling the giant scorpions.

"You all right?" he said to Lailani.

She fired at another scum and shivered. "It's here. We're above him." Her voice was a strained whisper. "The emperor is right beneath us."

They were past the two mountain peaks, Marco saw. They stood in a crater the size of a soccer field. In its center rose what looked like a giant anthill the size of a palace.

"The entrance to a hive," he said.

"*His* hive," Lailani said, clutching her gun. "And he knows we're here."

CHAPTER NINETEEN

They gathered in the crater, thousands of soldiers. Hundreds of tanks surrounded the crater in a wall of metal, and hundreds of Firebirds flew overhead. In the center of the crater rose the entrance to the hive, a hill of dirt and stone. When Marco looked up and hit the zoom function on his visor, he could just make out a distant shard of light orbiting the planet: the HDFS *Terra*, the flagship of the invasion where Admiral Bryan was overseeing the battle.

"Are you sure, Corporal de la Rosa?" Lieutenant Ben-Ari was standing before Lailani, along with several intelligence officers.

Lailani nodded. "Yes, ma'am. I'm still connected to the scum hive. They keep trying to contact me, to hack into me, to control me. Always they're screaming in my head, but they can't break through, not with the blocker in my skull." She touched the back of her head where the surgeons had implanted the chip. "The signal is strongest here by far. The hive of the scum emperor is right beneath us."

After two devastating days of battle, the Human Defense Force and its allies had claimed this crater and the mountains around it. They had dropped explosives into every crack and hole, aside from the one here in the crater, and sealed them with reinforced concrete. Firebirds had carpet bombed the canyons and hills again and again, flattening the land, destroying any hiding place for the scum.

But Marco knew that most of the creatures still lived, still lurked underground. Still waited for them.

An intelligence officer punched controls on his wrist, and a hologram appeared before them. "Our sonar detectors have revealed a part of the hives. Not an accurate map, and not all the way down, but here are the tunnels we know about." The hologram spun, revealing hundreds of forking paths. "It's a fucking big hive. If you ask me, we should just fill the whole damn thing with napalm."

"No." Ben-Ari shook her head. "Admiral's orders. The scum emperor would just burrow deeper. Napalm won't work. Nor would chemical or biological weapons. The scum can breathe anything we toss their way. Only one thing to do. We crawl deep. We find the emperor. We shoot him at point-blank range."

"All right!" rumbled Gunnery Sergeant Jones. "Time to go burrowing." The beefy NCO hefted his Fyre rifle. "You kids ready?"

"No," said Marco. "But we'll go anyway."

"Atta boy."

"So how do we do this?" Addy said, pulling up her visor to spit into the sand. Blood dripped from a cut on her forehead, and she wiped it clean before slamming her visor shut. "Same as on Corpus?"

"Corpus," said Ben-Ari, "was easy."

Her exoframe clanking, the lieutenant began to climb the hive. The rest of the platoon followed. A hole gaped open atop the hill like a volcano's mouth. Scum claw marks marred its rim.

"Corporal Linden?" Ben-Ari said. "Some fury?"

"Fire in the hole!" Addy shouted and lobbed a grenade down into the hive. An explosion sounded deep within, and the hive shook. Smoke blasted out. Once the dust settled, Marco, Addy, and a handful of others arranged themselves around the hole and blasted down plasma from their guns. The inferno filled the hive. A few scum tried to flee from within, only to burn in the flames, shrivel up, and fall back in.

"Cease fire!" Sergeant Jones said, and they all stood for long moments, waiting for the dust to settle. They peered down inside. The tunnel delved into the shadows.

"I'll lead the way," Ben-Ari said. "Follow close behind. Keep your rifles on semi, and fire only bolts, not streams. Friendly fire can kill us down here as easily as the scum."

The lieutenant leaped down into the hive, vanishing into the shadows.

Standing on the rim, Marco glanced at his friends.

"Let's get this over with," Marco said. "We can do this. We can--"

"No time for speeches," Addy said and shoved him.

"Damn it, Addy!" he shouted as he tumbled into the hive.

He fell for several meters, finally thumping down onto a tunnel's floor and sliding. He grabbed the walls for support, digging his gauntlets into the stone to slow his slide. Finally he was able to climb down, gripping the walls, and found Ben-Ari standing in a cavern the size of a living room. The other soldiers joined them. Several wounded scum twitched on the floor, filled with shrapnel and burnt with plasma.

"We go deeper," Ben-Ari said. "De la Rosa, you hanging in there? You feel it?"

Lailani was shivering. Inside her helmet, her face was pale, and she was biting her lip so hard it bled. But she nodded. "I can feel him. He wants us to come to him. He's right below us."

"How many enemies are down there?" Ben-Ari said.

"They're everywhere," Lailani said. "Millions of them filling this planet. This whole world is full of them like maggots in an old block of cheese."

"Marco, don't eat the planet," Addy said. "You know cheese disagrees with you."

"Addy, why don't you take off your boots and gas the scum to death?" Marco said.

They walked through the hive, plunging deeper. The tunnels were just large enough to let them walk upright. Scum were longer and heavier than humans, but as crawlers, they needed only thin tunnels, no larger than pipes. Yet these tunnels were larger. They must have been carved for bigger bugs. Marco shuddered to think what new breed of creatures would need tunnels the size of human corridors. His suit included an air filtration system, but with his visor cracked, he could smell the place. It stank like a burrow of worms.

Soon their gauges reported that they were a kilometer underground. Behind the Spearhead Platoon, other platoons were following, and thousands of soldiers filled the mines. The tunnels forked every hundred meters. Whenever they reached a fork, Lailani stood with eyes closed like a dowser, listening to invisible voices, finally pointing and choosing a path. Their flashlights, built into their helmets, were their only source of light.

As they walked deeper, Marco frowned. He thought he heard a voice ahead. At first he thought it only like the voices he had been hearing at night, a mere illusion brought on by stress. But as he stepped closer, he realized it was real, coming from farther down the tunnels. He climbed down a shaft, emerging into a horizontal tunnel, and approached the voice. It was louder now, speaking in a foreign language.

Marco's exoframe came with an automatic translator. The translation was projected across his visor in glowing letters.

"Help . . . me. Help . . . me."

He glanced at Ben-Ari. The lieutenant walked at his side, dust and blood coating her exoframe. Both soldiers raised their weapons and advanced together, the others walking behind.

They entered a round chamber. Several fleshy bulbs clung to the ceiling, glowing like strange lampshades made of skin. Their light illuminated an alien that hung on a wall, its limbs bound with sticky membranes. The creature was about twice the height of a man, cadaverous, and green, and eight eyes blinked on its bulbous head.

Ben-Ari gasped. "It's an Altairian. The scum destroyed their homeworld a century ago. I thought all the Altairians were extinct."

Marco approached the green alien. "We can help you. We--" He winced and fought down nausea. The alien's belly had been slashed open, and tiny centipedes, perhaps some race of miniature scum, were breeding within the host. "He's wounded!" Marco said over his shoulder. "We need a medic!"

He and Ben-Ari drew their knives and worked for long moments, cutting the membranes that held the alien to the wall.

"Scum coming!" Addy shouted and fired a blast of plasma.

A centipede squealed and died. More scum came scurrying up from a tunnel. Addy and the others fired their guns while Marco and Ben-Ari lowered the wounded alien from the wall. Medics rushed forth with a stretcher, then had to add a second stretcher to fit the large alien. As the soldiers slew the centipedes, the medics carried the alien back to safety.

"His planet was destroyed a century ago," Marco said. "Has this creature been hanging here for that long?" He shuddered, then fired a plasma bolt, killing a last scum that scuttled toward him.

"Let's keep going," Ben-Ari said. "De la Rosa, show us the way."

But Lailani was standing still, her armor clanking as she shook. Her eyes were sunken, her face ashen, and her hair clung to her forehead with sweat.

"Lailani!" Marco approached her and held her hands. "You all right?"

She nodded. "Almost. It'll be over soon." Tears flowed down her cheeks. "I could hear the green alien inside me. He was screaming into the hive for so long. His misery fed the scum. How they savored his pain!" She took a shaky breath. "Let's keep going. This way. We have to kill the emperor. We have to kill him now."

They kept descending. Lailani led the Spearhead Platoon, but many other platoons were taking other paths, filling the hive. Gunfire sounded from across the tunnels. As the Spearhead walked, they sprayed plasma, killing the scum who approached. They had descended another kilometer when Marco heard another voice--weak, pained, begging.

They stepped into another chamber. A stone table stood here, and an alien lay on it, strapped down with fleshy sheets. It was a bloated white creature, all rolls of fat and tufts of hair. Perhaps once it had been graceful, but tubes now thrust into its veins, pumping yellow liquid into its corpulent form. Maggots lived inside it, breeding. Marco had to struggle not to throw up.

"Osiris," Ben-Ari said, "do you recognize this species?"

The android approached, the only member of the platoon not wearing an exoframe suit, not even battle fatigues. She still wore her blue service uniform, and not one of her synthetic platinum hairs was out of place. She placed a hand on the quivering white alien and tilted her head.

"DNA analysis confirms: It is a member of the Klurian species of the Alpha Pavonis system. The scum destroyed them over two hundred years ago, ma'am. This individual is even older."

Marco felt sick. At his side, a soldier lifted his visor and vomited.

"Fuck," Addy said. "The scum have been collecting creatures from planets they destroyed and keeping them here. Some kind of weird trophies."

"And weird hosts for their parasites," Marco said.

Lailani nodded. "They're harvesting the DNA of these aliens," she said. "I can hear what they're thinking. Even the little maggots are in the hive. They're learning. They're trying to understand the aliens they encounter. They want to take their traits, to think like them, to grow stronger. To absorb the galaxy, to take a part of every conquered species into their own DNA. The way some species collect technology or resources from worlds they conquer, the scum collect DNA."

"Well, they messed with the wrong species this time," Addy said. "Because the only DNA they'll get from humans is Devastating Nuclear Ass-Kicking."

"That would be DNAK," Marco said.

"Ass-kicking is one word!" Addy insisted.

"And we're not even using nuclear weapons," Marco said.

"Poet, shut up!"

They freed the bloated alien, and medics carried the poor creature back to the surface. The platoon kept delving deeper into the hive.

Through their communicators, they heard updates from other platoons. They too were finding aliens imprisoned here, dozens of species once thought extinct. Marco found some small aliens, no larger than butterflies, trapped in translucent boxes of skin-like material. There was one massive alien the size of an elephant, bound to the floor, bellowing in misery. The animal wept in joy as the soldiers freed it, leashed it, and squeezed it through the tunnels toward the surface. One alien looked almost human, a beautiful woman with glimmering indigo skin, golden eyes, and fairy wings. Another alien was a mere blob of slime with eyes and a mouth; they carried it out in a bucket. Chamber by chamber, they freed these poor souls. And chamber by chamber, they encountered the scum--and they killed them.

And as they traveled deeper, more scum emerged.

From one tunnel raced giant centipedes woven of fire, crackling and spurting out flame, and the plasma could not hurt them. The platoon had to fight with grenades, with blades, with metal fists. The flames washed over them, and one soldier screamed and fell, his armor melting.

In another chamber, the scum took on strange human forms, the centipedes' tails split into clawed legs, and they stretched out spiky arms. Marco fired his gun again and again, burning the creatures. Several of them swarmed over a soldier by his side, ripping off the woman's helmet and spitting acid into her face, melting the flesh down to the skull.

Tunnel by tunnel, hall by hall, the horror grew. The scum were experimenting here, evolving, engineering. In a grand hall flew giant insects with wings, and the platoon filled the place with plasma. Still the blazing insects swooped at them, clawing. Stingers thrust out from their abdomens like the stingers of bees. The creatures managed to stab one soldier, tearing through her armor. Inside her exoframe, the soldier swelled up until she burst, coating the inside of her visor with blood and brains. Two more soldiers died, infected with venom, their flesh leaking from their suits, before the platoon managed to slay these monstrous hornets.

Chamber by chamber, more creatures slain.

More soldiers dead.

They had begun the invasion with fifty soldiers in their platoon. In the tunnels, they lost life after life, dwindling to thirty, to twenty, finally to only ten soldiers. They fought on. More soldiers joined them. Platoons shattered and reformed. Across the hive, thousands died.

Thousands of scum emerged from the depths, bugs of every kind. They tossed grenades. They fired plasma. Soldiers kept racing from behind, delivering more ammo, and they fought onward. The corpses of centipedes coated the tunnels. The hives shook madly as tunnels collapsed, burying entire companies. Marco had to dig himself out from under boulders, to carve a path through, to find another chamber, to pull his friends in.

Those with exoframes survived; those without perished under the stones. The Spearhead Platoon moved on, guns firing, deeper, always deeper.

Here was an entire civilization underground. In vast halls the size of starships, eggs lay in piles, maggots writhing within. The soldiers burned them. In other halls, captives--some alien, some even human--hung from the ceilings, their abdomens engorged to obscene size, filled with nutrients the scum were sucking on. There were halls full of rancid meat, halls of dripping honey, halls where scum mated in the dirt, halls where their dead rotted. There were scum nurses, scum builders, scum slaves and masters. The soldiers burned them all.

Ben-Ari and Marco led the way. Addy and Lailani followed. Gunnery Sergeant Jones. Osiris the android. Several others, sergeants in black. They were all that remained of Spearhead, but still they fought, cutting down the enemy, plunging deeper and deeper, kilometer after kilometer, moving underground through the hive.

"There are too many!" Addy shouted, retreating from a tunnel. "Fuck, there are a million down there." She lobbed a grenade.

"Go this way!" Lailani shouted, pointing down another tunnel. "There aren't as many down there. I can feel it."

They raced down the other tunnel, a tighter squeeze, so low they had to run hunched over. The rattle of scum rose from ahead.

"Incoming!" Addy shouted, firing her gun.

Marco stared ahead and gritted his teeth. A chill flooded him even in the heat. It sounded like thousands of scum were racing up from below.

Lailani closed her eyes and stood still. Marco could see her eyeballs moving under her lids, and her lips moved silently. Suddenly the scum in the tunnel ahead turned and took another path. Lailani opened her eyes and breathed out in relief.

"I did it," she whispered. "I sent them a signal through the network. I sent them another way." She cringed. "Toward another platoon."

Screams and gunfire rose from the other tunnel.

"Come on," Marco said. "Lailani, you keep using your brain to send those scum away. The other platoons will deal with them. Our job is to find the emperor."

They fought onward. They fought for hours, for a day, for a night. They were ten, then twenty, then thirty kilometers underground. From all across the mines, the reports came in of soldiers slaying the scum, dying in the hives. Thousands were dying. Entire brigades, famous brigades who had fought in many battles, who had become legends--they perished in the hive. Two more of the Spearheads died, consumed by larvae the size of horses. Other soldiers replaced them. The survivors fought on.

Every hour, Lailani grew weaker. It was not just the physical exertion. She spent almost all her time now with her eyes closed, living inside the scum network, choosing paths, sending commands. Sometimes Marco saw a hundred scum racing toward them, and he would begin to fire, only for Lailani to send the bugs a message through their invisible network. Every time, the scum would take another path. More than any grenade or gun, it was Lailani who was their greatest weapon. Lailani, genetically engineered by the scum, placed into the womb of a homeless woman, grown to become an agent of the enemy. Lailani, only ninety-nine percent human. Lailani, that one percent inside her, that little bit of *scolopendra titania* DNA, letting her control the creatures, understand the creatures. Today she led humanity.

And finally, after thirty hours of battle here underground--thirty hours with no sleep or rest--Lailani stopped walking and nodded. She pointed down a shaft. And she said, "He's there. The emperor. We found him."

CHAPTER TWENTY

The shaft plunged down, and through the cracks in his exoframe, Marco felt cold wind and smelled rot. He stood on the rim, staring down below. Lailani's words echoed.

He's there. We found him.

Marco stared down the dark shaft. His flashlight showed nothing but shadows. Did he truly lurk down there? The scum emperor? The creature they had to kill to destroy the hive, to topple this cruel empire?

Marco tried to peer through the shadows, seeing nothing, but he heard a low rumbling, barely audible, almost like breathing. It was the voice he would hear lying on his bunk at night, a murmur, muffled, only his imagination giving shape to words.

Marco . . . Marco . . . They're waiting for you, Marco. Come join them . . .

Marco inhaled deeply. "I'll lead the way." He placed one foot over the chasm.

"Let me," Ben-Ari said, holding his shoulder.

Marco shook his head. "You've led us through many battles, ma'am. You've placed yourself in the path of danger too many times. Let me take the lead this time."

"Wait," Addy said. "Fire in the hole!"

She tossed a grenade down the shaft. They waited for the dust to settle, and Marco climbed into the shaft. He dug his gauntlets and steel-tipped toes into the walls, descending slowly, peering down into the depths. His flashlight illuminated nothing but shadows, but he could still hear it. That breathing. That muffled grumble of a voice, perhaps no more than creaking stones and wind in the tunnels.

Marco . . . Come to me . . . I see you, Marco . . .

He climbed down faster, jaw clenched.

Enough, he thought. *Enough! Enough of this shit.* He inhaled sharply, and his rage surprised him, flowing over his fear. *I've suffered these scum for too long. It's time to end this.*

He reached the bottom of the shaft, walked down a tunnel, and entered a vast hall.

It was a chamber the size of a cathedral, and lamps of skin and flesh shone on the craggy walls. Skulls covered the floor, thousands of them, each from a different race, a lurid collection of conquests. Marco couldn't even see the human skull here, if there was one. He saw skulls the size of marbles, skulls the size of cars, skulls with horns, round skulls, elongated skulls, black skulls, red skulls, anguished, furious skulls, some staring with two eye sockets, some with a hundred. Here were the trophies of a galaxy, rising knee-deep, a sea of bones. In the center of the hall, many skulls had been stacked and fused together with sticky membranes, forming a tower, and upon the tower rose a throne of bones, but the seat was empty.

The warriors entered the hall. Lieutenant Ben-Ari. Marco. Addy. Lailani. Sergeant Jones. A handful of others. They were all that remained of their platoon. Marco kept waiting for more soldiers to emerge, warriors from other units, but none came. He heard battle above--screaming, screeching, gunfire, flesh ripping.

Lailani inhaled sharply. "Thousands more scum are leaving their burrows above," she whispered. "*Hundreds* of thousands. They're coming in from other hives, from hives all over the planet--coming here." She glanced up the shaft they had just descended. "They'll be here soon. We must hurry."

The chamber began to shake. Dust rained from the ceiling. The sea of bones rattled.

"It's a trap!" Addy said.

"Calm down, admiral," Marco said to her. He took a deep breath and turned to Lailani. "Do you sense anything here? Do--"

Lailani was staring at the pillar of bones. "There," she whispered. "There!"

Marco stared back at the tower woven of skulls and bones, at the throne at its top. The throne was large enough for a giant, but he saw no occupant. Marco squinted, trying to look closer. Wait! There. Something moved in the shadows on that throne. Something small, pale gray, peering with black eyes.

The bones rattled louder across the floor. The walls shook. A voice rose from the tower.

"Marco . . ." A dry cackle sounded. "Einav . . . Lailani . . . Addy . . ."

The voice rose louder, louder, calling out their names. It rose to a shriek, to a demonic laughter. It was too loud. Too loud! Marco couldn't stand it. He placed his hands on his ears, realizing he still wore a helmet, and it was too loud! He screamed. At his side, Addy ripped off her helmet and covered her ears. Lailani fell to her knees. The chamber shook.

"Kill it--it's on the tower!" Marco shouted. He aimed his plasma gun and fired a bolt. More bolts flew from his fellow soldiers' guns.

The creature on the throne scurried away, maybe just a shadow. It couldn't have been larger than a baby. The plasma hit the throne, melting the bones. The cackling echoed through the chamber.

"I knew you would come." The voice seemed to come from all directions at once. "I lured you here. I've been calling you all your lives."

"Kill it!" Ben-Ari shouted. "There!"

She pointed. They saw a creature on the wall, clinging, glistening white like a wet, naked cat, scurrying away in an instant. Their plasma hit the wall, melting stone.

"Einav Ben-Ari . . ." said the voice, but it was like a hundred voices speaking at once, some high-pitched and demonic, some impossibly deep. "The girl with no home. The girl who was born on a military base. The girl who ran away, who fucked men twice her age, who drank, who hated herself. The girl with no nation, the girl who will never be as admired as her father, her grandfather, the heroines before her. The girl with a barren womb, who can grow only monsters inside her. The last, shriveling leaf of a dying tree."

Ben-Ari had tears in her eyes. "Kill it!" she was screaming, firing her gun everywhere, but the creature leaped from place to place, appearing, vanishing, a ghost. Marco couldn't catch more than a glimpse of it, couldn't see what it was.

"It's the emperor!" Lailani said. "He's there! He's the whole room! Kill him!"

"Lailani Marita de la Rosa," said the creature, this emperor of arthropods. "The girl born to a child-whore. The girl born infected with our sweet blood. The girl who ate from landfills, who danced for men for a handful of pesos, who cut her wrists, again and again, pleading to die. The girl who murdered her friends to prove her loyalty to me. The girl who came back to her master. Who will be mine again."

"I will never be yours again!" Lailani screamed, weeping. "Never! I will never kill anyone for you again!" Her tears flowed. "I never killed Elvis--you did! You did! I cut myself only to get rid of you, and now I'm going to finally cut you out!"

She grabbed a grenade and hurled it across the room. A shadow fled, and the grenade burst, showering the chamber with shrapnel. Hot pieces dug into Marco's armor. His ears rang. Skulls shattered across the floor. Dust rained from a crack in the ceiling.

"And you . . . Marco," said the shadow. "The boy whose mother my warriors consumed. Oh, I tasted her flesh too, Marco. I was there. I was in my soldiers' minds as they feasted. And I was in your mind. When you were a child, afraid of me lurking under your bed. When you were alone. All those years, when you were alone, hurting, grieving, when the clouds were so dark, the pain so great, I was there with you. When you read those dirty magazines as a boy, so ashamed. When you betrayed Kemi, the woman you loved. When you betrayed Lailani, taking Addy into your bed. When you realized that you were a traitor. When you watched your friends die while you lived on, too cowardly to fight with them. But there is no guilt here. There is no treachery in the dark. Soon you too will be one of the hive. Soon you will savor the tastes of countless flesh, of endless conquest."

"We'll never join you!" Marco shouted. "Mock us all you like. You are the coward now! You are the one hiding! You think yourself brave and powerful, oh mighty emperor? Then show yourself! Face us."

The creature laughed. Marco glimpsed the white thing above, fired his gun, but it vanished again.

"Tell me, Marco," the emperor said in a thousand voices, some mocking, others twisted beyond understanding. "Do you miss your friends? The friends that you killed? I tasted them too. I savored the sweet flavors of them. I took them into my hive. I remade them for you, Marco. Your new friends." The emperor laughed. "Rise! Rise, my children! Let Marco see what he will become!"

And from the sea of skulls across the chamber, figures rose.

Marco and his fellow soldiers raised their guns.

"God," Addy whispered. "Oh God."

Nausea rose in Marco's throat. At his side, Ben-Ari was clutching her Star of David pendant and praying. Lailani gasped and crossed herself, tears on her cheeks.

"Stop this!" Marco shouted at the emperor. "Stop this mockery!"

But only cruel laughter filled the chamber, and the figures stepped closer.

They were somewhat human, maybe mostly human, but centipede too. They rose twice Marco's height, created from many human torsos stitched together, forming bizarre centipedes. From each torso emerged two human arms, the hands tipped with claws. Not scum. Not human. And yet Marco recognized their faces.

They were the faces of his friends.

There was Beast, his head bald, his eyes white, slithering forward like a cobra prepared to strike, most of his body still under the skulls. Beside him advanced Corporal Diaz, Marco's old squad commander--or at least a creature with Diaz's face. Sergeant Singh was here too, still bearded. Marco spun around, panting, head spinning, unable to believe this. It had to be an illusion. Had to! Yet they were all here, all those the scum had slain, had eaten. There was Corporal Webb, the commander from Fort Djemila with no legs. There was Caveman who had died on the tarmac. And there--there in the distance, staring with blank eyes--there was Elvis, there was his dear friend Elvis, and he scuttled forward on many legs, and his mouth opened with a hiss. The faces of his friends. The bodies of deformed centipedes formed from human parts.

"Hello, Marco," Beast said.

"Hello, friend," said Elvis.

"It's nice here," said Diaz.

"Join us," said Singh.

"Join us!" they all chanted.

Marco wanted to fire his gun, to kill the creatures. But he couldn't. He couldn't do it. The other soldiers stood by him, their own guns raised, their faces twisted in disgust. They too couldn't fire.

"It's . . . it's really them," Lailani said. "I can feel it. It's them. Their DNA. The scum took their DNA when killing them."

"Fuck!" Addy said. "Oh God, what do we do?"

The creatures kept advancing, reaching out their claws, surrounding the remaining soldiers.

"No, it's not them," Ben-Ari said softly. "Maybe they have the DNA of our friends. But that doesn't mean it's them. They were never babies. They never grew up in loving families. They know nothing but hatred, a mockery of life. These are not our friends, just zombies cobbled together from our friends' flesh." She raised her gun. "And we end this now."

Ben-Ari fired. A stream of plasma shot out and slammed into the centipede with Sergeant Singh's face.

The creature screamed.

Singh's face melted, revealing the skull, and Ben-Ari kept firing, tears in her eyes, and her lips kept moving, and Marco could read her words. *I'm sorry. I'm sorry.*

The other creatures leaped toward them.

The monster with Caveman's face charged toward Marco. Its hands swung. Its claws stretched out, long as daggers, and slammed into Marco's armor. The graphene and steel tore open like a tin can. Marco fell onto the skulls, his side bleeding. The centipede with Caveman's face stared down at him, drooling, eyes mad.

"Marco . . ." it said. "Marco, why did you leave me to die?"

Its claws thrust down again, ripping metal panels off Marco's leg, cutting his skin.

"You're not him!" Marco shouted.

"You killed me, Marco," Caveman said, rising higher, many torsos stacked together, many arms spreading out. "You'll be like us. You--"

Marco fired his gun. The plasma shot out, washing over Caveman. The creature screamed, and as it screamed, as it burned, it sounded less and less like a monster to Marco, more and more like a human. Like his old friend.

And he was begging. He was begging for his life.

Marco held his fire, and the creature that was half Caveman collapsed, dead.

"I'm sorry," Marco whispered. "I'm sorry."

Then he shouted in sudden rage, tears in his eyes, and fired his gun again. The others fired with him. And they burned the creatures. Some of the soldiers--those who had joined their platoon in the tunnels, who wore no exoframes--they died, cut by the creatures' claws. More and more of the hybrids kept emerging from the sea of skulls on the floor.

Three of the creatures leaped onto Osiris, tearing off her uniform, her synthetic skin, exposing the crackling, sparkling innards. The android looked at Marco, met his gaze with lavender lights in a white plastic skull, and then her lights darkened, and she fell.

Sergeant Jones tossed aside his gun, out of plasma. The beefy NCO bellowed, drew a knife, and leaped onto the centipede with Elvis's face. The creature swatted aside the knife, grabbed Jones's head, and crushed the helmet, crushed the skull. Blood spurted. The massive warrior, the platoon's second-in-command, fell onto the bones, his head cracked open.

Marco screamed, weeping, and fired his gun, letting the plasma wash over Jones's corpse, wash over Elvis, wash over his deformed friends, wash over this whole damn war and all his grief and memory and loss. And they burned. He burned them all, firing again and again until the entire chamber was smoke and charred meat and melting bones.

Marco fell to his knees, panting.

The creatures were all dead.

Marco. Ben-Ari. Addy. Lailani. They were all who remained. Four living souls, trapped in this chamber of death.

The four of them . . . and him.

The emperor sat on his throne, staring down at them. When Marco had first landed on this planet, he had imagined a giant bug, as large as the king he had fought above the mines of Corpus. But this creature was small as a baby. Finally Marco could get a good look at it. He could not determine its species. It was not scum, not fully, at least. Mandibles thrust out from its jaws, but that was the only feature of an arthropod. Its body was humanoid, wilted, the white skin pressing against the ribs. Gills opened and closed on its neck, and rudimentary wings thrust out from its back. Each of its limbs was different: a hoof, a claw, a tentacle, a leg, a tail, an arm and hand.

"It's a bunch of different creatures," Addy said. "All mixed together."

Marco nodded. "The scum don't use tools, don't build technology like humans. They're genetic engineers. Their ships, their soldiers--all built by engineering DNA they steal across the galaxy. This isn't an emperor so much as a scientist. An experiment."

The creature on the throne laughed. "I am the cosmos. I am life. Every species in this galaxy is weak. I take from them all. I make myself strong. The best traits of every civilization quiver through my body. Humans . . . Ah, humans. So clever. So cruel. So ready to kill. I have taken much of your cunningness and cruelty into myself."

Marco noticed that the creature was wounded. One of their plasma blasts must have hit it. Its side was burnt, bleeding, perhaps the reason it no longer scurried through the chamber. Marco raised his gun and pointed it at the emperor.

He fired.

Yet the creature was still fast. It leaped from its throne and clung to the ceiling. Addy fired her own gun, and the emperor leaped down, dodging the blasts. It snarled, scurried aside, avoiding a bolt from Ben-Ari's gun. It was like a rabid dog, hissing, sneering, and it began to grow. Its body bloated, thrusting out spines, and drool dripped from its fangs. Soon it was the size of a man.

"Now . . . it's time to die."

The emperor howled and charged toward them like an enraged bull.

They fired. The emperor dodged the bolts. It leaped toward them, growling, reaching out claws and fangs, whipping from side to side at incredible speed, then jumping into the air and--

The emperor froze.

It hissed.

It fell down, cracking the skulls beneath it, only feet away from Marco.

Lailani walked up toward the emperor. She pulled off her helmet and stared down at the creature, which was shrinking, soon the size of a baby again.

Tears flowed down Lailani's cheeks.

"You placed the hive inside my brain," Lailani whispered. "You made me a part of this corrupt web. But they fixed me. The humans fixed me. You can no longer control me." She pointed her gun at the emperor. "But I can still control you."

The emperor tried to rise, screaming. It managed to reach out claws, but Lailani stared at it, snarling, and the emperor fell again. Lailani twisted her hands, and the emperor's limbs twisted too, creaking, snapping. The creature screeched so loudly skulls shattered on the floor.

"That's right," Lailani said. "Be afraid. I was afraid for so long. You were able to control me before. When my brain was yours. But there's a little chip inside there now. A chip placed there by my people. I am human. Do you hear me?" She was shouting now. "I am human! You cannot control me! With the weapon that you gave me, I can hurt you. I can reach you through the web. I can feel your brain--so weak, so afraid. You are nothing." Lailani was shaking, tears falling. "You are not any of the beings you stole. You are nothing but a thief, just a thief cloaked in others' clothes. But I'm human." She looked at Marco, smiling through her tears. "For the first time, I'm fully human."

The emperor wailed and leaped toward Lailani, fangs bared.

Lailani fired her gun.

The plasma bathed the emperor, and the hybrid fell, howling in agony.

The other soldiers added their flames. The plasma washed over the emperor, and the creature wailed, wept, begged. It twisted on the ground, reaching up claws. It grew to the size of a man, then the size of a horse. It shrunk to the size of a mouse. It became a writhing centipede, still twitching, still screaming.

"Mercy!" it cried. "Mercy!"

But still they burned it.

They burned it until it crumbled. Until it was nothing but ashes. Until it moved no more.

Addy's gun ran out of plasma first, dying with a clicking sound. Ben-Ari and Lailani's guns followed. Marco removed his hand from the trigger to see just a single bolt of plasma left in the charge.

The scum emperor was dead.

They lowered their weapons, and from across the tunnels, they could hear a great ruckus, millions of screeches and voices. Ben-Ari's communicator crackled.

"The scum!" rose the voice of a soldier somewhere far above in the hive. "They're fleeing! They're fleeing the hive!"

Marco approached Lailani, and they fell to their knees together, holding each other, shaking, weeping.

"It's over," Lailani whispered. "It's over. It's over. It's--"

A crackling sounded.

They turned toward the pillar of bones that rose in the center of the chamber.

Skulls rolled down the structure, and from within, emerging like an animal from its burrow, stepped an old woman with long white hair, her eyes haunted.

CHAPTER TWENTY-ONE

The soldiers stared, eyes wide.

The old woman stepped toward them, eyes sunken into her deeply wrinkled face. Scraggly white hair hung down to her waist. She wore only wisps of cloth, and tubes were attached to her veins, running into the floor.

The human prisoner, Marco thought. *The scum emperor had every kind of alien species as a pet. Here is the human.*

The woman reached toward them, her limbs shriveled down to the bones. Her mouth opened, toothless, but no words came out. She looked, Marco thought, like those old photos of Holocaust survivors after the camps had been liberated. He rushed toward her, as did the others. Addy pulled a blanket out from her pack, and they wrapped it around the old woman.

The prisoner tried to speak again. Only a hoarse whisper left her mouth. She fell to her knees, wept, and clung to Marco's legs.

"Thank you," she seemed to be saying, her voice slurred. "Thank you."

A choked sound rose from behind them.

Marco turned and gasped.

Admiral Evan Bryan himself--the hero of the war fifty years ago, the general who had led this massive invasion--stepped into the chamber.

Tears were running down his cheeks.

The silvery-haired admiral ran across the chamber and knelt before the old woman.

"Helena," the admiral whispered, eyes wet. "Helena, I'm here. I'm finally here. I came back for you."

The old woman touched Admiral Bryan's wrinkled cheeks with trembling fingers. "Evan. Evan, it's you. It's really you."

Evan embraced the woman, weeping. "I've got you, my wife, my love. It's over now. Your captivity is over. I'm taking you home."

The old woman--Helena Bryan--trembled with sobs. "My husband. My husband. For so many years, I waited. For five decades, I waited. But I always knew you'd come back for me. I always knew. I never lost hope. I love you."

The soldiers watched them, standing around the couple. When Marco glanced at the others, he saw that Addy, Lailani, and even Ben-Ari had tears in their eyes.

"His wife," Addy whispered. "His wife was captive here all these years. Since the Cataclysm."

"I'll call the medics," Ben-Ari said, reaching for her helmet's communicator. "She needs help. I--"

"Hold it right there," Admiral Bryan said, and suddenly the old man was pointing a gun at Ben-Ari. "Stop that call."

The soldiers all froze, staring at their general.

"Sir, I--" Ben-Ari began.

"Remove your helmets," Admiral Bryan said. He took a step away from his wife, gun still pointing at Ben-Ari. "All of you. Toss them aside. No communicators. Do it!"

The soldiers glanced at one another.

"Sir, she needs help," Ben-Ari said. "Why--"

Admiral Bryan fired his gun. A bolt of plasma slammed into Ben-Ari's chest, piercing through the metal armor, burning through her. She fell.

"Ma'am!" Marco cried, making to run toward her. "Lieu--"

"Freeze!" Admiral Bryan said, pointing his gun at Marco next. "Drop your weapons and helmets, all of you. Do it or I'll shoot this one too."

Addy and Lailani froze, hissing, guns raised halfway.

"Toss them!" Bryan shouted. "That is both an order and a threat."

Grumbling, Addy and Lailani tossed down their guns, then their helmets with the built-in communicators. Marco did the same. Ben-Ari lay on the ground; Marco wasn't sure if she was still alive. The three corporals--Marco, Addy, Lailani--stood before their admiral, their weapons and communicators gone. Helena knelt farther back, staring with wide eyes, trembling.

"You fucking bastard," Addy whispered, staring at the admiral. "You killed Ben-Ari. You fucking killed her. Why?"

"Why?" Bryan said. "Don't you understand? Don't you know anything about love?" Suddenly the admiral's eyes were damp again. "Helena is my wife. And I love her more than anything. More than the cosmos. And nobody can know. Nobody can ever know she's my wife. I'm going to take her to a medic myself, and all they'll know is that I found a prisoner here. A stranger. A stranger whom, in a few months, I will marry. Nobody will ever know the secret, that fifty years ago, my wife flew with me to war against the scum. That the aliens captured her. That for fifty years, I've been trying to get her back."

"Why are you doing this?" Addy shouted. "Why keep it a secret?"

But Marco understood. He spoke in a low voice, and his shoulders slumped. "Because this war could have been avoided. Because millions of lives could have been saved. Because we could have had peace."

The admiral nodded. "Yes. This one understands. Emery was always intelligent. I saw that in him early." Bryan stared at a wall, seeming to stare back in time. "Fifty years ago, the scum dealt a devastating blow to Earth. They killed billions. It's what we call the Cataclysm. A few of us brave pilots flew to war. I was only twenty-one years old, more balls than brains. Only days before, I had married Helena, a fellow pilot, the love of my young life. I nuked the scum's world, destroying millions of them. But Helena crash-landed onto the planet. The scum captured her. And then, as they buried their millions of slain . . . the scum offered us peace."

"Peace," Lailani whispered, kneeling over Ben-Ari. "We could have had peace fifty years ago?"

"But not with my wife," said Bryan. "Helena had come to bomb them. They would not release her as part of any peace treaty. They were determined to keep her in this dank, dark cell for the rest of her life. And so I refused their peace offer." His eyes hardened. "And I would do it again. And again. A million times over. And so, for the past fifty years, every time the scum offered peace, I refused. Every time the War of Attrition deescalated, I launched new attacks on their hives. I had to keep the war alive. I had to make the war worse. Four years ago, the scum sent me a message: that Helena was ill, nearing the end of her natural life." He took a shuddering breath. "And so I withdrew the defenses from Corpus, allowing the scum to take that world, to breed there. And so I withdrew the defense system from Vancouver, allowing them to destroy it. And so I made sure that our conflict escalated into full war, that the United Nations and the HDF's Chief-of-Staff would authorize this invasion, that they would grant me a hundred thousand ships and ten million troops. To come here. To kill the emperor. And to save her, my wife, my beloved, at the very end."

"Millions of people died!" Addy shouted, eyes red, fists clenched. "My parents died! Marco's mother died! Millions of people on Earth died. Millions of soldiers in space died. We could have had peace! They could have been saved. You let them die. You killed them!"

Admiral Bryan had tears in his eyes, but he squared his shoulders and raised his chin. "Yes. I let them die. I could have saved millions of lives. But I sacrificed them all to save just one life. To save the woman I love. That burden will forever be mine to bear. And now . . ." He pointed his gun at Marco, then at Addy, then at Lailani. "Now I must sacrifice three more lives. Three more who know the secret. Three more before it all ends."

The admiral pointed his gun at Marco and pulled the trigger.

"No!" Helena shouted, grabbing her husband's arm, yanking the gun aside.

Marco leaped sideways, and the blast of plasma seared the top of his shoulder.

"Evan, no!" Helena cried. "Let no more die for me!"

Admiral Bryan tried to shake her off. He fired again, but Helena tugged his wrist again, and the blow hit the wall. Marco leaped, grabbed his fallen rifle, and fired his last bolt of plasma.

The bolt tore through Admiral Bryan's chest, emerging from the other side.

The admiral fell to his knees, then to his side.

Marco stood still, panting, staring down at the old man.

Bryan reached up and held his wife's hand. Helena knelt above him, tears falling.

"Helena," the admiral whispered. "I'm sorry. I'm sorry . . . I love you . . ."

As his wife held him, Bryan's breath died, and his glassy eyes stared at the ceiling.

Marco rushed toward Lieutenant Ben-Ari. She lay on the skulls, a hole in her chest, but she was still breathing. Marco grabbed his fallen helmet and hit the communicator.

"We need a medic!" he shouted. "Medics in the lower cell! Hurry!"

Fingers shaking, Marco placed a bandage on Ben-Ari's wound, and he held her hand. His commander looked up at him, eyes sunken, her skin gray. She blinked, tried to whisper something, could not speak.

"It's all right, ma'am," Marco whispered. "You're all right. Help is on the way."

Ben-Ari placed her bloody hand on his. She smiled softly. Her eyes closed.

CHAPTER TWENTY-TWO

They were going home.

After months of war, of heartache, of loss, of pain, they were going home.

Marco stood in the lounge of the HDFS *Terra*, flagship of the human fleet, staring out the viewport. Below him lay the ravaged world of Abaddon, planet of the *scolopendra titania*, a planet in ruin. Its hives had been destroyed, filled with concrete. The emperor was dead, his connection to his soldiers lost. Already across the galaxy, hives of scum on other worlds were disoriented, fleeing, dying, no central power to command them.

The war was over.

Humans won.

But we won at a terrible cost, Marco thought.

The remains of the human fleet gathered behind the *Terra.* They had flown here with a hundred thousand vessels; only ten thousand remained. Ten million troops had come to battle the emperor; only a quarter million were flying home. Only a handful of the alien allies' ships remained; the rest would never return to their planets. In future history books, Marco knew, they would name this the most devastating battle since the Cataclysm.

From Earth, the news was scarcely better. As the human fleet had attacked Abaddon, the scum had been attacking Earth. The Iron Sphere defense system had stopped most of the assault, but not all. Entire cities lay in ruin. Millions lay dead. A new Cataclysm, they were calling it.

"We will mourn those who fell," Marco said softly. "We will never forget, never forgive, forever grieve. A second Cataclysm has shattered our world. But again we will rise from the ashes." He looked at the phoenix stitched onto his uniform, symbol of the Human Defense Force, perhaps of all humanity. "Like the phoenix, we will rise."

Lailani stood at his side, slipped her hand into his, and leaned her head against his arm. "We will rise."

Addy stood at his other side, and she placed a hand on his shoulder. "We will fucking rise."

Marco watched a squadron of Firebirds flit between the warships outside. He recognized Kemi's Firebird, saw her in the cockpit as she flew nearby on patrol. The larger ships were already warming up their azoth engines, and their turbines glowed blue. Within a couple of hours, the fleet would be blasting into hyperspace, beginning the three-week journey back to Earth.

"I wish the others could be here with us," Marco said. "Elvis. Beast. Diaz. Singh. All of them."

"We will remember them," Addy said. "Always."

Marco thought about the last survivor of their platoon. About a leader, a woman he had come to love deeply--as a friend, as family.

As the fleet gathered, making the last preparations for the journey home, Marco left the lounge. He walked through the carpeted corridors of the *Terra*, this ship the size of a skyscraper, and took the elevator several floors up. He reached the ship's hospital, and he walked down bustling corridors where nurses and doctors rushed, pushing gurneys. Through the windows of many doors, he saw doctors performing surgeries on the wounded. And he saw many orderlies pushing wheeled beds with the blankets pulled up over the dead.

Finally Marco reached the door he had sought. He knocked and stepped into the small room.

Inside, Ben-Ari lay on a bed, hooked up to an IV.

Marco saluted.

His officer smiled weakly at him. "No need to salute here, Marco. I'd rather save my strength."

He nodded and sat beside her. Her eyes were sunken, but some color had returned to her cheeks. Bandages covered her wound.

"How are you feeling, ma'am?" Marco asked.

"He shot me right through the lung," Ben-Ari said. "Missed my heart by only two centimeters, missed my spine by just a bit more." She coughed weakly. "I'll need a new lung. With so many fallen, they'll find me a good one."

Marco nodded. "I'm so glad you're all right, ma'am." He thought for a moment, then asked the question that had been on his mind all day. "I shot him. I killed him--our admiral. They'll know one of us did it. They--"

"They heard everything," Ben-Ari said. "My communicator was on the whole time. I turned it on just before Bryan shot me. His confession is recorded." She sighed and turned her head, looking out the viewport at the fleet. "His legacy is forever tarnished. For fifty years, he was our hero. Now he'll be remembered as a monster."

"I don't think of him as a monster," Marco said. "Not fully. I've wondered: What would I do if the scum had Lailani? Would I be willing to sacrifice others to save her? And I don't know. I don't envy the choices he had to make." He thought for a moment longer. "But I don't regret killing him."

She clasped his hand. "You did well, Marco. I'm proud to have you as my soldier. As my friend."

Her uniform hung by the door, and Marco noticed that new insignia topped the shoulder straps, three golden bars where two had once shone.

"And I'm proud to have fought for you, Captain Ben-Ari," he said. "And to be your friend." He hesitated for a moment, then asked the second question that had been on his mind. "Ma'am, what happens now? With the Human Defense Force? With our service?"

"Our military service will continue," Ben-Ari said. "We defeated the scum. But there are ten thousand technological civilizations in our galaxy alone. Some will rise to fill the void the scum left. Some, perhaps, will challenge humanity. There's still a need for the HDF. For us. It's time for peace, to holster our guns, but not yet to lay them aside." She stared into his eyes. "Have you reconsidered the offer I made to you once? About going to Officer Candidate School? I would still write you that recommendation. You can be leading a platoon of your own within a year."

"I've thought about it," Marco confessed. "But I still must refuse your generous offer, ma'am. Officers have military careers, sometimes lifelong." He sighed. "I joined for five years, the mandatory time, and I've been doing my best to be a good soldier. But I don't think this life is for me, not forever. I'll remain enlisted. And maybe, with the war over, they'll even shorten our service. Maybe I can spend the rest of my life at peace. At home. With my family."

Ben-Ari looked at him, a small smile on her face, then turned to look out the viewport. "Look, Marco. The stars are spreading out. We're leaping into hyperspace."

Her hand tightened around his. He sat by her side, holding her hand as the stars spread into lines, as they began their journey home.

*****

They were home.

After long months of war, they were home.

They took the rocket here together. Marco. Addy. Kemi. Lailani. All four wore their service uniforms, the navy blue of

Space Territorial Command. Marco, Addy, and Lailani wore the insignia of corporals, while Kemi wore the rank of ensign. All four carried Fyre rifles. In the aftermath of the war, all had been given a week off from the military. All had come here to Toronto. For a week of healing. A week of home.

The city had been spared the brunt of the scum attack, suffering a thousand casualties and still standing. From above, as the rocket descended, it looked like the same Toronto they had always known, the place where Marco, Addy, and Kemi had been born and raised. Lailani, who had never been to North America, stared through the windows with wide eyes.

"It looks . . . less crowded than Manila," she said, then nodded. "I like it, but I'll still miss home."

Sergeant Stumpy sat at their side in a crate. The dog, rescued from the scum-infested mine of Corpus, looked out the viewport and huffed in approval.

Marco's father was waiting for them at the starport. Carl Emery hugged his son--a long, crushing hug.

"You've lost weight!" he said. "You need to eat!"

"I'm fine, Dad!" Marco laughed, but Father would hear none of it. The librarian insisted on stopping by the nearest burger joint, a greasy little hole-in-the-wall with tattered booths and a sizzling griddle. Trying to hide his damp eyes, Father ordered onion rings and cheeseburgers for the lot of them. Kemi's parents were there too, and they all ate, and then Father bought a second round of burgers, insisting they needed to fatten up, couldn't even wait for the drive back home. Music was playing on the radio--a new pop tune, one Marco hadn't heard before. A few kids were in the burger joint too, laughing and playing on their phones. A mother was cooing to her baby.

It was the world. It was the real world again--with good greasy food, and music, and civilians, and family, and life.

But Marco was silent as he ate.

And Addy, and Kemi, and Lailani--they were silent.

Sometimes Marco caught his friends glancing up at him, then looking away quickly. And he knew that they were remembering too, like he was. Remembering the mines of Corpus. The hybrids underground. The millions dying as the fleet shattered. The music seemed too loud, and when the baby cried, Marco jumped.

The bathroom was out of order in the burger joint, and Marco stepped behind the restaurant to pee in the alleyway. When he zipped up his pants, he thought: *What am I doing?* He should have held it in, would have only months ago, but in the army he had always sneaked off to pee in some alleyway or behind some boulder. And he realized that he had stuffed half his second burger into his pocket, saving it for later, for days of hunger, though months ago he'd have just tossed it out. And he didn't know who he was now, who he had become during the war.

Before her parents drove her to their apartment, Kemi kissed Marco's cheek, and he stood for a while, watching her car drive off. Marco's father drove the rest of them back to the library.

Home seemed familiar but smaller somehow, their apartment above the library just somehow *wrong*, too clean, too neat. It almost felt like being in hyperspace again, when everything was just a little bit off. Father insisted on feeding them again at home, cooking spaghetti, even when Addy complained that he'd turn them all into blimps. They played old Beatles records, then drank some beer, then watched a hockey game. Sergeant Stumpy fell asleep on his back, hogging half the couch and snoring. It was what they had waited to do for so long, what they had dreamed of, what had gotten them through the hardest of times. They sat silently on the couch, staring at the TV, making no noise or movement when a goal was scored.

That night, Addy and Lailani shared the pull-out bed in the living room. Marco lay in his old bedroom, alone, staring up at the dark ceiling.

The scum were scuttling through the tunnels.

Elvis was dead, his heart on the floor.

Ships burned.

All night, Marco was still fighting that war, cold sweat trickling, breath panting, until gray dawn scratched at the windows.

Marco and Lailani walked through the city that day, leading Stumpy on a leash. In six days, they would return to their service, to four more years of the army. This day, Marco showed Lailani his home. They walked down Yonge Street toward Lake Ontario, and they watched ships from the boardwalk. They bought steaming cups of coffee and jelly donuts. They fed the geese. But they were silent a lot, glancing at each other furtively, then quickly away, daring not maintain eye contact. And this was no longer Marco's home.

There were no more guards with guns at every street corner. Civilians no longer carried their gas masks. The scum were defeated, and there were parades of victory across Toronto. People waved flags of Earth. They sang, they danced. A group of old men sat on a bar's patio, giving Marco and Lailani a standing ovation as the two soldiers walked by. But Marco did not feel honored. He wanted to shout at these men, to shake them. How dared they applaud, how dared they congratulate him? How dared people dance on the street and sing? How dared they be joyous when countless had fallen, when countless had come home alive but broken, dead inside?

"Our generation is lost," Marco said, standing on a street corner, watching a victory ceremony on a nearby stage. "People like Admiral Bryan. Like our president. The generals and politicians. They sent us out to die, or worse--to break. To shatter. An entire generation--lost."

"We're not lost," Lailani said.

"I feel lost," said Marco. "Millions of us are. Our ghosts came home, but we died out on Corpus, on Abaddon. In a senseless war."

"I'm not a ghost, Marco." Lailani held his hands, staring into his eyes. "Look at me. I'm *alive*, Marco. I'm hurt. I'm broken inside. You are too. But we're *alive*. We can still find a life now. Even with our scars." She glanced down at the scars on her wrists, then back into his eyes. "Some scars don't heal, those on the body and those on the soul. Our scars won't heal. Our wounds won't stop hurting. But we're still a long way from dead. I intend to *live* the rest of my life."

Live. Marco looked across the city. The towers. The lake. The parks. A city that had suffered so many dead, a thousand slain only last month. A city in a world still lying in ruins, millions dead across its charred landscapes. A city still alive.

To live, he thought. *To rise again.*

"Can we still find joy?" he said. "Even after seeing so much pain? Can we ever still laugh, dance, see beauty?"

"I don't know," Lailani said, and her eyes were damp. "But maybe we just have to take breath by breath. To live day by day. To be grateful that we're alive. And maybe we won't find joy. And maybe we'll always hurt. And maybe that's the sacrifice we had to make to our elders, to the cruelty in space, to the next generation, and if that is so, then that is so, and we'll live on, and we'll see that next generation live in a world that we never had. A world that is good. And maybe that's not enough, but if that is what we have, that is what I'll take."

Memories, Marco thought. *Pain. A broken world. Haunting dreams. If that is what we have, that is what we take.*

"So that is what we take," Marco said softly, voice hoarse.

Lailani embraced him. "Forgive, Marco. That's all we can do. Forgive our leaders, our parents, our enemies. Forgive our lives. Forgive all the pain and cruelty and shit and unfairness in the world. Just to forgive. Just to accept. Just to let it all flow over us. We tell ourselves that we're strong, that we can control our own destinies, that we can make our own choices. But we can't. We're only dust. Just dust. So forgive, Marco. Forgive what happened to us. Forgive yourself for hurting. Forgive yourself for remembering. Forgive me."

He held her close, tears falling. "Always."

She smiled through her tears and poked his nose. "Also, remember, I'm still going to marry you and give you beautiful mixed-race babies. Not just yet. In a few years. But it's coming. It's something to wait for. Something good."

May our children have a better world than we had, Marco thought, holding her. *May they never know war. May they never know loss. May they never know horror and pain and memories that don't die. May we build a new world for them, a good world. May a lost generation create a generation of peace.*

They walked down the street to the boardwalk. They stood by the lake, gazing at the water. Ships were sailing by, and seagulls cawed above.

"I love you, Lailani," Marco said.

She leaned her head against his chest. "Ruv you too."

They stood together, holding each other, watching the ships sail by.

* * * * *

Lieutenant Kemi Abasi flew in her Firebird, traveling several times the speed of sound, gazing down upon the world.

Earth lay in desolation.

In her small jet, she flew over India, where entire cities lay in smoldering ruins. Tanks and battalions of infantry were still moving through the wreckage, picking out the last scum who had invaded during the great war. She flew over Tibet, where temples lay shattered on mountaintops, where monks were performing sky burials for their fallen, carving up the dead for the vultures. She glided over ancient Chinese cities, their glory lost. She flew over Japanese castles where flags rose, defiant, above seas of ruin. She flew for a long time over the water, then over a field of rubble that had once been Vancouver.

So many gone, Kemi thought. *Millions dead.*

Night fell, and as she flew over the dark plains of Saskatchewan, she looked up through her cockpit. The stars shone above, and among them, she could see the lights of the Iron Sphere. It was the largest, most expensive missile defense system ever built. Thousands of its satellites surrounded the Earth, armed with missiles, manned by teams of gruff gunners, ready to fire at any enemy pod swarming toward the Earth. As Kemi had been bombing Abaddon five hundred light-years away, the brave soldiers of Iron Sphere had been firing at the scum invaders. They had destroyed hundreds of thousands of scum pods . . . but thousands had still made their way through.

Thousands of pods had slammed into Earth at once, not just a war of attrition but a massive assault. Blazing with fire, excreting poison, spilling out centipedes, the pods had devastated so much.

Millions gone, Kemi thought, flying over the good earth. *Cities wiped out. We won. We defeated the scum. But at what cost?*

The world was in ruin--and so was her life.

She had lost Marco, the man she loved. She had lost her brother to the war; he had died in a starfighter like the one she now flew. She had seen such horrors. She had seen the hybrids screaming in the scum hive, twisted into creatures half human, half alien. She had stared into the soul of that hive, had become a part of it, connected by tubes and pheromones to its cruelty. She had gazed into the eyes of a million scum, and she could not forget that horror. Kemi had not slept the night through since the terror on Corpus, waking up every hour drenched in cold sweat, struggling for breath, dreams of centipedes racing through her mind.

Yet as Kemi kept flying, she saw hope among the despair, life among the death.

Tractors were moving through ruins. Cranes were rising. People were rebuilding.

"Like a phoenix, we rise again and again from the ashes," Kemi said.

And she too would rise from ruin. She too would build a new life.

Kemi nodded. Perhaps every generation suffered a tragedy. Her grandparents had fled Africa as refugees during the Cataclysm. Her parents had grown up during the War of Attrition, had lost a son to the violence. She, Kemi, had seen this new destruction. But every generation had risen up.

Because we are human, she thought. *And that's what we do. I'm no longer the naive young girl, chasing a boy halfway across the galaxy. I'm an officer in the Human Defense Force. I'm a pilot. I'm not just a survivor; I am one who will thrive. I am one who will rebuild her world and her life.*

"Red Bird, do you copy?" The voice emerged from her headphones.

Kemi turned her head to see the rest of her squadron, fourteen other Firebirds, flying toward her. She was now flying over Houston, where her home airfield was located.

"I copy," she said. "Patrol completed, skies are clear. It's good to be home."

The other pilots came to fly around her. The starfighters formed a vee in the sky. They were defenders of Earth. They were heroes of the war. They were her new life.

* * * * *

Marco walked through the desert, wearing drab fatigues and a helmet. A T57 assault rifle hung across his back, and magazines jangled in pouches in his vest. He passed along a barbed wire fence, around a rusty tap, and toward a group of tents in the sand. The sun beat down on this North African wasteland, a forgotten hole somewhere between mountains and slow death.

He remembered coming to such a base, only a few hundred kilometers from here, a year ago--a frightened kid, disoriented and green as grass.

A thin smile touched Marco's lips. It was strange to see things so differently now, so clearly, so calmly, a bird's-eye view even from here in the dust.

He looked at his friends. At Addy. At Lailani. They walked at his side. Once more, they too wore the green of Earth Territorial Command. Sand rose around their heavy boots.

"You guys ready?" Marco said.

Addy nodded. "Fuck yeah, time to fry up some fresh meat."

Lailani nodded too. "Fry 'em up!"

Marco's smile grew. He had a feeling that Addy's and Lailani's soldiers would suffer a lot more than his.

A platoon of recruits awaited them by the tents. The boys and girls stood at attention, their sergeant scrutinizing them, holding an electric baton. They were just kids. Just goddamn kids, eighteen years old, terrified. One of them, a thin boy with thick glasses, was shaking. Another, a girl with red hair, had tears on her cheeks. Fresh meat indeed.

"All right, you fucking maggots!" shouted the sergeant. "Here are your squad leaders. These bastards have battled the scum more times than you've jerked off. They will whip you into soldiers! Corporal Marco Emery. Corporal Addy Linden. Corporal Lailani de la Rosa. They will turn you into killers, or by God, I will bury you under the sand myself."

Marco tried to stifle his smile. The last thing he had expected was to end up here, to train recruits for battle. He had wanted to serve in the archives, to spend his five years in a shadowy room, poring over computer screens. He had even tried it for a few months before requesting a transfer. In that shadowy room, he had remembered the war too often. Had felt imprisoned, anxious, even afraid. He had seen too many reports of alien species across the galaxy fighting for pieces of the scum's empire, fighting to become the next threat, to spread from star to star--and to Earth.

So no, he had not expected to end up here. But as Lailani had once told him, nobody expected the Spanish Inquisition.

Marco looked at the recruits before him.

I hope that you never have to fight, he thought. *I hope that you never know war. I hope that Earth will forever live in peace. But in case you must fight, in case a day comes again when the sons and daughters of humanity must fly into battle to defend the Earth . . . you will be ready.*

The platoon divided into three squads, standing in new formations by Marco, Addy, and Lailani. The recruits hadn't even received their weapons yet.

One of the recruits gasped and pointed at Marco and his friends. "I know them! They're in the *Why We Fight* newsreel! They're the ones who killed the scum emperor!"

The other recruits stared with wide eyes, whispering amongst themselves.

"Right now the only scum here is you!" Addy shouted, pointing at the recruit who had spoken. "You will not speak without permission again. Down and give me thirty!"

The recruit dropped into the sand and began his push-ups. Marco thought of the time he had come here as a boy, a tattered paperback and photograph in his pocket. A boy who had wanted nothing more than to hide in his library, to read, to write, not to become this man. Not to become this soldier. Not to have these memories.

Forgive, Lailani spoke in his mind. *Accept. If that is what we have, that is what we take.*

"All right, recruits!" Marco said to his squad. "Follow me. It's time you learned how to shoot. It's time you became soldiers."

They followed him across the sand, through this training base in the desert, and Marco prayed that they would never follow him through fire, never follow him to war.

May you never know what I did, Marco thought. *May you never see your friends die. May you never come home broken. May we build a better world for you, a world led by poets rather than generals, by healers rather than killers, a world that will never more burn. May you know nothing but peace.*

CHAPTER TWENTY-THREE

In the darkness, he peered.

In the shadows, he waited.

In the night's forest, he lurked.

Before him spread the cosmos. Before him burned the light of a million stars. Before him danced a million worlds. Before him waited a realm that had fallen, a realm that must be filled.

He was the watcher. He was the weaver of webs. He was the master of strings. He was ancient. He had only just hatched. He hungered. He was Malphas, the one with many eyes.

The hiss and clatter rose behind him. "The . . . centipedes . . . have . . . fallen."

Rasps. Scrapes. Guttural vibrations. Malphas reached out one of his six legs. His long digits unfurled, tipped with claws. His saliva dripped down his fangs, sizzling, seeping through his web. He grabbed a strand. He pulled. His web quivered. Another leg reached out, the claws made for disemboweling, for carving open bone, yet here in his dwelling they glided, so delicate, lovingly tugging. Glass spheres moved. Lenses came into place, ringed with dew. And Malphas saw.

He saw the stars. He saw the empire of the centipedes burn, crumble, vanish into ash. He saw the vastness of the cosmos. He saw the great empty spaces and the fusion in the heart of stars where all creation was forged. He saw the whispers of life quiver in mud across a billion worlds, trying to rise, fading away. He saw creatures emerging from the ooze. He saw them reaching into the emptiness. He saw them crave. He saw them fear. For he had many eyes.

And he saw a great web, strands extending from world to world, his claws woven of light, tugging, delicate, loving, pulling the strings.

The voice rose behind him again. One who served him. One who would fight. Who would feed.

"The . . . humans . . . will . . . rise."

Malphas turned from the cosmos, web trembling. He fixed his four terrestrial eyes upon his slave.

The creature stood before him on the web, jaws opened and drooling, large enough to swallow one of the humans whole, claws long enough to skewer them. Upon his abdomen gazed the eye sockets of a hundred skulls claimed in battle, glued onto the body, forming clattering armor. This servant was inferior to Malphas in every way, yet mighty enough to devour the greatest human warriors, even those who had defeated the centipedes in their lairs. And Malphas knew their faces, knew their names, for he had many eyes and his gaze was long.

Malphas opened his jaws, letting the clattering, the grunts, the scraping emerge, a rumble of his dominion.

"Then . . . we . . . will strike them down."

His slave hissed. "We . . . will . . . feed."

Malphas's abdomen twitched with hunger. His own trophy skulls, the mementos of a hundred vanquished enemies, clattered across him. Feed? Yes. Soon his brood would feed. Soon they would spread across the darkness. Soon they would breed upon the endless worlds. Soon they would rise, and soon the humans would fall.

But now, on this world of murk and mist, it was time to whet his appetite.

He moved across his web, six legs rising, falling, tugging, cutting. He descended, the dark trunks dripping around him, moving down through the primordial forest, skulking, hungering. Always hungering. He left the stars above, plunging into the deeper, thicker darkness, where mist rose from the cold soil, where ancient roots grew in unholy cathedrals, where the air was rich and rank with sweet rotting things.

There, in the murk, she waited. His morsel.

A human woman, female, young, just blooming into her full ripeness. Webs embraced her pale, naked flesh. Malphas inhaled, savoring her sweet scent, the aroma of her skin, her fear.

"Please," she whispered. "Please, sir, whoever you are, I mean you no harm. Our species can be allies. We--"

Malphas stretched out a leg, and he caressed her cheek with a claw. She shut her eyes, trembling, and oh, the smell of her, how it mingled with the richness of this air. He could already taste it.

"You . . . are . . . afraid." He licked his fangs.

"I am," she whispered, one of her tears rolling onto his claw.

"Good." His nostrils flared. "Fear enhances the flavor."

He lashed down another leg, and he gripped her head firmly in place.

She screamed.

She kept screaming as his claws cut, sawing through the skull, as they peeled off the top, exposing the quivering brain within. How she screamed!

"Please," she said. "Please, I'm scared, I'm scared . . ."

Malphas could wait no longer. His tongue unfurled from his jaws. It reached into the skull. He scooped out the brain and lapped it up, felt it wriggling down his throat, rich with terror. Rich with nutrients. Rich with the full, pure flavor that only sentient prey could give.

His hunger sated, he worked in silence, cutting the rest of the skull from the body, then licking the flesh and blood until it was clean. Soon the skull was pure. He added it to the armor on his back, his first human trophy.

But not the last.

He climbed his web.

He climbed through mist and roots.

He returned to the sky, and he tugged his strings, and he gazed through his lenses.

There, in the distance, he could see it. A small, distant sun. Orbiting it--a pale blue dot.

"We hunger," said his slave.

Malphas grinned. "Soon we all shall feed."

The story continues in

EARTH FIRE

EARTHRISE, BOOK IV

NOVELS BY DANIEL ARENSON

Earthrise:

Earth Alone

Earth Lost

Earth Rising

Earth Fire

Earth Shadows

Earth Valor

Earth Reborn

Earth Honor

Earth Eternal

Alien Hunters:

Alien Hunters

Alien Sky

Alien Shadows

The Moth Saga:

Moth

Empires of Moth

Secrets of Moth

Daughter of Moth

Shadows of Moth

Legacy of Moth

Dawn of Dragons:

Requiem's Song

Requiem's Hope

Requiem's Prayer

Song of Dragons:

Blood of Requiem

Tears of Requiem

Light of Requiem

Dragonlore:

A Dawn of Dragonfire

A Day of Dragon Blood

A Night of Dragon Wings

The Dragon War:

A Legacy of Light

A Birthright of Blood

A Memory of Fire

Requiem for Dragons:

Dragons Lost

Dragons Reborn

Dragons Rising

Flame of Requiem:

Forged in Dragonfire

Crown of Dragonfire

Pillars of Dragonfire

Misfit Heroes:

Eye of the Wizard

Wand of the Witch

Kingdoms of Sand:

Kings of Ruin

Crowns of Rust

Thrones of Ash

Temples of Dust

Halls of Shadow

Echoes of Light

KEEP IN TOUCH

www.DanielArenson.com
Daniel@DanielArenson.com
Facebook.com/DanielArenson
Twitter.com/DanielArenson

Made in the USA
Lexington, KY
16 November 2017